D0938293

WHILE i LIVE

MERRY XMAS
MOLLIE " 2003 "
LOVE DAD xxx

WHILE i LIVE
THE ELLIE CHRONICLES

JOHN MARSDEN

MACMILLAN
Pan Macmillan Australia

John Marsden's website can be visited at:
www.macmillan.com.au/pma/marsden
or johnmarsden.com

First published 2003 in Macmillan by Pan Macmillan Australia Pty Limited
St Martins Tower, 31 Market Street, Sydney

Copyright © Jomden Pty Ltd 2003

All rights reserved. No part of this book may be reproduced or
transmitted in any form or by any means, electronic, mechanical,
including photocopying, recording or by any information storage and
retrieval system, without prior permission in writing from the publisher.

National Library of Australia
Cataloguing-in-Publication data:

Marsden, John, 1950– .
While I live.

For young adults.
ISBN 1 40503554 4.

I. Title. (Series: Marsden, John, 1950– The Ellie chronicles).

A823.3

Set in 12/14.5 pt Legacy Serif by Post Pre-press Group
Printed in Australia by McPherson's Printing Group

Poems and songs appearing in the text:
p. 5 'The Man from Snowy River' by Banjo Paterson; pp. 24 and 30
by John Marsden; p. 25 'The Lover Tells of the Rose in his Heart'
by W. B. Yeats; p. 26 'Daisy Bell' by Harry Dacre.

The characters and events in this book are fictitious and any resemblance
to real persons, living or dead, is purely coincidental.

For Sam Harper,
just because . . .

Thanks to Sarah Alexander,
Michelle Mitchell, Warwick Kirk, Susan Kirk,
Charlotte Lindsay, Anna Higgins, Ronda Gawley,
Rachel James, Des James, Maureen Wiltshire.

CHAPTER I

WE WERE HALFWAY up the spur when we heard it. Homer and Gavin and I, just the three of us. The spur was steep and the rocks were loose; we slid back two metres for every three we climbed.

It was about 1.15 p.m. A warm afternoon in May. It had been a hot autumn. Surrounding us was the bush, an army of twisted trees standing to attention. They wore grey-green uniforms and waved their bunches of leaves in endless useless motion. They were the army that never went anywhere, never did anything. They were the army who cared about nothing.

Sometimes the bush is quite silent. Not often. But sometimes, around noon on a January day, when the temperature is in the high thirties and the gumtree leaves are hanging tired and limp, and the birds stop flying and the insects hide in shade, then all you hear is the cracking of stones and the grizzle of a lost fly and, if you're in a paddock, the shuffle of a steer as he moves slowly to a better patch of grass.

But on this May afternoon there were the usual background noises, none of them loud, just humming away. Bees and wasps and beetles; tree branches rubbing against each other; magpies and rosellas, wagtails and wrens. Mum had a friend from the city come to stay once; I think she'd had a nervous breakdown or something, and on the third day she ran into the house with her hands over her ears crying, 'I came here for peace and quiet and it's nothing but noise noise noise.'

This particular day we were making so much noise ourselves that I hardly noticed the sounds of the bush. The clicking and rattling and clatter of sliding stones blocked out nearly everything else. And then there was the puffing and panting, from Homer especially. He was getting pretty unfit lately.

He stopped and leaned against a tree; half a tree really, because it had lost most of its upper branches. He grinned at me. His face sparkled with sweat. I stopped and grinned back. Ahead of us Gavin, head down, relentless as ever, ploughed on.

'You're getting slack,' I said to Homer.

'Race you,' he said. But he didn't move.

I walked on a dozen steps. Now I was just ahead of him.

'I win,' I said.

'Remind me again why we're doing this?' he asked, wriggling his shoulders to make his pack more comfortable.

'Fun,' I said, as firmly as I could. 'Fun, pleasure, recreation, sightseeing, enjoyment.'

He sighed. 'Some people swallow a dictionary,' he said. 'You have to swallow a bloody thesaurus.'

It was on the word 'thesaurus' that the shots began.

They came from the bottom of the valley, echoing up the hillside, then around the valley. To be mathematical about it, I'd say there were fifteen shots in the first volley, evenly spaced, lasting about twenty-five seconds. Then there was a pause of maybe ten seconds before three ragged groups of shots that went for a minute. After that there were occasional random ones, probably thirty in all, for about five or six minutes.

Five or six minutes. By the end of five or six minutes we were halfway home again. It seems incredible when I think about it. After all, we'd taken about two and a bit hours to get that far. Of course that was uphill and this was nearly all downhill, but even so, considering I lost at least half a minute going back for Gavin . . .

Gavin's profoundly deaf, which doesn't mean totally deaf, but then according to his teacher, hardly anyone's totally deaf. All I know is that Gavin's very deaf. He can hear loud yells, semitrailers going past, explosions, and helicopters at close range. He can't hear TV or music or conversation. He definitely can't hear anyone telling him to clean his room or do his homework or set the table. He can't hear me telling him he needs to get a move-on or he'll miss the bus, but he can hear me saying, 'Gavin, get your ass in gear right now or I'll kick you all the way to the bus-stop,' which I tend to say fairly often.

He can't hear shots that are a couple of kilometres away. I'd forgotten that. I remembered it after I'd turned and run down the spur a hundred metres. When I remembered I stopped, irresolute. I've always liked that word. I've just never had a chance to use it before.

I had a flash in my mind of the scene in *The Silver Sword* where Jan abandons his dog Ludwig in order to help the girls save the little boy Edek. The author says that this is the point at which Jan begins to grow up. When I was a kid and I came to that moment in the book I hated Jan, I hated him for leaving his dog to die in terror and loneliness and the knowledge he had been betrayed. Now I had a similar problem. Similar but even more difficult. I knew, as surely as I know winter follows summer, that the shots came from my place. I knew they meant something terrible was happening, and that I had to get home as fast as I could, in order to help my parents, perhaps even to save their lives.

But I also had to remember that Gavin was only a kid, tough little bugger though he was, and I couldn't leave him to walk on up the spur, not knowing where we'd gone, not knowing what was happening, certainly walking into loneliness, possibly walking into danger.

Because suddenly nothing was safe now, and these mountains were alive with frightening possibilities again.

So tearing at my heart with my hand, literally, grabbing at it as though I wanted to pull it out of my chest and throw it on the ground, hating every step I had to take in the wrong direction, I turned and ran back up the spur.

Ahead of me Gavin walked on and on and on. When I got within twenty metres I grabbed a handful of pebbles and chucked them. Every single one missed. Frustrated and desperate I bent and picked up another handful but as I did Gavin saw one of the first lot bouncing past. He turned around.

I didn't know how to communicate to him what Homer and I had heard but one thing about Gavin, he's quick on the uptake. Boy is he quick. Or maybe it's just that I was such a scary sight. One look at my face and he was bounding down the boulders towards me. Apparently I didn't need to say anything. I swung around again and started down the hill. It seemed like only a couple of seconds before Gavin reached me and actually passed me. I stopped worrying about him then, and put on a sprint.

He sent the flint-stones flying, but the pony kept his feet,
He cleared the fallen timber in his stride,
And the man from Snowy River never shifted in his seat –
It was grand to see that mountain horseman ride.
Through the stringy barks and saplings, on the rough and
 broken ground,
Down the hillside at a racing pace he went;
And he never drew the bridle till he landed safe and sound
At the bottom of that terrible descent.

Well, unlike the man from Snowy River I didn't have a horse, but we all had a terrible descent. I don't know how we didn't break six ankles between the three of us. Seven ankles even. The rocks that had slid under our feet as we climbed slid even worse as we came down. In the first couple of minutes there were waterfalls of stones cascading away from me. As I concentrated on them I was nearly wiped out by a fallen tree at the height of my neck. I ducked that, but only at the last second: I scraped my forehead going under it.

Lower down the spur were a few damp areas that never saw the sun. I skidded on one of those and went down on my haunches, feeling my knee crack – my left knee of course, it always had to be the bad one that took the punishment. My right knee bore a charmed life. I skidded two metres or so trying to keep my balance, and somehow I did and I was up and off again from the squatting position, instead of rolling sideways, which would have cost more time.

Bends in the track, rabbit holes, and then a series of fallen trees, four trunks, one after another, just a metre or so apart, and all the masses of dead branches that went with them. We'd laughed as we struggled over them on the way up. Now I hurdled the first one, jumped onto the second one, took a leap from there onto the third one, then had to get down and wrestle my way over the last. That's one thing the bush is good at: passively resisting human beings.

Quite early on I'd left Gavin well behind, and at some point I passed Homer and then I was on the flat and running through a paddock, Burnt Hut, with sweat flying from me. The paddock felt airless and the heat was stealing my energy. I started to wallow, to run heavily, that horrible sensation that you're running on the spot, running like crazy but not getting anywhere. All the way down the spur I'd heard the scattered shots, getting closer as I got closer, and all the way down I tried to think of reasonable explanations for them, and I couldn't think of a single thing that made sense.

Not one single solitary thing. My father didn't do a lot of shooting. He was a bit allergic to it I think. All he had these days was a .222 and he used it for knocking off the occasional fox, or for putting down dying cattle, or to shoot kangaroos that had been hit and left for dead by cars. He didn't even have as much ammo as I'd heard in those five or six minutes.

Ploughing across the paddock I listened for more shooting but there wasn't any. I didn't know if this was good news or bad news. I took a glance over my shoulder and saw Homer and Gavin a hundred metres behind, and about level with each other. I didn't look again, couldn't afford the energy.

To get to our house, from where we were coming, you go across a cleared paddock, One Tree, and then into my favourite paddock, Parklands. Dad never liked Parklands, because it didn't have much feed for stock. That's because the old driveway to the house runs through it, and many years ago the drive was planted with European trees, so what with those and the gums that had been allowed to stay, the grass doesn't get much chance.

This time I loved those trees like never before, because they gave me good cover. I didn't know what I was running towards, what I was likely to find, but I knew with every fibre of my being that it would be bad. The war was over. It had been over for four months. But you don't get dozens of rifle shots four months after a war finishes without feeling sick to the bottom of your feet.

There's a vehicle bridge over the creek, but when I was a hundred metres away I thought it mightn't be a good idea to use that. Too exposed, too obvious. Already I was getting back into the ways of thinking that had kept me alive during the war. It's like riding a bicycle – you never forget. You click back into it without a moment's conscious thought.

So I swerved and crossed the creek a little further down, where there was a footbridge half lost among the periwinkle, an old yellow bridge where the boards had been rotting for years. It had been slippery with dampness and mould, but Dad had just replaced the planks. I could smell the creosote. Then I raced up the bank, at an angle, so I would keep the two big water tanks between the house and me as I approached.

At first I thought nothing was wrong. It seemed peaceful. It seemed quiet. There was no movement. But of course that was wrong. At this time of day it should have been quite busy. Mum should have been hanging out washing or weeding the herb garden or heading off down the drive to look for mail. My friend, Mrs Mackenzie, who'd been staying with us, should have been with her, keeping up the endless supply of chatter that Mum found so exhausting. Dad should have been drilling boltholes in the new rails for the cattle yards or servicing the ute or chainsawing the fallen blackwood down at the gate into Nellie's.

The silence that I talked about before, the silence you sometimes hear in the bush around noon on a hot day, that was the silence of my home now. It engulfed me. It felt so real that I could have been running into a huge wall of cotton wool. It felt so real that I almost bounced off it.

And there was something else. The smell. You always get a smell after you fire a rifle or shotgun. The strong, almost sweet smell of gunpowder, that drives out everything else, for a little while at least. The smell of rotting kangaroos, or petrol, or a hundred sheep in the yard, it drives them all out. And the roses and the lavender and the gum trees – they don't stand a chance.

Even though it had been, I don't know, a bit more than five minutes since the last shot, the smell was still heavy in the air.

I ran straight into the house. I knew the risk. I had a fair idea by now what had happened. I knew gunmen might be in there. I knew it might be an ambush. But when it's your family, what else can you do? It's like they say, 'You turn your back on your family, you're no good.'

'Girl turns her back on her parents, that girl's no good.'

Then every thought was driven from my mind. Even the fear of the gunmen. They could have come in and shot me as I knelt on the kitchen floor. I don't think I would have heard them. I don't think I would have even felt the bullet.

Funny, some things, even though you're expecting them, even though you've known for the last five minutes what's probably happening and what you're likely to see, when you're face to face with them you realise that nothing, nothing, nothing on God's earth can prepare you for them.

My mother was lying on the floor, on her back, twisted around and looking up at the ceiling. I could really only look at her legs. I thought, 'She's still very thin.' Everything above her legs was too terrible to see. Whatever bullets these people used were high-powered. They'd done a lot of damage. There wasn't much left. Blood and stuff had gone everywhere.

I stood up again. I felt myself falling apart, coming to pieces, right there on the spot. But I tried to hold together. I told myself it was too early to react, to feel anything. There were other things I had to do.

Homer and Gavin came bursting into the kitchen. I didn't look at them, didn't say anything, just turned away. I heard their gasps, could imagine their horror. I think Homer said, 'Oh Jesus, no.' Right there and then it was almost easier to imagine their faces than to have my own feelings. I saw Mrs Mackenzie's feet and legs sticking out of the pantry door. Steeling myself, clenching my fists, trying to find some kind of composure, I went over there.

As I looked at her body I felt something in my throat rise like it wanted to force itself up, like there was a slimy animal who'd been living inside me and now wanted out. It slithered up into my mouth and I had to clamp my teeth and swallow it again.

At least Mrs Mackenzie hadn't been torn to pieces like my mother. One bullet had been enough.

I guess I was in some kind of trance by then. I half ran outside to find my father. I suppose, looking back, I should have run flat out in case he needed first aid. But I was emotionally in a dead state. And I was physically wrecked from the run down the spur and across the paddocks. And I was terrified about what I might find. And I was . . . oh a thousand other things.

But I also knew I couldn't stay in the house and hide in my wardrobe, which a lot of my instincts were telling me to do. I had to find my father. For better or for worse I had to find him.

The men who had done this thing, who had attacked our farm, were professionals, no doubt about that. The odds were that they'd done the same thing to my father as they had to my mother and Mrs Mackenzie. I went to the shearing shed and ran past the empty stands, sobbing a little, my fists clenched, my stomach jammed solid, like I'd swallowed wet cement. I went past the old woolpress and the classing table, into each of the dusty little rooms. I went to the machinery shed and checked round the back of each tractor, and even the plough. I hesitated between the old barn and the new feed sheds for the turkeys and geese, the ones Dad had built as part of our short-lived attempt to diversify, and I chose the feed sheds.

I cut across the gully to get there and suddenly almost tripped over a body. It was lying face down. It wasn't in uniform but I knew where he was from. Blood still oozed from under him.

I jumped over it and ran up to the shed. Two other bodies lay in the long grass. I felt my throat block like two hands were closing around it to strangle me. Dad had gone down fighting. He was in the shed, his body in pieces, like Mum's. There was blood everywhere. Another body was in there with him, almost lying on top of him. It was hard to tell what had happened but I think somehow Dad had got one of their rifles off them and done what damage he could before they killed him.

CHAPTER 2

MY FAMILY HAD been cockies since before The Beatles even, back in horse and plough days. We had always been into cattle and sheep, but when the war ended and twenty million people had to be crammed into an area that used to hold six million, we lost a lot of land. My friend Fi's mother was appointed to do the redistribution for the Wirrawee area and we didn't come out of it all that well. That's my opinion anyway.

Dad decided to break with tradition and go into turkeys and geese. At first I thought it was a good idea but it turned out badly. No sooner had we started than the turkeys were hit by blackhead disease and we lost three-quarters of the poor buggers.

Dad was convinced the disease had come from the other side of the border but who knows? The truth is it happened so quickly that I did wonder if the turkeys were infected before we got them. It was hard to say. Before the war the government had been really strict on agricultural stuff, and being an island made that easier.

Anyone who brought in nasty diseases like fire blight was smeared with mustard and fed to sharks. But when the war ended, it suddenly became a whole different ball game, because here we were on one side of the border being strict about quarantine and there they were on the other side not giving a stuff.

As we cremated a couple of thousand dead birds on a huge bonfire, an event that put me off cooked chicken for a long time – and I've never been keen on raw chicken – Dad realised that turkeys and geese weren't his scene. I suppose the blackhead disease almost did us a good turn in that way.

Equally it was obvious that three of the four families who'd gotten large bits of our farm in the land redistribution weren't going to make a go of it. One lot had never been on the land before, another lot were lazy, and the third were on the grog. So Dad sat down with them and did a bit of negotiating. I was proud of him, because negotiating didn't come naturally to him. But after nearly a week of bargaining he'd leased back three-quarters of the land that we'd lost, and even though I didn't like the fact that we had to pay these people a lot of money just to get our own property back, I started to hope that maybe we could return to the way it had been in the old days.

The other good thing was that we got rid of three of the families, because we'd had to give them housing. One of the rules with the new arrangements was that we'd had to provide their accommodation while they tried to get houses built and launch their farming operations.

The ones left were the Sandersons, who were nice. They were quite a young couple with two kids. Unlike the others they'd already built their own house, in a paddock called Hillside, and moved into it about a fort-night earlier. Pretty fast going, considering how hard it was to get building materials, let alone stuff like electrical cables and poly pipe.

But Mrs Mackenzie, Corrie's mum, was still with us. No wonder it had seemed like a small township around my place for a while there. Corrie was my friend, who was killed in the war. Well, one of my friends who was killed. Mrs Mackenzie was nice, but she was pretty depressed most of the time. No surprises there. I mean, she'd lost her only daughter, and then her husband shot through, and for someone who'd put all her energy and time and love into her husband and her daughter, suddenly Mrs Mackenzie had nothing to do, and nowhere to go. Except to our place.

At least my mother had got most of her old spirit back. The war had knocked her around pretty badly. One of the invisible victims. I've never been quite sure exactly what a nervous breakdown is, but I think that's what my mother had. These days she was still thin, and she'd aged a lot, but I knew she was back to normal when she charged into my room one Sunday morning and told me to take down a poster that said 'For people with dyslexia, UFKC OFF', and to take the pile of washing behind my door to the laundry and put it through the machine (the pile wasn't as big as Uluru, she definitely got that wrong), and to clean up my room in the next sixty minutes or I'd be grounded till Christmas.

It was a relief in a way, because for a while there I'd been feeling like I was the mother and she was the daughter.

So much had happened, so many changes to our life. But things had started to settle down a bit. God they needed to. In the last month or so I'd been getting to school every day, and even doing a bit of homework. A lot of homework some nights. It felt weird doing assignments on ancient Egypt and immunology and the poems of Philip Hodgins after what we'd been through. But I quite liked it. It gave me, I don't know, detachment.

Dad had taken delivery of forty scrawny cows who were meant to be in calf, and twenty skinny steers. Stock was hard to come by but he was hopeful of getting a couple of hundred wethers and ewes from a mate near Stratton. It was going to be a long hard haul to build things up again, to get back to the way it had been for so many years, but I think we felt like we were heading in the right direction at last.

For all that, there was still plenty of stuff that kept everyone on edge. In particular, the stories about border raids. It was hard to know exactly what was going on, because we only had one newspaper and one local television station. Nearly all of our TV now came from America.

Some people reckoned a lot of the local news was censored. The government didn't want us to get too depressed, or scared. Mr Purvis, at the Mitre 10 in Wirrawee, told me he'd written thirty-eight letters to the paper since the war ended and not one of them had been published, and that proved there was censorship, but I thought it was more likely that he wrote crap letters.

There were certainly heaps of rumours. Wirrawee these days was a regular gossip factory, spewing out stories the way the Stratton Smallgoods Factory spewed out sausages. But border raids were one of the biggest talking points, almost from the day the war ended. Some of them were reported in the news but there were plenty of people to tell you that the media only mentioned one in every ten. It was impossible for us, living so far out of town, busy trying to rebuild the farm, to know what was really happening.

It seemed pretty clear though that there were people from both sides sneaking across the border for all kinds of illegal reasons. I would say that from our side people were doing it for thrills, to steal stuff, to get revenge for the war, and looking for unreturned prisoners who were rumoured to be hidden in hard-to-reach places.

From their side, I'd say they were doing it for thrills, to steal stuff, to get revenge for the war. And some of them were pissed off about the peace settlement, and thought they should have kept the whole country.

Come to think of it, maybe that's another reason people from our side were going over the border. Maybe they thought we should have got the whole country back, so they decided to take it a little bit at a time. A lot of people on our side, Mr Purvis included, were sure that we should have got more land. They even said we'd ended the war too early, accepted peace terms that were one-sided. I don't know about that. Seemed to me like neither side won this particular war, but the big New Zealand counter-attack at the end got us the best terms we could have hoped for. Without that we'd have ended up with Flinders Island. Twenty million people on Flinders Island. Could have been tricky. Anyway, what would I know?

But considering the experiences I'd had in the war, hanging out in the bush and fighting like a tiger cat, staying alive even with half an army chasing us, I can hardly believe, looking back, that I didn't take more care. Dumb, dumb, dumb. You make a lot of mistakes in life. You leave your bus pass at home, you forget to take the scones out of the oven, you lose a library book, you call Mrs Mackenzie 'Mum' in a moment of absent-mindedness. None of those things matter an awful lot.

You don't take the idea of a raid on your place seriously, and as a result your parents and Mrs Mackenzie are killed.

I knew a lot more about guerilla fighting than my parents did. I should have been the one to think this through.

I don't know how to describe those first few days. I don't know how to describe those first few minutes. Gavin went into shock. I mean real, serious shock. I'd seen a kind of shock before, during the war. My friend Kevin had it, especially when a group of us, as we ran feral and loose around the countryside, blew up Wirrawee Airfield as a contribution to the war effort. Kevin had been a mixture of catatonic, sulky and terrified while that was happening.

Now Gavin was a complete mess, lying on the verandah like he was having a fit, white-faced and shaking, his eyes way back in his head, his teeth chattering. It was completely distracting, coming back towards the house, trying to get my head around what had happened, trying to come to terms with the bodies and the blood and the death and the way my life had changed, and in the middle of all that suddenly realising that I had to look after Gavin. He didn't reply to anything I said. He wasn't unconscious, but he might as well have been. I had to make myself function, go to the linen press and get a blanket, and then another blanket when he still didn't stop shaking, and sit with him and hold him and talk to him and sing to him.

I don't suppose he heard any of what I said but I don't

think it mattered. There were times when I resented Gavin's arrival in our family, even though I was the cause of it, but this wasn't one of those times.

From time to time I had glimpses of Homer. He was holding Dad's rifle and first I saw him hurrying through the kitchen, then prowling around the outside of the house, eyes searching the garden and the trees, occasionally stopping to poke into a bush or throw open the door of a shed and look inside. It was brave that he did that: if anyone was there, they would have got him pretty easily I think.

The phone in the house rang but I didn't answer it and eventually it stopped.

After a while Gavin got some colour in his face and his skin felt a bit warmer. He'd more or less stopped shaking and I thought he might have gone to sleep. I got up. It was hard: my legs had certainly gone to sleep, and I didn't seem able to walk properly. Gavin moved when I got up, but he didn't open his eyes, so I took a few steps away. When he still didn't move I hurried back into the house. Homer burst in from the other side, giving me a fright because for a moment I didn't know who was coming through the door. He had a second rifle, obviously taken from a dead soldier, and he gave it to me and together we carefully checked each room. I was in automatic mode; I think I quite liked having something to do so I didn't have to think, didn't have to feel.

But then I couldn't postpone it any longer. I went back into the kitchen.

Homer and I still hadn't exchanged a word. I took another look at the two bodies in there, as if I wanted to see whether they might have come back to life. Then I went to the linen press again and got two more blankets.

'Do you want to go after them?' Homer asked. He meant the soldiers. I don't know why I call them soldiers. They were murderers. I shook my head. I was even angry at him, that all he could think of was punishment and revenge. It was unfair, but I was filled with such rage and despair that anything would have made me angry. To be honest I was angry that he'd even spoken. A house spider ran across the kitchen bench and I slammed it so hard with an old copy of *Vogue Living* that its little black body disintegrated.

I sat down in Mum's favourite chair with my head on my arms. I stayed like that for a while then got up and called the police. I felt listless. When they answered I said, 'My parents have been shot. And Mrs Mackenzie. They're all dead.' Then, stupidly, I hung up. A moment later they rang back. I don't know how they worked out I was the one who'd rung them. And I didn't know the guy. I think his name was Elliott. He said, 'Is this right? There's been a shooting? At the Linton place?'

I gave the phone to Homer and went back to look at Gavin. He still seemed asleep. I took yet another blanket, from Gavin's bed this time. One thing we did still have was a lot of blankets. I went outside. All the time I could hear Homer's voice, low and urgent, talking to the cops. I wondered how he was feeling. He loved my mother and idolised my father. I went outside to my father and put the blanket over him. Blood was still seeping from his body but it seemed to be coagulating now. Surprisingly there was only one fly buzzing around him. I was grateful for that. I returned to the house.

I'm not sure what we did until the police came. It seems like it took them quite a while but I'm not sure about that either. Homer told me to sit with Gavin. 'Shock can kill people,' he said. 'Keep him warm. Look after him.' I guess he knew it was good for me to have something else to do.

After a while Gavin did wake up. He didn't say anything. I just sat there rubbing his head and stroking his hair. I knew how much he loved this, like a dog, and how it calmed him. I thought about the strange route he had taken, from the wild streets of Stratton to being on our verandah as a member of our family, and I wondered if I'd done him any favours. Maybe I should have left him back there to live or die on his own.

Occasionally a little tear ran down his face, leaving a track like a snail trail, and a fit of trembling shook his body.

The police arrived and the ambulance about a second later. I'm not sure if Homer rang the ambulance; I don't think he did. The police probably arranged that. There wasn't much for the ambos to do.

There were two police cars, three men and one woman. I had this feeling that I only wanted to talk to the woman so I stuck pretty close to her.

Not that there was much to say. We'd been heading up the spur for a picnic on Tailor's Stitch, just the three of us. First time we'd been up there for ages. Heard the shots, came running back. Found dead people everywhere. End of story.

There was a lot of activity. People moving around, talking in hushed voices, photos, and in the middle of it Homer got everyone coffee. I thought I didn't want it but he made me take it and maybe the caffeine helped.

The ambulance went away again. I had thought it would take the bodies, but it didn't, just left them. Bodies.

It seemed weird to think of my parents as being bodies. Like they had become objects. Homer's mum, Mrs Yannos, arrived, and other neighbours and friends, I can't even remember who they were. Gavin came in and tried to crawl into my lap but he was really too big and I didn't have enough compassion left for him now. Mrs Yannos gave me lots of hugs but I hardly felt them.

Two more cars arrived, station wagons, and some men in grey suits. They spoke to me in voices that were so hushed and oily that I felt a little ill, like I'd eaten a sausage that wasn't cooked properly. They gave me forms to sign and I signed them. It took me a long time to figure out who they were and what they wanted. Then I realised they were undertakers. I stood up and screamed at them, but Mrs Yannos grabbed me from one side and Homer from the other, and I had to stand and watch as they took what was left of my mother and Mrs Mackenzie away, on metal stretchers. Then to torture myself, or to do him honour, or for both reasons, I went out on the verandah and watched as they got my father. They came back for one of the killers.

'We haven't got room for the others,' they said. 'We'll pick them up in a couple of hours.'

Clutching myself around the stomach I nodded. I didn't want the murderer's body in the same vehicle as my parents so I made the man put him in with Mrs Mackenzie, which was totally gross of me.

Mrs Yannos, along with Mr and Mrs Sanderson, the people who were still farming part of our old property, starting cleaning the kitchen. I took a Chux thinking I would help them but instantly felt so sick at cleaning up my mother's life blood and fragments of her body that I had to go outside and gulp in fresh air. Homer came after me and put his arm around me and I leaned into him but I couldn't cry. On my other side Gavin was leaning into me and I suddenly thought, 'These are about the two most important people left in my life,' and I felt desperate at how alone I now was.

CHAPTER 3

THE NEXT FEW days passed like some gruesome dream.
Or a bad drug trip. Not that I've ever had a bad drug
trip. Or a drug trip full-stop. A dozen times a day I felt
revolted at finding yet another drop of blood or something worse in a corner or crevice or cranny of the
kitchen. I couldn't believe how far blood spreads, how it
splatters. I'd already learned during the war how much
blood there is in the human body but I'd never had to
live with the results of that before. I didn't want to go
into the kitchen. I shuddered every time I went through
the door, but I knew I had no choice. And every time I
felt like I could see the bodies of my mother and Mrs
Mackenzie, still lying on the floor.

Poor Mrs Mackenzie. In the middle of everything I
found time to think about her and her family. It was
almost easier to think about her than it was to think
about my own parents. Mrs Mackenzie had lost her
child, her husband, and now she had gone to join Corrie. It was like suddenly there was hardly any trace of her

on the planet. I hoped for her sake, as well as for my sake, for everyone's sake, that there is an after-life, and that she and Corrie had been reunited there.

Although I used the kitchen when I had to, I hardly ate anything. I picked up food and looked at it and felt sick and put it down. I had no appetite. At least I didn't need to cook. People left food, lots of it. Mrs Yannos and Mrs Sanderson came in every day, bringing casseroles and cakes and soups and sandwiches. And Gavin kept eating, so he had to be fed. I used the kitchen to make his breakfast and to heat up the food the neighbours left and to microwave hot chocolates for him.

Homer and the Anglican priest from Wirrawee sat down with me and told me we had to work out the details of the funerals. I said I couldn't do it but when they got up to go I changed my mind. I realised that if I didn't do it, they would. And I knew I couldn't live with myself if someone else made the arrangements. Homer probably would have started with The Vines, and finished with The Strokes.

So that evening I found it quite therapeutic to sit down and write out what I wanted. Father Berryman had left a bunch of poems and prayers, and there were a few that I liked. One of them started

Everything slips away. The river goes to the ocean
And joins that great mystery.
Now I too. You cannot hold me,
Any more than you can hold water. Let me go . . .

The trouble was that although I liked this one I didn't want to listen to it. Letting them go? I ached for them, hungered for them. My bones were sore with the pain of their not being here. I wanted to grip them to me.

I went looking in my mum's books, and found a poem that she'd marked with a little cross. Somehow it seemed to fit better, and I knew Father Berryman wouldn't mind.

*All things uncomely and broken, all things worn out and
   old,
The cry of a child by the roadway, the creak of a lumbering
   cart,
The heavy steps of the ploughman, splashing the wintry
   mould,
Are wronging your image that blossoms a rose in the deeps
   of my heart.*

*The wrong of unshapely things is a wrong too great to be
   told;
I hunger to build them anew and sit on a green knoll
   apart
With the earth and the sky and the water, re-made, like a
   casket of gold
For my dreams of your image that blossoms a rose in the
   deeps of my heart.*

Their deaths seemed to fit with 'the wrong of unshapely things'.

As well as the poem I remembered all the times my mum had told me about 'their song', the song Dad and she had first danced to, the one that always got them smiling when they heard it again. It was pretty well known I think.

Daisy, Daisy,
Give me your answer do!
I'm half crazy,
All for the love of you!
It won't be a stylish marriage,
I can't afford a carriage
But you'll look sweet on the seat
Of a bicycle built for two!

I got on a bit of a roll then and stayed up till late, looking for music tracks. It was hard because my parents sure as hell didn't have the same taste in music as I did. I didn't want to choose stuff they didn't like. But I didn't want to choose stuff that I didn't like either. So in the end I compromised, and went for 'Take It In' by The Waifs and 'There is a Mountain' by some old hippie called Donovan.

The day of the funeral started out wet and grey. Just like you'd expect. Just the way a funeral should be. I got Gavin into his best clothes, which was a big effort. In some ways it was a typical Gavin day, when you saw him at his best and worst. He took an hour and a half to get dressed, and he whinged and complained and cried and sulked pretty much the whole time. Did I have any sympathy for him, this little stray washed up to our doorstep by the war? Did I care that the only place in the world where he'd been able to find security had now been blown up in his face?

Well, yes I did. But after an hour and a half I was totally fed up with him. Although there had been people coming and going so much in the house ever since the shootings, at the end of each day it was still Gavin and me alone together, and I was finding that pretty hard to take. I guess he was too.

Then, the moment I'd at last got him into his clothes, he disappeared outside. I was furious but I couldn't be bothered chasing him anymore. If he got muddy, or worse if he disappeared altogether and missed the funeral, that was his lookout. I'd done all I could.

Then the next thing he's coming back into the kitchen with a bunch of flowers he's picked from the garden and I realise he's done it so he can take them to the funeral. There weren't many flowers in the garden at that time of year; he must have taken pretty much everything. A few late roses, a lot of white azaleas, a hydrangea leached of colour but beautiful in its dry coat, and even some early wattle.

Like I say, it was a morning of Gavin at his best and worst. I smacked a kiss on his forehead, which he immediately wiped off before he could catch girl germs.

Seeing Gavin walk in the door with his bunch of flowers really got to me. I was finding everything so hard to take. In particular the way in which my parents were everywhere I turned, as though they were still alive. Their presence was in every corner. This'll sound sick, but in the same way that my mother's blood had spread to every corner of the kitchen, her life spread through every corner of the house. Same with my father. I picked up a cookbook and there was a note in my mother's writing, with a recipe for beer bread; I opened a drawer and found my father's messy old address book; on the table in the dining room was the last bunch of flowers my mother had arranged, starting to wilt now. I didn't like going into their bedroom, couldn't go into their bedroom, because it was too unbearable. Their presence filled the room so strongly that for the first time in my life I felt there was hardly room for me in there. Maybe it was their smell, because the room was laden with that. The first time I went in after the murders I tiptoed around as though they had dissolved and spread through the room like a heavy invisible mist. I was scared to touch anything.

I got ready for the funeral myself. I wore my hair out, the way my mother liked it.

Homer arrived at half past ten. When I saw him from the kitchen window, walking towards the door, and realised that he had dressed up in clothes I'd never seen him wear before, a navy suit with a dark red tie and polished black leather shoes, I felt like I'd swallowed a small apple and it had stuck halfway down my throat. It wasn't just that he looked so handsome. It was the fact that he had put on clothes that I knew he would have hated. And there was also my awareness that in the last few days someone had been looking after the property, feeding the chooks and putting them to bed, checking the cattle, fuelling the vehicles and filling the woodbox, and I knew for sure who that someone was.

I felt a surge of love for my older 'brother' Homer and my little 'brother' Gavin. I'd practically grown up with Homer and I'd known Gavin for a lot less than a year but I could almost see the links between us at that moment.

We got in the car and off we went. I was so sick at the thought of what was in front of me. I didn't know if I could get through it. When I saw the crowd at the church I felt even worse. 'Don't these people have homes of their own to go to?' I muttered to Homer. It was a standard joke we'd been swapping for years. He squeezed my hand.

'What do you want to do? Sit here for a while?'

I had my head down. I couldn't look up. 'I guess not. I guess I'd better face it.'

'Hey, you've been through some tough spots. Remember the airfield? The prison? And the prison camp? You can do this.'

'This is worse.'

He didn't say anything. I waited a few more minutes, then, before it became impossible, got out, grabbed Gavin's hand, and in we went.

We got through it.

It was another, I don't know, a week I suppose before I started to function in any way again. I felt sort of guilty waking up at all, as though it was disrespect-ful to my parents, as though I should mourn them forever. Anything short of that and I wasn't a good daughter. If I smiled or noticed a song on the radio or took an interest in a programme Gavin was watching on TV I felt ashamed. If I didn't think about them every moment of every day, if I didn't keep their mem-ories alive by the power of my heart and mind, then I was disloyal. And worse than that, they'd go, they'd disappear into oblivion, and they'd be truly dead then. I was the only thing, the only person, standing between them and extinction.

I seem to be quoting a lot of poems here, but what the hell, here goes with another one. Mr Kassar gave it to us in Drama one day, back a couple of years. We had to pre-pare a Drama presentation based around it. At first we didn't even understand it but when he explained that it was about memory and the way when someone dies a lot of their experiences and stories and personal memo-ries die with them, suddenly I got it.

It was called 'The Old Man's Dead, the Baby's Dead'.

When the old man died there was no-one left to remember the little baby he and his wife gave birth to sixty or so years ago. So it's like now the baby's really gone.

> When he died and went to earth,
> All the thousand million memories he'd had since birth
> Went with him. The comet over Kakadu,
> The buttercup he waved for love in playground games,
> The Army Hall that fell in flames
> And the baby who drew a dozen breaths and died.
> No-one left now to read the words 'Always remembered',
> In faded brown on the granite slab.
> Good-bye old man! A lot went with you.
> And only now can it be said
> The old man's dead, the baby's dead.

I knew some of my parents' stories. My father's were all about farm life. The swaggies and Indian hawkers who called in to the property when Dad was a little kid. The silence in the shearing shed as the men sheared the stud rams with blades instead of electric shears, to avoid injuring them. The weekend rabbit drives, when the trappers gradually pushed the rabbits into nets in a corner of a paddock, getting over two thousand rabbits in a weekend. Drenching the sheep with bluestone-nicotine, and going out the next morning to see hundreds of huge white tapeworms all over the ground. The glut of cattle which led to well-bred Poll Hereford cows in good condition selling for ten, twenty, fifty cents each. And the fires and the floods. Always the fires and floods.

My mother's stories ranged a bit wider. Some were about growing up in the city, some were about her trip overseas when she was eighteen. And some were about life with Dad on the farm. Her father was an accountant and her mother did a few different things, including catering and landscape design and radio production. And raising a daughter.

So my mother's stories were about going to a private school where some girls were driven by chauffeurs each day, where Mum got caught putting a bra on a statue of the school's first principal (who to make things worse was a guy), where she saw a teacher get run over by a drunk on a bicycle. And later, after she'd left school, helping her mother design a garden for Monica Duran, who insisted on having a huge photo of herself on a courtyard wall, going to a dance and finding a girl dead in one of the toilet cubicles, seeing the pandas in the Washington Zoo, and a soccer riot in Barcelona.

And, later, the fires and the floods.

I really believe that our stories make us who we are. I don't think people are born as empty shells. They already have the makings of a personality and they have intelligence. But from the moment they're born, and maybe before that, they start accumulating stories and it's those stories that have the biggest effect on them.

Like the poem says, a thousand million memories. A thousand million stories. And then some.

I feel that in my short life I've already gone over the thousand million mark. Sometimes I have trouble believing that I've seen and done so much.

A week after the funeral Fi walked in through the kitchen door. I was at the table trying to show Gavin how to separate eggs, and I hadn't heard her coming. Gavin certainly hadn't heard her coming. He dropped the egg, shell and all, into the bowl with the whites and rushed to her like he'd been a calf on one side of the fence and she was his mum who'd been bellowing for him on the other side. Not that I've ever seen anyone less like a cow than Fi. She's more deer, more antelope, more your young wallaby, the most naturally graceful person I know.

Gavin hugged her and hugged her. It was hard for me to get near her. I actually felt jealous of Gavin, no, not jealous, envious. Somehow I was getting too old for the Total, Give It Everything You've Got, No Holds Barred hugs. They were the best hugs of all. But when I was finally allowed access to Fi we held each other for a long time. She felt very warm.

Soon enough I got her a cup of coffee and we sat down at the table, Gavin squished up next to Fi on the same chair, holding his glass of cordial. (Another pang as I got the bottle of cordial from the pantry – Mum had made it less than two months ago and it had her own label on it, with a little sketch of fruit, and the words 'Linton's Lemon and Orange' in cute printing.)

'How have you been?' she asked me.

'OK.'

'You looked terrible at the funeral.'

'Were you at the funeral?'

'You mean you don't remember?'

'No. I didn't think you were there. I was a bit hurt about it actually.'

'Oh my God, Ellie, we had a conversation, but you seemed so switched off that I didn't know if you wanted me to stay away or what. So I thought I'd wait a bit, until the first rush of visitors had finished. 'Cos Mum said that you'd be overwhelmed by them at first and the true friends are the ones who are still around when the others have gone back to their normal daily lives.'

'There's a book from the funeral, that people signed apparently, but I haven't been game to look at it yet.'

Fi continued. 'So I'm here if you want me, and for as long as you want, whether it's five minutes or a couple of weeks.'

'Oh, Fi, I'd love you to stay, for as long as you can. For life if you want.'

'Has it been terrible? Is that a stupid question?'

I nodded. I couldn't speak. Finally I gulped: 'Terrible.'

'You want to talk about it?'

'No. Not yet. Maybe later. I don't know.'

There was a bit of silence. 'Do you remember anything about the funeral?' she asked.

'Oh yes. Quite a bit.' I laughed. 'Even stupid things, like Mrs Mathers and Mrs Kristicevic wearing the same dress.'

'Yes, I noticed that. Of course they weren't actually wearing the same dress. That would have been a bit uncomfortable.'

It took me a minute to realise what she meant. Showed how slowly my brain was working. 'Oh very funny,' I said, when I did figure it out.

'Did you notice Lee fainting?'

'No! Are you serious? Was he there too?'

'God, you poor thing, you really were out of it.'

'Did he actually faint?'

'Totally. My father was one of the men who helped carry him outside. I've been talking to him on the phone just about every day. He's out of his mind. He's written about four letters to you.'

Lee. It doesn't seem right that someone with a one-syllable name of three letters could have caused me more than a year of complicated agonising confusing

33

wonderful sensations, and what was worse, he was still doing it. He loved me, he loved me not, I loved him, I loved him not. Last time I'd seen him we'd made love. But then in my mind the relationship slowly died. But then in my mind the relationship flared back to life. Then it didn't. Then it did. Didn't. Did. Now . . . I don't know. Yes, no, maybe, all of the above.

'I guess Lee would know what it's like.'

'I guess he would, except he never saw his parents' bodies. He just heard about it.'

I looked away and sighed. 'I haven't even opened the mail. There's so much of it and I think it's nearly all about Mum and Dad and I just think it's going to be so depressing reading it. I don't even answer the phone most of the time.'

'Yeah I've noticed. Well, that's one thing I can help with while I'm here. We can open the mail together and go through it and work out which ones you want to answer. If any.'

'Oh, it's going to be so good to have you here. I just don't think I should let you read Lee's letters.'

She grinned. 'That's better. You're getting a bit of life back. Can I have another coffee?'

With my back to her as I poured the coffee I said slowly, 'You see, Fi, what I keep wondering is, whether what's happened is my fault.'

A lot of people would have jumped in right there with the comfort hugs, and said reassuring things like 'Oh no, Ellie, whatever gave you that idea, of course it's not your fault, you have to stop thinking like that', and so on. Fi had more sense than that. She didn't say anything.

I brought the coffee back to the table and sat down again. Without looking at her I said, 'Why did they pick out this place? Of all the farms, all the properties, all the houses to choose, why this one?'

'You're close to the border.'

'We're on the border, more or less. Except for a bit of bush. But so are thousands of other people. There are plenty of places they could have gone for.'

'So you're saying this is deliberate revenge. That they picked you out because of what we did during the war.'

'Exactly. We did do rather a lot of damage.'

'I can't believe all the stuff we blew up.'

'Me neither.' One of them had been her house, which had been used by enemy officers as a base. But she didn't seem to be thinking about that, and I wasn't going to mention it unless she did.

'Well, you might be right about them targeting you.'

'Oh God, Fi, don't say that. I can't bear to be right. I don't want to be right. You're saying I killed my parents.'

'No, you're saying that. The truth is that you don't know, I don't know, no-one knows. No-one on this side of the border anyway. But even if it's true, what was the alternative? That you should have been a coward during the war? That you should have been able to look into the future and see this would happen and then, I don't know, what next? You should have surrendered to the nearest authorities and had yourself locked up?'

'Something like that.'

I knew it was irrational, but I couldn't stop the thoughts buzzing round in my head like dodgem cars.

Fi took a sip of her coffee and gave Gavin another back rub. After a while she said slowly, 'Of course if you're right, they could have been out to get you, not your parents.'

'Gosh, you're a comforting person to have around. But yes, that did cross my mind.'

'Have you done anything about it?'

'How do you mean?'

'Like, protecting yourself? And Gavin?'

'No, because if they come back, I figure it won't be for a while. They'll know the district'll be in an uproar and there'll be people ready for them. But it doesn't stop me jumping about a metre when I hear any funny noises.' I pushed my empty mug away. 'Oh, Fi, all I want to do is be normal again. Reverse the clock. Have Mum and Dad back, and Grandma, and go to school and muck around on the bus and tell stupid jokes and stir the teachers and play soccer at lunchtime and be in another drama production.'

'Does anyone really appreciate life while they have it?'

'Oh, what's that from? Where have I heard that before?'

'It's that play we did in Year 9.'

'Oh yes. *Our Town*. "The poets and philosophers, maybe they do some." Wasn't that the answer?'

'Something like that.'

'I think babies appreciate it too. Not babies: infants, toddlers, whatever they call them. You know what I mean? The way they play in water, or look at a butterfly. The way they go crazy if you take them for a ride on a motorbike.'

'And artists. Monet. When you look at his paintings you have to think, OK, he must have switched off the TV for an afternoon or two. He was right into it.'

'People who notice stuff.'

'I guess. Speaking of your grandmother, did you ever hear any more news about her?'

'No, nothing.'

'I never told you this, but I felt she was dead when we were hiding in her house during the war.'

'Really? You mean, like in a psychic way?'

'Yes.'

Homer came in, banging the kitchen door and making me jump. He twitched a bit himself when he saw Fi. They had a history and although they'd drifted apart they were still officially a couple. I always had an eye on Homer myself and I needed to know where he and Fi were going. I was a bit suspicious of Fi's claims that her feelings about him had changed. She was always totally fascinated any time she heard me or anyone else talking about him.

'You want a coffee?' I asked him.

'No thanks.'

He sat on one of the chairs. Of course he had to pick the broken one. He got up again in a hurry and looked at it in embarrassment.

'Don't worry, it's been broken since I got my first dummy. Dad was always going to fix it.'

'I'll have a look at it after.'

He took the last of the peanut cookies from the jar on the table and ate it slowly, a nibble at a time. I watched him, thinking, 'Another trace of my mother gone. There won't be any more peanut cookies.'

Fi said to Homer, 'Ellie's thinking the guys who did this might have been after her family in particular. Or her. Targeting people who did the most damage during the war.'

'It's possible,' Homer said, straight away.

I suddenly had the feeling they'd had this conversation already, out of my hearing. Maybe at the funeral. Maybe by phone. 'What you think?' I asked Homer.

'General Finley thinks most of them just target places at random, looking for stuff to steal.'

'Oh! General Finley! He sent the nicest flowers.'

General Finley was the New Zealand officer who organised some of our 'guerilla' stuff during the war. He was pretty important in the Army. I thought of him as a friend, even though we hadn't spent a lot of time together.

'Huh,' Fi said. 'You remember his flowers, but you don't even remember me being there.'

Homer said: 'Well, according to General Finley, there's been a pattern of killings, groups coming across the border in search of whatever they can find. And he reckons the media only report about a quarter of the cases.'

'So the rumours were true. I knew I should have listened to them.' I gazed at Homer, trying to process all this information. 'You've been talking to the General?'

'Only by phone. But we've had a couple of long conversations. Plus his son's here.'

'His son? Here in Wirrawee? You're kidding!'

'He is in Wirrawee at the moment. But he's been living in Stratton, and going to school there. His mother lives in Stratton – she's Australian, but she and the General are divorced.'

'How old is he?'

'About our age. I've been talking to him too. Good bloke. Got a bit of common sense. You could take him fox-shooting and be pretty certain you wouldn't get a bullet up your bum.'

Coming from Homer, this was high praise.

'So why aren't they doing anything about these raids? How come soldiers can just come over the border any time they want and kill anyone they want?'

Homer tapped a fork on the edge of the table and gazed out the window, frowning. 'I suppose it comes down to politics in the long run,' he said. 'These guys who killed your parents and Mrs Mac. You just called them soldiers, and we all know they are soldiers, everyone knows that, but how do you prove it? They don't wear uniforms, they don't carry any papers ID'ing them as military, and every time there's one of these raids their government says they're very sorry but they can't be responsible for criminal elements who take the law into their own hands. I mean, they say all the right things. They even say they'll track them down and bring them to justice but funnily enough they never seem able to do it.'

He leaned back on the chair. I thought that at any moment we'd have another one broken. 'Ellie, I don't know how you're going to feel about this, but the truth is that it's too dangerous to let you stay here anymore. We think you should sell the place and move into town. Somewhere safe. General Finley thinks so too.'

Trust Homer to choose words that were bound to stir me up and get the opposite result to the one he wanted. He did that every time. I blamed his Greekishness. He had to be the boss. Well, stuff that for a joke. I had to be the boss.

'*Let* me stay here!' I exploded. 'Since when do you decide whether you're going to let me stay here or not?'

He pushed the chair back about a metre. Gavin retreated towards the pantry. Fi stayed where she was but she kept her head down.

'That's the trouble with you, Homer, you think everything on this goddamn planet should be under your control. That no-one should eat breathe sleep or shit unless it's with your permission. You know how long my family's been here? You know what we've been through to keep this place? Homer, my family's eaten dirt and dug dams with their bare hands to keep it going. You think I'm going to walk out on it now, after my parents died to defend it? I tell you what, Homer, I'm not quitting. I'm here to stay.'

'Go Ellie!' Gavin yelled.

I looked at him in astonishment. How could he have lip-read all of that?

'Have you got the slightest idea what we're talking about?' I asked him.

'Sure,' he replied straight away. 'Homer wants you to quit the farm and you're saying "No way".'

I shook my head. I never could work out how Gavin understood so much of what was going on, but he had his ways. Maybe he had an aerial on his head, buried in his thick mop of hair.

'What do you think we should do?' I asked him.

Since my parents got killed, no-one had mentioned the problem of Gavin. I hadn't thought much about it myself. There'd been no time for that. Everything was still too fresh, too raw, too recent. Was I going to be left to look after him myself? In this new world, even that was possible. There were so many orphans, so many homeless kids. If there was a scale that gave a 'one' to kids living in dumpsters and a 'ten' to the Brady Bunch, Gavin still rated a three or a four with just me to take care of him, no parents of his own, and my mum and dad, his foster-parents, killed in a massacre.

'Stay here,' he said promptly.

'But it's dangerous,' I said.

'Life's dangerous,' he said, with a funny little shrug of his shoulders.

It was a breath-stopping moment. I realised how much I underestimated Gavin sometimes. It was too easy to forget that this boy, with nothing but the strength of his personality, had not only survived many months of the war in the ruins of Stratton but had held together a group of other feral kids under his leadership. He was something special.

'Well,' I said to Homer and Fi, 'you heard him.'

Fi looked distressed, Homer grumpy. They both began talking at once, in urgent voices. 'Ellie, you've got to listen to reason –' Homer started saying. 'Ellie, you might want to think about this a bit longer –' Fi said.

For the first time since the death of my parents I felt real strength. 'No,' I said. 'I'm staying right here. I don't care what I do. If I have to fight I'll fight. Don't you understand? You two, of all people?' I felt like I didn't need to shout anymore. I was certain now. 'Homer, Fi, my roots go as deep into this earth as any old redgum. That creek down there is my life's blood. These paddocks, I know them like I know my own skin. I can take you to the jumper ant nest in Nellie's, I can show you where the lichen on the southern side of the fenceposts is red and the eastern side is yellow. You know that gully over there beyond the shearing shed? Those willows in it are the ones my grandfather planted to stop the soil erosion. I know where the pink fingers flower and the coral-peas, and the sundews, and I know how to make them catch crumbs of bread.'

'The flowers?' Fi said, looking startled, but I wasn't going to let her interrupt me. I could hear that I was talking wildly but I couldn't shut up.

'I know the kind of moo a calf makes when it's got bracken poisoning. I know the cow whose udder looks good but whose milk is poor. I know the way Romneys graze differently to Polwarths. I can tell you how many bags of seed potatoes you need to the acre. Dammit, I can castrate lambs with my teeth.'

Gavin jumped away fast, holding his hands to his crotch. We all laughed then. Once again I had no idea how he followed such a long speech. Lip-reading is seriously hard! But he sure had understood that last sentence.

At least he'd broken the mood. We started talking more sensibly. And I began to realise just how serious the problems were. Fi spelt it out. 'Look,' she said, 'I don't know anything about farming. But if I've got it right, you're planning to keep going with school, keep running the property on your own, and somehow keep yourself and Gavin safe from guerillas who might come roaming through the countryside. And as if all that's not enough, you've got to try to cope with the death of your parents and Mrs Mac. It's a pretty tough order, Ellie. I mean, I can stay a while, like I said, because we've only got a week of term left, and then two weeks holidays, but after that my parents'll probably want me back. And I don't know how much use I'm going to be to you anyway. I can hardly tell the difference between a cow and a sheep.'

'You'd soon find out if you tried to castrate a calf with your teeth,' I said.

CHAPTER 4

I WANDERED LONELY as a cloud along the escarpment overlooking the house. I'd wanted to bury my parents up here, but the priest said it would break twenty-seven different laws and then some. So now they were in the old cemetery behind St Matthew's. I thought of their cold damaged bodies lying in that cold ground and shuddered. I'd been there a few times and put flowers on the grave and done all that stuff. I'd hoped I'd have some mystical experience when I was there, feel their spirits, hear them talking to me, get a bit of advice about the price I should ask for the twenty steers, or at least get a sense of peace, whatever, but so far I'd been sadly disappointed. I didn't feel anything. Just devastated and depressed, and I could feel that anywhere. Didn't need to go to the cemetery for it.

Gavin hated going there. The first time he'd come as far as the gate and the other times he wouldn't even get out of the car.

I wondered how long it would take Gavin to realise

that I'd snuck out the back door and come up this hill. He was more than ever my little shadow these days. I understood why. I was his last link to security, his last hope of a relatively normal life. I understood that but it didn't necessarily make it easier to bear. A lot of the time it didn't bother me, but sometimes it was just too much, too relentless, too suffocating, every sentence starting with the words 'I want', and I'd turn on him and, snap, 'Leave me alone! Give me a break! Go find something else to do.'

Then sooner or later – usually sooner – I'd be racked by guilt and start imagining Gavin scarred for life and how it was all my fault. Sometimes even that wasn't enough to send me looking for him to make it up to him though. And I think he was pretty scarred anyway.

I sat on a rock with my arms around my knees and gazed at the farm. I could see Fi's window, with the curtain drawn. She'd still be in bed. Talk about slack. She'd never make a farmer, even if she did eventually learn the difference between a sheep and a cow.

I was actually up on the escarpment because I was trying to come to terms with the idea that I wouldn't be a farmer for long myself. Yesterday I'd had an interview with Mr Sayle. He was a lawyer in Wirrawee. I didn't know him very well. Fi's mother used to do our legal work but when she moved to the city Dad had to find someone new, and he chose Mr Sayle.

I'd had a message asking me to see him, so off I'd gone, like a good Ellie. I left Gavin in the Wirrawee Library, which to his disgust was so crowded that they'd closed the waiting list for the computers, and I'd gone into Mr Sayle's office, across the road.

My first shock was to find that his receptionist was

Mrs Samuels, who used to deliver the mail to our place and various other farms. More importantly, she was the one who'd recognised me in a prison camp during the war. As a result she had caused me huge problems. I'd been in Camp 23 under a false name, knowing that if the guards found out my true identity, I'd be tied to the front of a missile launcher while enemy soldiers queued up to press the 'Fire' button.

Mrs Samuels hadn't meant any harm but she'd nearly cost me my life, by accidentally yelling out my real name. Since the war she'd been embarrassed every time she saw me so our conversations tended to be short and sweet. It was the same with this one.

'Hi, Mrs Samuels.'

'Oh, Ellie! Hi. Hi. Lovely to see you. Mr Sayle won't be long.'

Red-faced she went back to her desk, hunching over a knitting pattern book like it was the Dead Sea Scrolls.

'OK, thanks.'

I was relieved to be able to sit down and pick up a very old *Bulletin* magazine, from before the war, and start reading that.

Mr Sayle didn't look like a solicitor, more like a bull-dozer driver. He was big, filling the doorway, and dressed in clothes that could have been made by King Gee, even if he did wear a tie. He was balding, with a few strands of hair carefully plastered across the big bald area. He didn't even look at me.

'Mrs Samuels, call the Council, will you, and see what's happening about the planning application. You're Ellie. Come in, Ellie.'

I was glad he'd told me who I was. It's always a relief to know who you are.

Three minutes after I'd started the conversation with him the door opened a few centimetres and Gavin slipped in. That's what I mean about having a shadow.

Mr Sayle just ignored him and within the next few minutes I pretty much forgot he was there. Mr Sayle seemed like a nice enough guy, but he didn't muck around. First he explained that he was the executor for my parents' estate, then he explained what that meant, and then he told me that under my parents' wills I was the sole heir.

Then he told me I was bankrupt. Broke. No money. He wasn't quite that tactless, but he was blunt.

'Ellie, I've been through the books, and talked to the bank, and I'm afraid your financial position is very poor indeed. Beyond recovery, I have to say. As you know, a lot of savings were lost during the war, and the government is still negotiating to get some of that money back, but I think it would be unrealistic to put much faith in that. So once the war finished, your father had to start from a position of virtually no funds, and in the meantime he entered into a number of financial obligations that assumed there would be a long-term improvement in his situation.'

Gavin yawned and stretched and pressed against me. Mr Sayle riffled through the papers in his folder.

'Those obligations included a loan from the bank, to establish a poultry business. That loan was secured by a mortgage on the property. Then there was a second loan, secured by mortgaging various goods and chattels, to purchase cattle, and as well as those commitments to the bank, he entered into three leases totalling a thousand dollars a week with parties whom I gather had been granted pieces of land from your original property.'

He glanced at me from over the top of his reading glasses. 'Yeah, that's right,' I said, feeling a little dizzy. I hadn't realised the rents Dad agreed to pay those people were so high. No wonder he'd seemed stressed. No wonder he was always complaining about money. 'What's a mortgage?' I asked. I'd heard the word often enough but I'd never bothered to find out what it meant.

'It means that if you can't pay back a loan, you hand over some property instead,' he said. 'In your case the agreement was that the farm, the part of it you still own, would be given to the bank if the money could not be repaid.'

My head seemed to ring as though I had concussion. I sat there gaping at him. 'You're saying I might lose the land and the house?' I asked. 'Everything?'

'I'm saying you will lose it, yes. That's exactly what I'm saying.'

He glanced at me again and when I didn't reply he kept talking from his notes.

'Now, I gather the principal assets consist of the land with improvements, including the main house, machinery shed, shearing shed and various other outbuildings, three motor vehicles, two tractors, an ATV, three motorbikes, one in poor condition, approximately sixty head of cattle, and sundry other livestock, tools, and equipment. As well, there's just under eight thousand dollars in various bank accounts, and a small portfolio of shares, which at this stage do not have much value, as a result of the war. We can't factor them into the equation but they may eventually prove to be worth something again.'

He looked up, and waited for me to speak.

'What's he saying?' Gavin asked me. He was kneeling

on the coffee table, virtually in my lap now, looking intently into my face. He'd sensed the tension in me, and at the same time he'd obviously decided Mr Sayle was too much of a challenge to lip-read. If he wanted to keep up to the mark he'd have to rely on me.

'He's saying we've got no money,' I said bitterly. 'He's saying we're going to lose the farm and everything. That we'll have to find somewhere else to live.'

'Believe me, Ellie,' Mr Sayle said, 'I am very unhappy about this. I've looked at the figures from every direction, and thought and thought about how we can achieve a better result. But there's nothing else for it, I'm afraid. And you won't be left with nothing, not by any means. Land is in great demand, although unfortunately there's not much money around to pay for it.'

'So how much money would I get?' I asked, forcing the words out.

Gavin gave an angry sob and shook me by the shoulders when I said it.

'Well, the valuer has given me a rough estimate and he thinks the property should fetch around four hundred and fifty thousand dollars. The various vehicles and equipment, probably eighty to a hundred thousand dollars. The cattle, a hundred and eighty thousand.'

It sounded like a lot to me. But it was hard to concentrate, with Gavin clutching me and gazing up into my face, trying to pick up every word I said.

'So, say seven hundred and twenty thousand when we add in the money in the bank accounts. Out of that have to come various expenses associated with the winding up of the estate, including the funerals and my costs, the repayments to the bank, the costs and penalties involved with the premature termination of the leases, the costs of advertising and selling the property and chattels. So after all that there should still be about a hundred and sixty thousand which will come to you.'

He beamed at me. 'Not a bad outcome really.'

'That's easy for you to say.'

He wiped the smile off his face immediately. It was like a screensaver disappearing.

'So if I wanted to keep the place going, what would I have to do?' I asked.

For the first time Gavin turned and looked at Mr Sayle.

Mr Sayle grimaced. 'Well, it's just not feasible. You'd have to generate more income than is possible. There's the thousand dollars a week to cover the lease payments, plus seven hundred and thirty dollars a week to the bank. These payments had been made by your father up to the end of this month, which is next Tuesday. Plus of course there's also the normal running expenses of a property of this size. That would be everything from fuel to seed to pesticides to tractor parts to the food for your table and the clothes on your back. You and the youngster here. I've heard about him.'

Sitting on the escarpment and looking down at the house now, I could see the youngster emerge into the courtyard. He picked up a stick, which triggered instant excitement in Marmie, the new border collie. I assumed he was going to throw it for her. It was a game that could keep both of them amused for hours. 'He's such a kid still,' I thought, looking down at him.

He marched out of the courtyard, Marmie following eagerly. Instead of throwing the stick he carried it across his shoulder. Without a glance to left or right he went on down into the gully. The first yellow flowers of the broom infestation were already starting to show through. Gavin tossed the stick aside. Marmie reared back in excitement then pounced on it. But to her disappointment, and even though she paraded it right in front of him, Gavin ignored her.

'What is he doing?' I wondered.

He went to the fenceline, rolled up his sleeves, and to my utter astonishment pulled out a broom plant, then another and another and another.

I nearly fell over and rolled all the way to the bottom of the escarpment. Instead I watched with my mouth open as he pulled out plant after plant. He worked steadily and methodically. It was the perfect time to pull out broom, before it flowered and set its seeds, but also because the ground was soft. Pulling it out was the best treatment. Chemicals were expensive and toxic. Slashing caused it to come back the next year with three or four stalks that were much harder to pull, but in some places slashing was the only option. I couldn't get a slasher into this gully, though.

The thing about broom is that it spreads so quickly and takes over so much good pasture. Dad had always been trying to persuade Gavin and me to join his anti-broom campaign, but without much success, because it's pretty boring work.

'Oh, Dad,' I whispered in my head, 'come back and I'll pull out broom forever. I'll be your broom princess.'

I'd never really been his princess of anything, but I'd been his mate, his offsider, his advisor, his daughter.

After twenty minutes I couldn't stand it any longer. I walked down the hill. Gavin was so absorbed that he didn't see me coming but Marmie suddenly noticed me and came cavorting over to say hello. Empty-mouthed. She'd given up on the stick.

Gavin straightened up then. I'd noticed before how aware he was of any change in the environment. Although he had his back to Marmie he seemed to sense that she was reacting to something.

He took a glance at me and went back to work. That didn't surprise me. He'd hardly spoken to me the night before. He was furious that I'd given in to Mr Sayle.

'What are you doing?' I asked him. That was a waste of time as he had his back to me again.

I shrugged and found my own line of broom parallel to his and started pulling those out. After a while I almost forgot he was there. I got into a rhythm, the way you do. I reduced the boredom by counting the number of plants. I reached my first hundred in four or five minutes.

I was halfway to my second when suddenly I was attacked. A wild little whirling dervish was whipping me with a long broom plant. I backed off, defending myself with my hands, trying to grab the plant and pull it away.

'Gavin, what is this all about?'

'You're stupid,' he yelled. 'You're pathetic.' His eyes were full of tears.

I screamed back. 'What do you think? That I want to sell the place? You know I love it here. It's my home. I thought we'd always be here. I feel as bad as you do. Worse.'

'No you don't! You're not even fighting! You don't care! You're pathetic!'

He started ripping broom out of the ground, not caring whether he was getting the roots or not, sobbing as he did it. Suddenly he stopped and turned on me again. 'You're a coward! You don't have guts!'

'It's not a matter of guts! It's common sense. It's money. What would you know about it?'

'Dad wouldn't give in.'

I started to answer, then realised with a shock that he was talking about my father. Occasionally he had called him 'Dad', but it always seemed like an accident. It took me a moment to recover, then all I could say was, 'He would when things were this bad,' which sounded pretty weak even to me.

I walked away and went down to the lagoon. I stood there looking out over the water. This had been my father's dream. To the horror of my grandfather he'd resurrected this area, taking it out of production and turning it over to trees and native plants and birds. It was as though my father had brought life back to this tired and over-grazed area, as though the breeze that stirred the long green reeds was my father's breath. I felt then what I hadn't felt in the cemetery, like he was alive again, that maybe he hadn't died after all.

My shadow was beside me and he put an arm around my leg as Marmie wandered along the edge of the water, in it up to her knees, sniffing for nests in the under-growth.

'Gavin, we'd need to make two thousand bucks a week,' I said to him. 'That's so much money.'

He didn't answer.

'There's eight thousand in the bank. That'd only keep us going for a month.'

He frowned up at me.

'I don't know the first thing about money,' I said. 'Not a damn thing. Every time we play Monopoly I lose.'

He looked away.

'There's a hundred cents in the dollar, that's about all I know,' I told the back of his neck, which couldn't hear me.

He looked around at me again, impatiently.

I held him at arm's length and spoke straight into his face. 'Gavin, do you understand that we could end up losing everything? At the moment we'd have enough to get a little house in Wirrawee and keep us fed and clothed. Doing what you want, we could end up sleeping in dumpbins.'

He shook his head and hit me on the arm. He was strong enough; he really hurt.

'Fight,' he said. 'If you fight, you win or you lose. If you don't fight, you lose.'

I stood there gazing at the lagoon, my mind in an agony of indecision. Finally I turned to him.

'We'd both have to work like we've never worked before,' I said. 'If you're going to pull up broom for ten minutes and then get sick of it, well, say so now, so I know where we are. We're going to have to work before we go to school and work when we get home. You can forget about sleepovers with your mates and birthday parties and blue-light discos. You can forget about weekends and school holidays. You can forget about your social life. We can't afford to employ anyone. We'll have to do it on our own.'

He gazed at me with his face and jaw set in the bull-dog glare I knew so well. Then he marched away over the rise. I followed him, thinking we were heading home. But I got it wrong again. He swung left, back into the gully, and we both started pulling up more broom.

CHAPTER 5

THAT SAME EVENING my social life actually seemed to take a turn for the better. I was totally exhausted. We'd pulled broom for more than two hours, with a bit of help from Fi when she finally surfaced. Then we fed the cattle, and the surviving poultry, while Fi organised lunch. After that we put in a hard afternoon on the new cattle yards. The old yards had been OK, but they were built sometime before Captain Cook. While the farm was occupied by the enemy, during the war, it seemed like one of them had lost control of a vehicle, probably a tractor, and kaboodled it through the rails, smashing part of the holding yard. Then Dad had pinched a lot of the old timber crossbars for the turkey and geese sheds.

When we got the farm back he'd decided to start again from scratch and build the yards he'd always wanted. With double races, hot showers, cappuccino machine, satellite television, you get the idea. Nothing's too good for our cattle. He'd done some of the hard yakka already, but not enough of it. At least he'd dug the holes. We had a post-hole digger that was run off the tractor, so it wasn't really such hard work, but I wasn't sure if I could operate it without his help.

He'd also put in a set of scales, which was something he'd always wanted. I just hoped he'd paid for them. They cost around twenty thousand dollars but they were useful. Or so Dad said. When it comes to guys and gadgets I'm always a bit suspicious. But it's true that a 300 kilogram beast can lose twenty of those kilos after twelve hours in the yards, and at the same time it's compulsory to yard them for twelve hours before sending them in to be sold, so you do need to know what's going on in terms of their weight.

I'd spend twelve hours in the yards myself if I thought it'd knock twenty kilos off me.

I explained all this to Gavin as we worked, in the same way that Dad had always explained stuff to me. Gavin did seem like one of those kids who had a genuine interest in farming. By God he was good that day too. He stuck to his guns. He'd said he was going to work – not in so many words but near enough – and he did. He never complained once, hardly ever got distracted, only took a break when I did, and – this is the mark of the true worker, I reckon – started anticipating.

Dad always said there were three types of workers. The ones who stood there saying 'Is there anything I can do?', and did nothing. Most of our city guests were like that. The ones who said 'Tell me what you want done and I'll do it', and did. Most of our workers over the years had been like that. And the ones who didn't say anything but were always a jump or two ahead of you. When you were changing a flat tyre and you took the old one off and turned to pick up the new one they'd already have it in their hands, and they'd move in and put it on from your left while you were still turning round to the right.

Dad reckoned one of those was worth two of the second type and five of the first type.

And there were quite a few times when Gavin was like that. I'd be on my knees and I'd reach behind me for the ratchet wrench to tighten a nut, and he'd come in from the other side and be doing it while I was still wondering where I'd put the bloody thing.

I think I had my first glimmerings of the possibility of happiness that day. It wasn't the free light-hearted happiness I'd known as a child, because I'd never have that again. From now on any good feelings were going to be under-shaded by the awfulness of what had happened. My personal castle was always going to have a big dark basement. Guess it already did, after the war, and losing my grandmother and Robyn and Corrie and Chris and the others. But the basement had got a hell of a lot bigger recently. Maybe that day I had the first faint awareness that I could still live in the castle. It hadn't been totally demolished.

It got dark early of course, and we were both pleased to call it a day and stagger back to the house. I'd had plenty of hard days on the farm, but it was different now, because before it had all been just physical. I'd do the different jobs, sure, but Dad decided the important stuff. I'd be responsible for doing each of my jobs properly, but I didn't have the feeling of responsibility for the whole thing, the big picture. I didn't have the mental weight, back then.

Just as I flopped down in front of the TV, having put away a kilo of Fi's pasta, and made a few admiring remarks about the way she'd cleaned up the house, I heard a car outside. I was so jumpy that I lifted a metre out of the chair. Of course if the gunmen returned they wouldn't be likely to drive straight up to the house, but sometimes your mind doesn't function very calmly.

It turned out to be Homer, but not 'Homer alone', as I said to Fi, adding, 'Hey, good name for a movie.' That was my best joke of the year, which gives some idea of how badly things were going. But I was seriously annoyed when I saw that he'd brought a bunch of people. It wasn't just that I was still in a severe state of shatter over what had happened to my parents, but as well I was exhausted from the day's work, I was stressing over how I could tell Mr Sayle that maybe I didn't want to sell the property after all, I was grubby and smelly and in my work clothes because I'd been too tired to take a shower before tea. And now I was expected to be the host of a party.

I don't think Homer noticed any of that. He ushered them into the kitchen happily and introduced them to Fi and me. Not to Gavin, who as soon as he realised what was happening stomped off sulkily to watch TV. He was so jealous of me now, Gavin, and he didn't like sharing me with anyone. But a carload of teenagers was too much competition, and all he could do was retreat.

There were three of them, besides Homer. The one who first caught my attention was Jeremy Finley, the son of General Finley, who'd helped us so much during the war. General Finley had also caused us a lot of problems but, like the Chinese say, 'the cured patient forgets the pain', and these days I felt pretty good about him.

Jeremy was tall and skinny and seemed like a nice guy: and he had a sense of humour. He immediately handed me this plastic bag. 'Chocolate and avocados,' he said as I opened it to peer inside. 'My dad said that'd really impress you. And sorry, but they don't make Iced Vo-Vos anymore.'

I blushed a bit, with pleasure. General Finley had surprised me again. It was many months since I'd yelled into a radio to tell him how desperate I was for chocolate and avocados and Iced Vo-Vos. We'd been at the top of Tailor's Stitch, near our hiding place during the war, trying to get in touch with New Zealand, and General Finley had asked if we wanted anything. I couldn't believe he'd remembered my list of requests. Maybe he had it programmed into his computer, in the Ellie file.

'They don't make Iced Vo-Vos anymore?' I asked Jeremy.

'Yeah, I think the Vo-Vo trees got blown up in a guerilla raid,' he said.

'That's terrible.'

'Yep,' Homer said. 'War sure is hell.'

He introduced me to Bronte, who had one of those thoughtful looking, attractive faces. I like people with eyes like oceans, where you know straight away that even if you talk to them for a thousand years they'll still have secrets from you.

I already knew Jess, who was dark-skinned, with lively eyes that were forever scanning the room. She seemed like she noticed everything. Jess used to live in Stratton but they'd moved to Wirrawee. Their house had been bombed so they arrived in Wirrawee with whatever they had in their pockets, which wasn't much. At first Jess often wore a black top to school, a black top with silver edging. One day Bridget Allen, who can be a real bitch when she wants to be, and most days she definitely wants to be, told Jess how it was my top, which I'd put into one of the charity bins that we all gave heaps of stuff to, and funny about that, Jess never wore the top again.

Jess's father was an IT teacher and her mother had gone off to America with another woman, which by the standards of the old Wirrawee was spectacular gossip. These days people didn't take a lot of notice.

I did start to warm up a bit. I got three coffees, a tea, a cordial and a water, and we sat around the kitchen table. Bronte and Jess were at Wirrawee High. At the start of the year Homer and I had enrolled in a special accelerated course, but we couldn't do the workload, so we'd both gone back into normal streams. We were still a year above Bronte. There was a time when that wouldn't have mattered, I'd have known her anyway, but since the war Wirrawee High had suddenly grown to nearly twice its previous size, and there were heaps of people I didn't know.

Jeremy was from Stratton. I had the feeling that he and Jess might be an item, or were on the verge of becoming an item. Or they would become an item eventually but didn't know it themselves yet.

Bronte was pretty quiet. Jess and Jeremy did most of the talking, with Homer contributing an occasional grunt. Fi and I were both too tired, even with the caffeine hits. We probably needed a litre of caffeine intravenously.

Jess started asking me about the guys who'd killed my parents. Gradually she probed deeper and deeper.

'I think they just pick places at random,' I said, although I know I always went a bit white-faced when I thought about the alternatives.

'What do you think they wanted?'

'To steal stuff I guess.'

'Yes, I suppose. Did they steal anything?'

'Well, no. But with four of them killed, I imagine the others panicked and took off.'

'How many do you think there were?'

'I don't know. The police looked at the tracks. But I haven't heard anything from them for nearly a week. So I'm not sure if they came up with much evidence. I get the feeling that there's so much happening with border fights and everything, and so many new people moving into the district . . . I think they're just overwhelmed. And face it, what chance do they have of finding these guys?'

'Not much I guess. But there are a few rumours going around.'

'Like what?'

'Oh, you know, camps of renegade soldiers, right near the border. People say they're responsible for a lot of the raids.'

'Oh, I hadn't heard about that.'

She shrugged. 'It's just a rumour.'

'Jess is the Rumour Queen,' Jeremy said. 'You want to know who you're with? She knows it before you do.'

I blushed a bit, thinking of how a few minutes earlier I'd been thinking that maybe he was with Jess.

Jess came back to the murders again.

'Does it make you mad?' she asked me.

I nodded. Our eyes locked together. It was weird, like I was being interrogated almost. She asked me a series of quick questions.

'What do you think should happen about it?'

'It has to be stopped of course. How can we live like this?'

'Stopped by who?'

'I don't know. The Army. The police.'

'What if they can't? Or won't?'

'If they really won't, I suppose people have to protect themselves.'

'The law of the jungle?'

'I don't know. I know that's not the best way. But we can't let them just wander around killing anyone they want.'

'So people have to defend themselves?'

'Maybe. Seems like it.'

'How far do you reckon they should go to defend themselves? Across the border, for example?'

I leaned back and sighed and pushed my hair out of my face.

'I'm sorry. It's too early for me to think about all this.'

Jess immediately switched off. 'Oh yes, sorry. I didn't mean to throw so many questions at you. You're in such a horrible situation.'

'What are you going to do, Ellie?' Jeremy asked.

'Depends on which day you ask me. A couple of days ago I would have said sell up and move out. Today it looks like I'm going to try to make the place work.'

Homer rolled his eyes. 'Make up your mind,' he said. 'I thought you were broke?'

'I am. But, I don't know, I don't want to give up without a fight.' I was too embarrassed to admit that Gavin had talked me into staying.

'Fair enough,' Homer said. 'Shame in one way. My old man was all fired up to buy your place and expand his empire. But he'll cope with the disappointment. Count on me for any help you want.'

'Thanks,' I said. 'If things go like I'm expecting, you'll

probably hear our pathetic fingernails scratching on your door one night, and our pathetic voices crying out for a crust of bread.'

Gavin came swinging into the kitchen, went to the fridge and got himself some Linton's cordial. I tried to introduce him to the three visitors as he poured the cordial into the glass, but he deliberately wouldn't look up. Somehow though he managed to spill half the drink onto the bench. I sighed and went for a Chux.

That night I lay in bed staring up into the darkness. I couldn't sleep a wink. It wasn't just the worry of how we were going to make two thousand bucks a week, although God knows, that was enough to keep anyone awake. I couldn't understand how my father had ever managed to get a peaceful night's sleep in his life. But it was also Jess's questions. I knew what she was getting at of course, but up until then I'd managed to avoid thinking about it.

I put a lot of energy into avoiding thinking about things these days. Since the murders I hadn't slept much. It wasn't only that the vastness of night gave room for dark and sad and awful thoughts. It was also that a lot of memories of my parents were associated with night-time. Lying in bed as a little kid I would hear the sound of their voices washing down the corridor and over me, my father's chuckles, my mother's dry laugh, my father reading articles from the latest issue of *Inland Outback* and my mother commenting from time to time. I'd hear my father going outside to check the dogs and I'd hear his footsteps on the gravel, then on the dust, then echoing along the verandah as he circumnavigated the house, just a habit he had before he went to bed, making sure everything was 'shipshape and Bristol fashion', as he called it.

I heard a sound in the corridor, and a moment later Gavin came into my room, his feet padding across the floor. I shifted over and let him in. He grunted like a koala. Couldn't even have my bed to myself these days. But he made a nice hot-water bottle.

He went back to sleep within a minute but I still couldn't. I started wondering what my parents would have said, what they would have wanted me to do. I'm not necessarily a big fan of that approach though. It's like those Grand Prix car races – when a driver or a spectator is killed they always go on with the race, because they say 'That's what he would have wanted'. Well, I'll tell you now, if I'm ever stupid enough to be a spectator at a Grand Prix and I get killed, I want the race stopped there and then. I want everyone to go straight home. I want three days of mourning, make that three days minimum, and I want all the cars painted black for the rest of the season. And five minutes silence before every race from then on. And the drivers to dedicate their future victories to Ellie Linton. Stuff the 'She would have wanted us to keep going like normal' approach.

When it came to the farm, I think my father would have said 'You don't have to carry it on if you don't want to', but all the time he'd be hoping like hell that I would. I think my mother would have said 'You don't have to carry it on if you don't want to', and she would have meant it. When it came to getting revenge for their deaths, going after the people who'd killed them, both of them would have said 'Don't worry about that, don't put your life in danger, we just want you to stay alive'.

Well, I was quite keen to stay alive too, but you've got to do what you've got to do, and although I hadn't had time to think it through, I was quite certain that something severe had to happen to the people who'd killed my parents and Mrs Mac.

And yes, if I had to get involved in bringing that about, I would do whatever I had to do.

I gave a big sigh and rolled over. Against my back Gavin wriggled and made a few mumbling noises. I still hadn't faced up to the other big issue, and I didn't want to. But it seemed like I wasn't going to get a choice. Like a monster this huge fear had sneaked out of the cupboard and even now was tiptoeing across the room towards me. This would have to happen in the middle of the night. I felt my tongue go dry. The monster was all around the bed now, sucking the air from the room. I heard myself make a whimpering noise. The monster was leaning over me, I could feel the heat of its body. I took a deep breath. My eyes were wide open in the darkness, but not seeing anything. If it had to be faced, I'd face it. I worked my throat a few times, trying to get some moisture back in my mouth. OK then. If these people had come to the farm deliberately, if they were looking for me, if this was a revenge attack because of what I'd done in the war . . . that was what Jess was getting at of course. It was the thought that kept creeping into my mind on a daily basis.

And now I could give up any thought of sleeping for this or any other night.

When would they be back? How could we protect ourselves? Maybe they wouldn't be back. Maybe they'd feel that they'd achieved what they wanted. They'd killed the two most important people in my life. They'd ended the lives of the two people I cared about more than the rest of the world put together. I would have sacrificed my own life for those two people, no questions asked.

Wouldn't that satisfy them? Wouldn't they be thinking 'Well, we got her a good one, that'll teach her a lesson'?

Maybe. Or maybe they were specifically out to get me, and my parents had died to stop that happening. Maybe these people had sentenced me to death and they'd return sometime soon to carry out the sentence. If it wasn't that, if it was a raid aimed at hurting me in whatever way possible, then the fact that they had lost four of their own men might have left them thinking that it still hadn't worked. They still hadn't achieved the clear-cut victory which would 'teach me a lesson'.

So if it were one of those two things, they would be back.

Oh God. I hadn't wanted to come to that conclusion. I turned and twisted in the bed, until I felt that I was making Gavin restless. I had to calm down.

What were we to do? Give up the farm? After the scene with Gavin this morning, and all the hard work we'd done since, I knew now that I didn't want to do that.

Have sentries? Couldn't afford it. Carry rifles everywhere? Well, we already were. But it wasn't likely to be very effective. It's hard to help with calving, keep a lookout in every direction and have a finger on the trigger all at the same time.

Fight back? I didn't want to even start thinking about that.

At some stage I did drift into sleep. But in the morning, at the kitchen bench, waiting for the toast to pop, my mind returned to the monster of the night before. A monster confronted is a monster defeated, that's what I've always believed. But this time it was more complicated. This monster was capable of recreating itself, of coming back in a different form and shape on each visit. As a group of renegade soldiers with guns, last time, arriving in daylight and shooting everyone they saw. But next time it might be as a sniper up in the rocks on the escarpment, or as a gang sent to kidnap me. Or maybe they were really smart, and they'd figured out the best way of all. Maybe they'd come back time after time and kill Gavin and Fi and Homer and Lee and anyone else I was close to, so that I'd end up with no-one to love me and no-one for me to love. That would be smart all right.

With such thoughts tormenting me, and no easy answers, no obvious path to follow, I was faced with the problem of deciding what to do.

And like a lot of people in an impossible situation I did nothing.

After breakfast Gavin and I went out with a load of hay for the cattle, then checked and fed the poultry, then fuelled the vehicles, and all the time I was tense and watchful, but I didn't actually change anything. Normally I like to make things happen, to be proactive, but for once I was in a position where I didn't know how. I was waiting for someone else to make a move, so I could figure out how to respond.

CHAPTER 6

MR SAYLE WAS thunderstruck. Lightning-struck even. If he'd climbed to the top of an electricity pole with wire between his teeth and flown an aluminium kite on an aluminium string, he couldn't have been more struck. He gaped at me for what seemed like three minutes before he could answer.

'But . . . what on earth . . . ?' he finally stammered. 'Have you gone completely mad? You'll lose everything. I'm not even sure that it's legal. You're underage, remember?'

It was hard to keep my nerve in the face of this attack, which was as bad as anything I'd imagined. I tried to stay calm. I knew the worst thing I could do would be to act like a stupid emotional kid who wasn't mature enough to make big decisions.

'Well,' I said, 'the way I figure it is that my father made these business decisions, leasing the other places and borrowing the money and buying the cattle, because he knew it could work. So that means it must be possible to make the place pay. I mean, the only thing that's changed is that he's not here anymore. The farm's the same and so are the stock and so's the financial situation.'

'That's true on the face of it,' he said. 'But . . .'

I wondered how long an adult could talk to a kid without using the word 'but'. About forty seconds'd be the record for most of them, and that's on a good day.

'But that's a very superficial analysis. I'd have to say, and I don't know how to put this kindly, your father did not make prudent decisions. I mean, the exercise with turkeys and geese was misjudged, and as I said to you before, it's resulted in the property being saddled with debts, which in my professional opinion are more than can be sustained.'

'But,' I said, thinking it was about time I used the magic word myself, 'land has suddenly become more valuable, now that there's a lot less of it. And food is getting dearer by the day, especially food that needs a lot of space to produce, like beef and lamb.'

'In the first place,' he said, 'your land has no value unless you sell it. Until that time it's not worth anything in cash to you. In the second place, livestock production is a very chancy business. Disease, drought, theft, fire . . . there are so many slips twixt cup and lip. And the costs are enormous.'

'I know that,' I said. 'I've been on the land all my life.'

'There are lots of things on the land,' he said. 'Including manure.'

I didn't like him very much after that. He went on though, without noticing my reaction. 'For example, how do you plan to keep going in the next few months?'

'Use the money in the bank,' I said. 'That'll give us another month. After that, I'm not sure. Sell some cattle I guess.'

'Well, there you are,' he said in a tone of disgust, pushing himself back from his desk. 'The cattle are your future profit. If you sell them now, so soon after buying them, where do you get your income after that? Anyway, that eight thousand dollars in the bank'll soon be swallowed up. You have to eat and drink, remember. And pay electricity bills, and gas, and doctors' bills if you get sick, and vet bills if the animals need attention. What about the funerals? I've just received the invoices for those.'

I'd forgotten about those. I was losing confidence fast. 'How much are they?' I asked, in a small voice.

'It depends,' he said. 'Are you planning to pay for Mrs Mackenzie's as well as your parents'? I gather you did sign an authority, although again, being underage, it's probably not enforceable. I don't think the undertakers realised how young you are.'

'How much would it be if I paid for all three?' I asked.

He consulted his notes. 'Twelve thousand dollars,' he said. 'Twelve thousand, three hundred and eighteen dollars. And fifty-five cents.'

He had an air of triumph, as if to say 'See, you stupid little girl, you have no idea of how the real world operates, do you?'

Twelve thousand dollars! I tried not to show any reaction, but the words 'twelve thousand dollars' echoed around in my head as though I were inside a huge empty silo.

But Mr Sayle went on, and I had to force myself to concentrate. 'As it happens, a client of mine is interested in the property, and I believe he might be willing to pay as much as four hundred and twenty thousand dollars. I know that's not quite as high as we were hoping for, but it's a good price, and by selling to him you save all the costs of using a stock and station agent, and advertising.'

I sat there feeling furious, and stubborn, as stubborn as a kid on a computer. I folded my arms and glared at him. 'Mr Sayle, I don't want to sell the place, or give up the leases. A couple of the paddocks are about the best in the district. Dad always said that. Those cattle were pretty poor when we got them and they're fattening up nicely. Sure it's going to be rough for a while but in the long run it'll come together. I'm not being stupid about this. I know I can make it work.'

He shook his head as he fingered his lips. 'It's a lovely idea,' he said, 'and I don't blame you for feeling this way, when you're still so emotional about what happened. But it's simply not feasible. I'm sure you'll come to see that eventually. My problem is what to do in the mean-time. The longer you stay out there the more debt's going to accumulate.'

He went back to his folder, gave a heavy sigh, and picked up yet another piece of paper. 'I see here that under your parents' will, your guardian until you turn eighteen is . . . oh –'

I already knew what he had just found out, that my guardian was Mrs Mackenzie. Showed how much homework he'd done.

He went very red in the face. 'Well, I'm not sure what the situation is for a minor who . . . I'll have to talk to my colleagues. I imagine a court will say that . . . Who are your nearest relatives now?'

'There's my aunt, Mum's sister, but she lives a thou-sand k's away. They came to the funeral, but my uncle's got cancer. And there's my dad's brother, Uncle Bob, but he married a Canadian lady and they live in Calgary now. He couldn't get a flight for the funeral because of all the restrictions on the airports, but he's rung a few times.'

Mr Sayle pulled hard on his bottom lip. 'It's a very unusual situation,' he said at last.

'Why do you want to know anyway?' I asked. 'I don't need a guardian.'

He stared at me. I could almost hear the gears of his brain operating at maximum revs. Finally he said, 'Legally of course you must have a guardian. But from my point of view it seems as though the only way to bring you to your senses is to have your guardian make the financial decisions on your behalf. An older person will see the force of my arguments.'

'You mean,' I said, taking a deep breath, 'that my guardian could agree to have the property sold and I wouldn't have a say in it?'

'Well of course. Your guardian is in the role of a parent. Until you reach eighteen he or she makes all the decisions a parent would normally make for you.'

I picked up Gavin from the library, where I'd left him under threat of instant death if he came looking for me again, but this time he was on a computer, so he'd been happy enough to let me go to Mr Sayle on my own. I was still speechless with rage when I tapped him on the shoulder and told him we were leaving. As I did I caught a glimpse of myself in the reflective glass in the window, and I could see the two angry red spots on my pale face.

Even Gavin had the sense not to ask me anything until we were well clear of Wirrawee.

Back home I headed for the phone. At times like this I needed friends, and I was lucky that one of my friends had a mother who was a lawyer.

Fi's mum has always been a good listener and she had plenty of opportunities to practise during this phone call. I guess I still hadn't let loose with much in the way of emotions since my parents were killed. I hadn't even cried. There were people around, visitors before the funeral and after the funeral, people at the funeral too, who seemed to be waiting for me to cry, who actually kept saying, 'Go ahead and cry, Ellie, you'll feel better,' as though it were somehow incredibly important to them that I cry. They were like spectators at a car wreck, slowing down to get a good view of the blood.

I didn't cry when I was talking to Fi's mum either. I was too angry to cry. But the words poured out of me, like at least one dam inside had broken, even if the others kept firm.

Finally though I ran dry, and stood there in the kitchen, leaning against the wall, phone held to my ear, waiting for her to say something.

It was kind of reassuring to hear that she was as calm and together as ever.

'Ellie, I don't know if it's a good idea to try to hang on to the farm. I can't tell at this distance. But I can see how you have an emotional need to stay there, in the short term at least. Mind you, I'm not sure if it's good for you. But those are the kinds of decisions a guardian can help you with.'

'But I don't know who they're going to give me as a guardian,' I wailed.

'Well, it doesn't work like that. Not at your age. If you were a six-year-old, that'd be one thing. But you're old enough to have a lot of input. If you come up with someone you especially want, and it's someone reputable, then the court will probably go along with you. They're so busy nowadays. They'll grab at any solution that saves them time. Do you have anyone in mind who you think would be good, who you'd like to ask?'

'You?' I said hopefully. Then Fi and I would be even more like sisters.

She paused. 'It's very flattering that you ask me, Ellie. Thank you. And you know I'll help you in every way I can. But now that we live in the city, I don't see how it would be in your best interests to have me do it. I think you would be better off getting someone local. Someone who can be of practical help. Take a few days to think about it if you like. And when you come up with a name, let me know, and I'll make the application on your behalf, rather than going through Mr Sayle.'

I didn't think there was that much time, given the big hurry that Mr Sayle seemed to be in. And in the end there was really only one choice. If Fi couldn't become my sister, Homer had to become my brother.

Mr and Mrs Yannos were really nice about it. I sat in their huge kitchen – a kitchen bigger than most people's houses – and told them the full story, and they signed up on the spot. The thing about Mr Yannos is that he's really got attitude. He's always hated 'them', the government, the authorities, whoever 'they' are, and once he got it into his head that 'they' were out to get me, he was well and truly on my side. I don't know if Homer was serious when he said his father wanted to buy our place, but Mr Yannos never once mentioned it. He took me into his office and made me go through all the figures Mr Sayle had given me, and he sat there nodding and nodding and writing it all down. When I'd finished he looked at the figures for a long time then he suddenly turned to me and said, 'Ellie, you definitely need a lot more money. Do you know what cash flow is?'

'Yes. The amount of cash that flows through each week, to pay the bills and keep the place going.'

'That's right. Ellie, your cash flow is terrible! Terrible! What was your father thinking?' He shook his head and sucked the end of his pen. 'I don't know if it can work or not. But there are a few things we can do. We can't let these bastards win! I think you gotta meet these people you pay rent to, and tell them they have to wait a bit for their money. What they gonna do? Move back onto the farm? I don't think so. They don't want to farm. They on the piss, yes? I remember your father saying.'

I nodded and grinned. 'One lot were.'

'So. You got them over a barrel. They can drink less piss for a while. Anyway, they don't need three hundred bucks a week for their piss. Now, next, you gotta go back to the bank, borrow more money.'

'But don't I have to give them a, what's it called, mortgage? I've got nothing left to do that with.'

'Hey. You got sixty cattle, yes? Very good security, sixty cattle. Bank love that. OK, next thing, you go to government, ask for this aid they give. They got millions! They tell everyone it's for people starting farming again after the war. That's you! Your father, he say to me, I never ask no government for help, I do it on my own, but things are different now. Okay, number four, you get more stock. Sixty head, not enough. Sure, you put your eggs in one basket, but you need money fast. This way you either win big or you lose big. Lastly, start planning next crop. Start planning now! I think lucerne is nice. But we talk to man from Elders.'

On the way out, something strange happened. Homer wandered over to me just as I was heading home.

He handed me a rolled-up copy of the newspaper. 'Page three,' he said and wandered away again.

When I got home I opened the paper. There was a lot of stuff on page three but apart from the stories about the girl streaker at Wimbledon and the launch of a new brand of beer, I could see only one that Homer might have wanted me to read. It was an article about the rescue of a guy who'd been kidnapped and taken over the border.

> The controversial organisation known as Liberation has claimed responsibility for the rescue of 28-year-old Mason Dwyer.
>
> Dwyer, reunited with his family two days ago, has confirmed that the group snatched him from terrorists who had held him for nearly four weeks.
>
> Dwyer has alleged that he was to be executed 'within days' if the demands of the kidnappers were not met. 'I'm very grateful to Liberation,' he said yesterday from his parents' home in Stratton.
>
> The group has also claimed responsibility for several other rescue missions.
>
> Rumours that the group has links to the military have been denied by Army commanders. The Minister for Post-War Reconstruction, Mrs O'Shane, said yesterday that while she was happy for Mr Dwyer's family that he had been recovered alive and well, she was concerned about groups who crossed the border illegally.
>
> 'There are people who for the best motives want to engage in cross-border activity,' she said. 'It is not helpful in the long run, and they should leave the recovery of prisoners or kidnap victims to the

appropriate authorities. Amateur groups may not realise what they are getting themselves into. The government will not be held responsible for this kind of vigilante behaviour.'

I finished the article feeling quite confused. What was going on? Why was Homer so interested in this stuff? What kind of message was he trying to send me?

CHAPTER 7

WHEN YOU'VE ONLY got sixty head of cattle, each one suddenly becomes very precious. The cows started calving three days after my visit to Mr and Mrs Yannos. From checking them once a day we went up to three times a day. It wasn't just a simple matter of driving round the paddock and admiring the nice cows. You have to decide whether each one is better or worse than the day before, how close she is to calving, whether she's showing signs of distress, if she's gone off on her own, if her fanny's all floppy and she looks uncomfortable. At the same time as you're doing that, you're also looking for weeds or insects in the pasture, you keep an eye on the fences and gates, you make sure the drinking troughs have got water, and you clean them out if they need it. And so it goes on.

At least the cows still weren't too fat, which was a good thing. For some reason that I don't understand, cows who are too fat often have trouble calving.

Most calves drop without problems, but there's

always a few that won't behave. The trouble was that if my father hadn't been killed, the new yards would have been finished. As it was they were a long way from being finished. That meant we were faced with having nowhere to hold a cow who needed help. So Gavin and Fi and I put in a frantic twenty-four hours to get the crush done at least, and a race into it, which meant we could look after one cow at a time. I just hoped there wouldn't be half a dozen suddenly demanding admission to the Maternity Ward.

What you look for is a calf that presents with two front legs and its head coming out first. They seem to find every imaginable way of twisting and turning around though. Different signs show you that the mother's in trouble. You usually see her acting strangely, and when you get a close look you see that the little hoofs are pointing upwards, for example. Or you see dry yellow hooves sticking out. Or you see nothing, even though the cow's been in labour a long time.

There are times when you have to pull the calf to get it into a good position to be born, and there are times when the only way to pull it is to tie a rope to a hoof at one end and at the other end a car or a tractor. This is very bad news though. The death rate is high for calves who need that kind of drastic treatment. Can't say I'd like it done to me.

The second calf looked like a shocker. He was bum first, which is a big problem. You don't get any warning of that. I moved the four wheel drive in and told Gavin to get the winch ready while I pushed my arm in and started working the calf's leg around. Eventually I got the chain on, then the same with the hook, into the socket. I gave Gavin a wave and away we went with the winch, nice and slowly. It went well. Within a few minutes we had a new little wet and wobbly calf. And the cow eating the placenta, which is not the most attractive sight in the world. This sloppy big thing, about the size of a family pizza, rolling around in its mouth.

I'm glad it worked. If it had been a disaster I might have lost confidence, which would have been dangerous with the calving just started.

Fi, to be honest, was pretty hopeless with the cattle, because she was too scared of them. She thought they'd bite her. 'Fi,' I kept telling her, 'they don't even have upper teeth! They can't do you much damage. They might gum you to death.'

But she made the cattle nervous so I gave her jobs she could do at a safe distance.

The neighbours were great. Mr Yannos came round every day, or else he sent Homer, or Homer's big brother, George. Mr Sanderson, who'd got the other part of our farm, never missed a day. He didn't know a lot about cattle but he was a fast learner. Other people called in regularly or occasionally.

I carried a couple of rifles in the ute these days. One was my father's .222, the other had belonged to the dead soldiers who'd killed my parents. Homer had knocked off their rifles before the police came. I don't know what he did with the other three; I didn't ask. I knew I was breaking about a dozen laws, but I guess I had different attitudes to stuff like that since the war. Laws were for the stupid, the immature, the irresponsible. The inflexible and the narrow-minded. The prejudiced. The obsessive. The lazy and careless and selfish and spoilt. The violent. I knew that if the killers came back I wouldn't be getting any help from the police or the Army: not help that would come in time. And I knew I was responsible with guns. I kept the ammo in a locked tin behind the seat of the ute and I kept the key around my neck, so Gavin couldn't get it. But I had to have some protection, even though it probably wouldn't be enough if the time came.

The calving finished. Out of forty cows I got thirty-six calves. For a while I thought I had thirty-five. One of them, who was only a few days old, died. I found his body in the cold wet grass one morning so I picked him up on the forks of the tractor and took him down to the tip and dumped him. Two days later I'm down there again with the usual rubbish from the kitchen and there's the calf tottering around on weak little legs yelling for his mother. I felt like a complete idiot at the same time as I was ecstatic to see the impossible. How did it happen? I have no idea. I could have sworn he was dead. For a moment I wondered if it meant that maybe my parents would come walking across the hilltop, hand-in-hand, but although I tried I couldn't link up the two things.

Some cows were good mothers, a lot weren't. It figured. The first cows every farmer wants off his place are the poor mothers. By picking up this mob at low prices we were pretty much guaranteeing that there'd be a high ratio of second-rate mums. So, some accepted their bubbas with instant enthusiasm, others had to be talked or tricked into it. Some had to be put in the crush and tied, and then we'd lead the calf in to her, hoping that if he sucked hard enough she'd let her milk down and it'd be a happy ending.

We set about castrating the bull calves, and ear-tagging both boys and girls. Gavin seemed to find the idea of castrating the boys a bit off-putting. I think it made him feel insecure. We used an elastrator, which has four prongs, that expand a little green rubber ring when you squeeze the handles. You get the ring over the scrotum, making sure you've got both the balls, then release it. The ring snaps tight. Very tight.

The calf goes off with the ring around its bag, cutting off the blood supply, so the scrotum gradually perishes and drops off. It was a good method and it worked well, a tad better than biting, but it took a while.

Any time I had trouble with Gavin I just waved the elastrator at him and he backed off fast.

At least things were quiet on the financial front, and the legal front. I'd rung Fi's mother and told her I wanted Mr and Mrs Yannos as my guardians, and I wrote a letter to Mr Sayle telling him the same thing.

By the time we were through with calving it was time to go back to school. Gavin and I had missed the last two weeks of the term, and now the holidays were over. Some holidays. The jolly old holidays. There should be a new word for holidays like these.

The last night Fi and I watched a video. Not a rented one, just *Grease* that I'd taped off TV ages ago. Fi sat on the floor. I was behind her, doing her hair, Gavin was sound asleep. Sandy, the Olivia Newton-John character in the movie, reminded me a bit of Fi. I'd never have said that to her though. She hated people saying she was 'sweet' or 'innocent'. But knowing she was leaving the next morning was getting to me. When Sandy sang 'Hopelessly Devoted to You' I was struggling not to cry. Not that I was hopelessly devoted to Fi, but I felt hopelessly shattered by all the stuff that had happened, and hopelessly lonely at the thought of her going back to the city.

Fi heard one of my muffled little noises that could have been a sob. She twisted around and bent back her head and looked at me.

'Don't,' I sniffled. 'You'll need a physio.'

'You want me to do your eyebrows?'

'No.'

She faced around again. After a bit she said, 'Knock knock.'

'Who's there?'

'Omar.'

'Omar who?'

'Omar goodness, I got the wrong address. Knock knock.'

'Who's there?'

'Max?'

'Max who?'

'Max no difference. Knock knock.'

'Who's there?

'Sarah.'

'Sarah who?'

'Sarah doctor in the house? Knock knock.'

'Who's there?'

'I love.'

This was an old joke between us. I groaned but asked anyway.

'I love who?'

'How am I supposed to know? You tell me.' She paused. 'Is this helping?'

'No.'

'I didn't think it would. I'm not very good at telling jokes.'

I asked her one. 'Knock knock.'

'Who's there?'

'Moo.'

'Moo who?'

'Make up your mind. Are you a cow or an owl?'

Fi clapped. 'That's the first funny knock knock joke I've heard.'

'It must be funny if you laugh when I tell it. I'm hopeless at jokes too.'

'There are more important things in life. Those boys who do nothing else but tell jokes . . . I just want to cover my ears and run screaming out of the room.'

And then 'Look at Me, I'm Sandra Dee' started and we were suddenly doing a dance number in front of the TV, and even though we hadn't done anything like that for more than a year we synchronised perfectly. We didn't need a choreographer. Our friendship was our choreographer.

The funny thing was that Gavin actually started kicking up a fuss when I told him we'd go to school on Monday. I thought I'd given him such a bad time, making him work so hard all day every day, that he'd be out to the bus-stop Monday morning at the rate of knots. But round about Friday I realised he didn't want to go. Amazing. He wouldn't say why. I thought it was a mixture of all that security stuff, wanting to stick close to me, and somehow the fact that he was so bloody useful and important on the farm. I mean, if he hadn't been there I would have sold up, not just because of the financial pressures, but because you simply can't run an operation like ours with one person. You've got to have someone else to be on the other side of the mob when you're moving them into a new paddock, to inch the tractor forward when you're pulling a calf, to start the engine of one car when you're jump-starting the other, to help cut an injured steer out of the mob, and so on and so on.

And even more importantly, it's the company. When you see a cow accept a calf that she's been rejecting for hours, there's got to be someone you can turn to for an exchange of high fives. When you see Marmie eating cow poo, there's got to be someone to share your groans of disgust. When you watch the little yellow robins bopping around your feet as you dig up a rock in the new cattle race, there's got to be someone to watch them with you.

I never said anything corny to Gavin about how important he was, how much I needed him, but he must have known it. He must have known it from the time we got up in the morning to the time we went to bed at night. And I thought maybe that's why he preferred being on the farm to going back to school. After all, in secondary school you get treated like you're eight years old. I guess it follows that in primary school you'd get treated as though you're three years old.

I couldn't treat him like he was three years old. A three-year-old was no good to me. I treated him like he was sixteen years old, because that's the only way the farm could survive.

Mind you, there were still plenty of moments when I treated him like he was four years old.

On the wall above my desk I've got a quote which says 'Don't treat people as you think they are, treat them as you think they are capable of becoming'. These days with Gavin were maybe the first time in my life that I'd actually done what the quote said. To be honest, I didn't do it because of beautiful principles but because it was the only way we were going to make it.

Fi left on the Saturday morning to go back to school in the city. It'd been great having her there. She'd helped me like no-one else could have. I stood in Wirrawee watching the bus disappear down the highway, wondering when I'd see her again. I felt awfully lonely that day. For all that Homer and Gavin were like my brothers, and I loved the big brat and the little brat (not counting the days I wanted to kill them), nothing beats a girlfriend who speaks your language and knows what you're thinking. And nothing beats a girlfriend like Fi.

After Fi left I went in to Elders with Gavin, to pick up some bags of concrete. We needed to cement in the posts for the new cattle yards. But the trouble with places like Elders is that you see all this stuff, and you know it would make your life so much easier, but you can't afford it, so all you can do is gaze and drool. For instance they had a post driver with a hands-free automatic auger. Dad would have loved that for the cattle yards.

The next day, Sunday, Gavin and I were sitting looking at the yards as we ate our lunch. I'd brought sandwiches, in an Esky, to save time. We'd done a pretty good job with the cement, considering. I said to him, 'Why don't you want to go back to school?' I'd already tried to have this conversation, but this time he seemed more open.

He got a terrible frown on his face. 'I don't like school.'

'Well, of course I am totally in love with school.'

'No you're not.'

'It was a joke.'

'Well, I don't care. I don't like it.'

'Yeah, you've made that pretty clear. But why?'

'It's boring.'

'Schools have to be boring. It's against the law for them to be interesting.'

'You're stupid.'

'Seriously, why don't you like it?'

He did get serious then. He gave me a long sideways look, as if trying to figure out whether he could trust me or not. I didn't say anything. If he hadn't worked that out by now, there wasn't much more I could do.

Finally, looking away, he said, 'The other kids don't like me.'

That did surprise me. I knew he'd had trouble early on, but I thought he'd been travelling quite well since then.

I waved to get his attention. 'They don't? Are you sure?'

After a long pause, looking away again, he said, 'They call me "Deafy".'

'Oh.' My sandwich suddenly coagulated in my mouth. I put the rest of it down. 'Oh. I didn't know that.'

'It doesn't matter.'

'Yes it does.'

He shrugged.

'Those little creeps.' I was starting to get angry. 'What do you do when they call you that?'

'I used to punch the crap out of them. But I got in trouble. So now I don't do anything.'

'Oh.' I felt both angry and helpless. It was typical of Gavin to have kept all this to himself. He might have told my parents, but I didn't think so. I wanted to tell him to go back and punch the crap out of the other kids again, but I realised that mightn't be the best advice. I couldn't think what to tell him. 'Sticks and stones may break my bones'? Yes, but being called names can break your spirit, break your heart. Which was worse?

I'd rather have a broken arm than a broken heart any day.

'What would happen if you dob on them?'

He looked offended. 'I'm not doing that.'

'Have you got any friends?'

'Yeah. Mark.'

I knew Mark. He was famous for being the naughtiest kid in Wirrawee. Naughtier than Homer even, when Homer was in primary school. In fact next to Mark, Homer would have been school captain.

I could see how Gavin might have ended up with Mark as a friend. I'd noticed even back in primary school that although the other kids laugh at what the naughty kids do, naughty kids usually don't end up with a lot of close friends. Homer was the exception.

It struck me that living wild on the streets of Stratton during the war might have been a good time for Gavin. He had a gang, a group of feral lost and homeless children, and he'd ended up in charge, so there was no question about his popularity. Away from school, in a situation where deafness was just a minor inconvenience, all his strengths had been shown to maximum advantage.

The next day he came to the bus with not much more than the usual amount of grumbling, complaining, whingeing, dawdling, sulking, and insulting remarks directed at me. Querulous, that's another good word. I can definitely say he was querulous.

It was my first day back since the funeral, and it was a little weird, the way the other kids treated me. I hadn't thought about what it would be like. We're nearly at the start of the run, so when Gavin and I got on the bus there were only the Sanderson kids, Jamie Anlezark, and Melissa Carpenter. They were just the usual 'Hi, Ellie', 'Hi, El', but they did look at me that little bit longer than normal, and their faces were that little bit redder.

The next stop is Homer's and he sat next to me as always. To my absolute astonishment no sooner had he sat down than he pulled out a book, turned to a bookmark near the end and settled down to read. I lifted it up as he read to see what it was. It looked old and dusty. The name was *The Scarlet Pimpernel*. I put it down again, gently, feeling really disorientated. This would be something like Van Gogh playing full-forward for the West Coast Eagles.

After Homer got on, there was a long haul to the Boltons, at 'Malabar', then the Grahams and the Pereiras, then the Young twins at 'Adderley', and then the bus filled up so fast you couldn't keep track of them all. There were lots of new kids on the buses these days, but we were lucky; we still had a friendly group, and once we got the Young twins it was like a party every morning. Shannon and Sam Young were a laugh a minute – no, sorry, take that back, a laugh a second. It didn't matter how sleepy you were in the mornings, when they came bouncing down the aisle of the bus everyone woke up. Even Brad Davis, who slept through parties, footy games and exams, sat up to attention when the Young twins climbed on board.

But today it was different. Everyone was so quiet. Everyone glanced at me as they got on and everyone waved or nodded or said hi or all three, but then they just sat in their seats murmuring away like magpies very early in the morning.

In the seat ahead of me Sam Young picked up a black beetle on a tissue and was about to chuck it out the window. Before he did though he knelt up and showed it to me over the back of his seat. 'Hey, Ellie,' he said, 'look what came out of my nose.'

I laughed. But the laugh strangled itself in my throat when I saw Shannon frown at him from across the aisle. They were treating me like I was an emotional cripple. Well, maybe I was, but I didn't like to be reminded of it.

We got to school. I noticed that Homer had finished his book. 'Can I borrow that?' I asked as he went to put it away.

'Sure.'

I had no idea what it was but an old book that fascinated Homer was worth a bit of a look.

Wirrawee High was a different place these days. There were so many new kids! The population of the school had gone from three hundred and fifty to six hundred and fifty. We didn't have nearly enough teachers or buildings anymore. Every class had at least forty students and every bit of space was a classroom. Walk into the gym anytime and there'd be at least four classes going on, with each teacher trying to stop her kids from distracting the others.

Some things hadn't changed though. I smiled as I walked down the corridor every day, because every day I passed the window we had broken during the war. The school, deserted and silent, had been a good hiding place for us back then. We had smashed a window to get in, then stuck masonite and tape over it to make it look like old damage. No-one had touched it since. Maybe we should have offered to pay for new glass but what the hell, money was short, and schools were meant to have a budget for repairs, weren't they?

These days, luckily, being seniors, we got the best conditions, but even so, it was hard. There was no hope of getting any work done in your frees because the library was so crowded and noisy.

The first few days back I got no work done. I sat through period after period and they could have been talking about making drugs out of pineapples or a school excursion to the top of Mount Everest or World War II being caused by someone popping a paper bag. I didn't hear a word, didn't learn a thing. Now that I wasn't physically active, now that I wasn't racing around pulling calves or cementing posts into the cattle yards, I could think of nothing but my parents.

Time and time again the memory of their bodies, and the feelings of desolation, washed backwards and forwards, like a great internal tide. The way everyone avoided me or treated me like I had the Ebola virus made it all the worse. There's nothing lonelier than grief. Sometimes I wanted to cry out to them all, in the middle of History, 'Please, please, look at me, help me, can't you see how unhappy I am?'

But what would have happened? They would have gathered round, making soothing noises, helping me out of the room maybe, offering me tissues . . . And none of that would touch the deep dark ocean that circled silently inside. They could not see it, touch it, stop it. I didn't know any way to do that.

It was a relief to get home in the afternoons and get physical again. I actually felt good when I saw Gavin on the bus each afternoon. It was like he and I shared something that no-one else could understand. It was like we were linked by blood: literally, my parents' blood, that had stained our hands and our clothing, and in another way the same kind of blood link that brothers and sisters, or parents and children, share.

I can't imagine that before the war he would have been left in my care but now things had changed so much that no-one even came enquiring after him.

The first few days though, Gavin was so exhausted by being back at school that I stuck him in front of the TV with a bunch of cushions and left him to it. That first afternoon he slept for two and a half hours. I felt guilty, that I'd worked him so hard, but what choice did we have?

Gradually the kids on the bus and the atmosphere at school started to go back to normal. During the war there'd been so much grief and loss that now people were more used to it maybe. I think if my parents had died in such a way before the war it would have taken months for our friends and neighbours to get back on track. But now, by the second week of school, the bus was a mobile comedy and gossip club again and people were no longer treating me like I was contagious. I even started to absorb a skerrick of information from my classes.

I got to know Bronte a bit too. The night she had come out to my place with Homer and Jeremy and Jess she'd hardly said a word. And because she was a year below me at school we didn't share any classes. But I noticed her in the queue at the canteen one day and we smiled at each other. I waited for her to get served and then we walked to the elm tree that looks over the footy oval.

We'd just had a History lesson before lunch and somehow, instead of talking about History, the conversation had swung around to a story from the radio that morning, about prisoners who weren't released at the end of the war. These rumours came along every few days, and a lot of people believed them. I simply didn't know if I did or not. There were so many people 'unaccounted for', and the theory was that they were still being held in secret out-of-the-way places. It was an emotional issue for anyone with friends and rellies who hadn't been traced. There were four people in our class with family members who'd disappeared during the war and hadn't been heard of since.

Jake Douglass, whose father had been one of the Wirrawee cops before the war but was now a security consultant or something, had been shooting off his big mouth, talking about raids across the border to find prisoners, and how he and his mates were ready to fight back any time.

I'd been pretty upset myself, listening to Jake going on and on, and I wanted someone to talk to. I told Bronte what Jake had said. She listened in silence.

'Things are still so dangerous,' she said at last. 'Especially around here. Some of these boys are dangerous to be around.'

'Jake Douglass thinks he's such a hero. What did he do in the war? Let down a few tyres.' She didn't say anything to that and I had to add, 'I know I sound like I think we're the big heroes, when I talk that way. But the truth is, we did do a lot, and now all I want is to try to make some sort of normal life for myself, and the way these boys talk, I'm like you, it really disturbs me.'

I didn't know why I was saying all this to her but she

was one of those people you instinctively trust. 'On the one hand there's Jake Douglass, who's got about as much guts as a disembowelled guinea pig and who's so stupid he's dangerous, and on the other hand there's Homer, who really is brave, but sometimes he seems to be dropping hints about some sort of gung-ho stuff too. Like Jess, when you guys came out to my place the other night. It's very confusing and I don't like things that are confusing.'

'I don't think we can expect things not to be confusing at the moment,' Bronte said, which, when you translated it, I think meant that things would stay confusing for a while yet. The way she said that kind of proved she was right.

Jess joined us. I liked Jess but I'd had the feeling the other night that Bronte wasn't so keen on her.

'Great History lesson,' Jess said.

'Yeah, I was just telling Bronte. Honestly, I don't know what's come over these boys. They're all out of their tiny minds. So many people seem like they haven't had enough war yet to satisfy them. I don't know how much they want. I've had enough for a few lifetimes. People like Jake Douglass make me paranoid. More paranoid than I already am, that is.'

'Hey, I'll make you really paranoid,' Jess said. 'You know what my father thinks? He says the enemy are sussing us out, getting ready for the next invasion.'

I couldn't cope with this conversation. I rolled away and started playing with a spider's web. I tried putting a leaf on it, to see if it would break. I heard Bronte ask, 'Why would they invade again?' She sounded calm, but she seemed like a calm person.

'Because a lot of their radicals are really angry with

their government. They say they gave in too easily, they shouldn't have compromised, they shouldn't have given so much away.'

'Given so much away!' I shouted back over my shoulder. 'It wasn't theirs to give away! It wasn't theirs in the first place.'

Boy, that Jess, she had an answer for anything. I put a piece of bark on the spider's web. It still didn't break.

'OK, OK,' she said. 'Keep your shirt on. Bad choice of words. Although I suppose it was theirs to give away, really, because they had a whacking great slab of it and we didn't. Possession is nine-tenths of the law.'

'So,' said Bronte, in the voice of someone who's had this discussion quite a few times before. It was like a teacher asking a class for the seventeenth year in a row, 'So, class, what do you think our rules should be for this year?' Bronte went on, 'What do you think they'd do if they invaded again?'

I stacked a twig on the web. It sagged but it held all that weight without snapping.

'Well, what they started doing in some places before. Resettle as fast as they can and turn us into fringe dwellers. We'd live in the crap places and do all the crap jobs and anyone who gave trouble would be locked up or they'd mysteriously disappear.' She paused, then added, 'According to the rumours, that's why they're not returning some prisoners. It's because they've identified certain people, certain prisoners, as troublemakers, the people who'd give them a hard time if they invaded again. They figure "Why create extra problems for ourselves? Let's just announce that these guys are dead, or we don't know where they are, and that way we'll make it all the easier when we launch the next invasion".'

'Next invasion,' I snarled back at her. 'No way is there going to be a next invasion. Not if I have anything to do with it.'

But even as I said that I knew I couldn't have anything to do with such a big issue. Nobody was going to come to me asking for permission to invade.

I karate-chopped the cobweb with my hand. It broke.

Chapter 8

I'VE NEVER FELT so young and inadequate as when I sat in the bank manager's office the next day. It was lunchtime at school and I'd belted down to the bank for this appointment. I was meant to be meeting Mr Yannos but he hadn't turned up. Much as I liked Homer's dad I had to admit he wasn't the most reliable person in the world. So suddenly I found myself in the manager's office having to explain why she should lend me a little matter of another hundred grand or so. For the first few minutes I could hardly get my breath to ask for anything except a glass of water but somehow my desperation to keep the farm got my tongue working enough to stammer out a few words. And once I started the words flowed a bit better.

I already owed the bank a breathtaking gobsmacking heartburning $480 000. Nearly half a million. But as I said to her, that was safe for the bank, because of the mortgages over the farm and the cars and machinery. Plus I had the cattle, which were now up to ninety-six head with the new calves. Before they'd calved, Mr Sayle had valued them at $180 000, but if I kept the calves a couple of years they'd be worth another $100 000 or so at current rates, and provided the market held up. So far it had risen like a ruckman taking a speccie.

I hadn't been game to go and see Mr Sayle or even to ring him, but I'd written him a quick letter to tell him what I was going to do. I hadn't heard back yet. I think lawyers were so overworked as a result of the war that they paid most of their attention to the urgent stuff.

'So what do you want to do with the extra money?' the manager asked.

'Buy more stock,' I said promptly. 'I need to build up the herd, in quality and quantity. These cows and steers were pretty poor when my father bought them, but they're putting on some condition. When Dad got them there was nothing else available. But there's some better stock coming onto the market now. I'd love to get one of these New Zealand bulls that they're shipping over but I don't know if I could afford them. They'll be fetching top dollar. But even if I miss out on them, I think I could get a decent bull from one of the studs that wasn't so badly affected by the war, and then another fifty or so cows.'

'Hmm.' She didn't look impressed. She sat back in her chair and started ticking off points on her fingers. She even spoke in point form. I don't think I'd ever met anyone who did that. She seemed to be talking to the wall, not to me. 'One, you're exceptionally young for such obligations. Underage to be signing contracts – guardian would have to guarantee it. Which reminds me, guardian also must guarantee existing loan. And he's not here now. Not good.'

She got up and stood looking out of the window, hands behind her back.

'Two, cattle market, unreliable at best of times. These are hardly the best of times. Three, cattle highly susceptible. Disease, bushfire, drought, all could take them out.'

She didn't seem to notice that she'd just rhymed. I gave a little grin but I was getting worried about the fate of my loan.

'Four, lack of experience in running operation like this. Five, no diversification. All cattle operation. Eggs in one basket. Hmm.'

Before I could start sticking up for myself she turned around, came back to the desk, sat down, took a pen from her pocket, and twirled it in her fingers. Now she looked at the ceiling.

'On the other hand, as you say, loans quite well secured. Repayments uncertain at best. Don't know how much more the bank wants to tie up in this property.'

I broke in, urgently. 'You know what everyone says about farming. Get big or get out. Ninety-six head means I'll always be on the borderline. You might as well close me down now as leave me on ninety-six head. We have good pasture, good paddocks. We've had good rainfall the last month. I could carry six hundred head through summer if I could afford them.'

She sat there staring. It was the first time she'd looked right at me. Finally she said, 'You know, loans depend on the borrower more than anything. More than security, more than paper, more than forecasts, more than promises.'

At that moment her phone rang. She picked it up and listened for a moment. Then she said to me, 'Your guardian is here.'

I didn't think it was necessary to tell her that he wasn't officially technically my guardian quite just yet. But I was massively relieved to hear that Mr Yannos had finally arrived. I'll never know whether the manager was about to give me my loan or not, but when Mr Yannos agreed that he would guarantee it she went ahead and got the papers and I had to sit there and watch Mr Yannos put his farm and his life on the line for me. I didn't like seeing him do it, but God I was grateful. People talk so casually about friendship, as though it's something you can pick up at the 7-Eleven like a Slush Puppy or a hot dog. But what Mr Yannos offered was the kind of friendship that you can only buy with invisible coins. I used to think that joining our farm with theirs would be a good idea, and maybe our parents would like Homer and me to get married just to create a super-farm. But despite Homer's jokes, that wasn't in Mr Yannos' mind. He did it for my mum and dad and he did it for me and he did it because of the war and most of all he did it because he was a good human being.

In the bus on the way home I finished the book I'd borrowed from Homer, *The Scarlet Pimpernel*. I really liked it! For an old book it was pretty cool. It is about a group of Englishmen who rescue prisoners from the French Revolution. The Scarlet Pimpernel is the nickname their leader uses, so he can stay anonymous. Like Superman is really Clark Kent, although I've never quite figured out why Superman has to hold down a second job as a reporter anyway. Maybe he needed the money.

The Scarlet Pimpernel's real name is Sir Percy Blakeney and no-one suspects him because he's the stupidest guy in Britain. Even his wife doesn't suspect him. But he's really diabolically clever. He uses disguises and quick thinking to stay out of the clutches of the enemy.

I couldn't help recognising similarities to Homer in the description of the Pimpernel. But I wasn't sure how far I could take it. The day my parents died, the day Homer and Gavin and I had been hiking up the spur, I'd have been willing to bet the whole farm and the cattle that Homer wasn't involved in any secret organisation or border raids. I just couldn't credit that he'd be in something like that without telling me, without at least dropping a lot of hints.

Since then, yes, I could imagine that he might be getting involved in something, but not as the leader. He wouldn't have been able to set up a whole network that quickly. It was very confusing.

I stopped thinking about it though when I got home and went to check the cattle. Oh God. The things that can go wrong on a farm. As soon as I saw the trampled fence near the south-west corner I knew there could be big problems. I raced down the hill, my heart drumming. Soon I was through the break, into the wetlands, and in among the first of the mob. They gazed at me in fascination, the way cattle do, and started crowding around. I ran on. A number of them were standing in the water and I couldn't tell yet whether some were caught or not. But there were at least four that looked to be in trouble.

I made myself stop and try to think what to do for the best. Marmie was still too young and untrained to be much use. I could try on my own to move the unbogged cattle back into their paddock but the mob was so scattered I wasn't sure I could do it. These guys were still pretty feral, and the mothers with calves wouldn't like me messing with them. They formed the bulk of the mob. I might end up with them scattered between heaven and earth, and half of them stuck.

Twenty or more had followed me down the hill and were now a lot closer to the water. In the time it took me to go back to the house and get Gavin we could end up with a major disaster. But I had no choice. I did a bit of yelling and huzza-ing to frighten away as many as I could, then ran up the slope and grabbed the bike.

They're always talking about farm accidents and farm fatalities, and you read some of the stories about how people get hurt or killed on farms, and you think 'How stupid of them', but you forget how when there's a crisis you go like stink and forget about safety. I just jumped on the Honda and took off. Halfway home I saw a ditch that had somehow dropped out of my consciousness. I hit the hand brake and the foot brake with everything I had but I must have been doing about eighty and the next thing I'm flying through the air and smacking the ground hard enough to rattle every bone in my body.

I'd hardly stopped rolling before I was up and running back to the bike. Between my chronically bad knee and the ache in my calf from a bullet wound during the war, plus all the new pains I'd now added, I wasn't running too fast.

Despite that I picked up the bike and got it going and was away again inside thirty seconds. But in the next few minutes I started to really hurt. I felt jarred and bruised and shaken and I had dust all down my left-hand side. I pulled up outside the house and staggered in, with only my right-hand side working properly.

Gavin was watching TV but his radar was in good

working order. One look at me and he was out of his seat and following me to the shed.

In the machinery shed, as we threw a winch and ropes and chains into the back of the ute, I told him the situation. 'The cattle got out of the paddock and some of them are bogged in the lagoon.'

Marmie was leaping around barking with excitement so I chucked her in the cab of the ute as well. Gavin got in from the other side and away we went.

This time I drove a bit more carefully, but not much. I was relieved to see when we got there that the cattle had spread out and were grazing peacefully again. But there were four bogged, two of them cows. Their calves were running backwards and forwards along the edge of the lagoon making that pitiful yearning noise that calves are so good at doing.

Trying not to stir up the other cattle we moved as many as we could back into the paddock. I did use Marmie for this. Once she was in the right place she did OK. In other words if I put her behind the mob and encouraged her to fetch them up and to let out a nice little bark once in a while she was quite effective. They say a good dog is worth three men. Ignoring how sexist that is, I'd say Marmie was worth as much as Gavin and me, this time anyway.

There were other times when she was as useful as a stuffed olive.

I left Gavin to put the fence back up as well as he could. I told him to tie Marmie to it when he was done; she would bark her little head off at any cattle who came within twenty-five metres. While he was doing that I ran down to the lagoon.

It was a cold afternoon and already the light wasn't

good. I dreaded going into the water but I didn't have a choice. I screwed up my face and waded in with the rope. I thought I'd deal with the cows first, but I realised as I got closer that one of them was in deep mud and was stuck more firmly than the other three. So I thought I'd try to get the other cow, and the two steers, and then worry about the worst cow.

I ploughed my way through the mud and water, making nice encouraging noises as the first cow eyed me suspiciously. You say such ridiculous things in situations like that, because you know no-one's listening. 'Who's a pretty girl then? Having a mudpack to make you look even lovelier? Hey, have I got a bull in the next paddock who'd be hot for you. Yeah, baby.'

I think it must have been the promise of the blind date with the bull that did it, because she stayed quiet and let me slip the rope around her. Then I reversed out, up the hill to the ute. I would have preferred the tractor but there hadn't been time to get it. The ute was a four wheel drive with a limited slip diff so I figured it'd be up to a job like this.

I looped the rope round the towbar and took off at eighty k's an hour. No, just kidding. But I was thinking of the ad on TV where the farmer pulls the cow's head off. I eased the ute up the hill, checking the rear vision mirror and wishing Gavin was back already so he could give me a few signals. But everything went OK. The cow popped out and started dragging her weary body to the edge of the lagoon. Her calf came towards her at the gallop.

I got the rope off her and left them to it. I would have liked to put them back in the paddock but there wasn't time. I had to hope she'd have the good sense not to bog herself again, although using 'cow' and 'good sense' in the same sentence is probably a bad idea.

I knew it'd be dark soon so I splashed in and roped up the first of the steers. As I sloshed back to the ute Gavin reappeared. I was extremely pleased to see him. Now all I had to do was watch his signals as I got the ute into gear and inched it forwards. Again we didn't have any problems. Gavin gave me the thumbs-up, with a big grin, and I was able to leave the ute and go back to the lagoon.

On one side of me was the calf frantically guzzling at the mother we'd pulled out, on the other side was a muddy steer shaking himself and looking pissed. But already he was grabbing huge mouthfuls of grass, tearing it off as fast as he could chew. That was a good sight: food can work miracles for animals in poor condition, giving them new energy. And these beasts could have been in the swamp all day while I was at school. In the cold water, weakened by their struggles to get free, they would have used up energy fast.

The second steer was not so easy. I knew this guy: he was a bad-tempered evil-minded mongrel. I had names for some of the cattle, even though they say you should never give names to animals you're going to sell for slaughter, because you bond with them too much. This one I'd called Major Harvey, after a man who'd tried to kill me during the war, so I was never going to bond with him.

As soon as I got close he started. Tossing his head and showing the whites of his eyes, snorting. If he could have he would have pawed the ground and taken a few steps towards me, in the charming friendly way that he had. Reminding myself that even if he was unpleasant and bad-mannered he was still worth at least a thousand dollars, I tried to get the rope on him. Soon though I was wishing he had less energy, were weaker, because I realised it was just too dangerous. I had to think of another strategy.

I backed off and used a bit of mime and a bit of lip-reading to ask Gavin to get me some hay. In the meantime I headed over to the last cow.

She at least wasn't interested in attacking me. She was rapidly losing interest in everything, even life. The trouble with her was that she was deep in mud, so deep I knew I could never get the rope under her and a rope around her head wouldn't be enough. I had to be careful I didn't get caught too. Fifty years ago an old lady on a farm in the Holloway Valley had died when she got bogged doing this.

The cow was shivering, with cold and distress. I was starting to shiver myself. As the sun sunk away and the shadows fell across the lagoon the temperature seemed to drop ten degrees in a moment. I got out of the water again and waited for Gavin. I jumped around and did a bit of jogging and waved my arms and then had the bright idea of running the two beasts I'd got out, with the calf, up the hill to get them further out of the way and closer to their paddock. It helped warm me up a bit and achieved something as well.

I was almost sorry when Gavin came back because I knew it meant I had to go in the water again. The only consolation was that it meant Gavin had to go in too. He didn't even blink though when I told him what I wanted, just marched down to the water's edge and started on in. 'By God,' I thought, following him, 'you're not bad sometimes.'

Being so short he had a problem getting to Major

Harvey and at the same time keeping the hay dry. He was virtually swimming when he was only halfway there. I could see that wasn't going to work. I got him to come out again and went up to the ute and got the smaller tarp and we put the hay on that. Then with Gavin pulling it and me following and pushing, we set off again.

We had the steer's interest now. It never fails to amaze me how cattle love hay. They'll do anything for it. To them, hay is like Neapolitan ice-cream, mangoes, Cherry Ripes, all of the above.

Major Harvey eyed it greedily, at the same time as he eyed me suspiciously. 'Meals on wheels,' I said to him as we approached. 'Hay to take away. What about a tip? Don't fool in the pool? I can't believe we have to go to all this trouble just to save your miserable life.'

He took a greedy grab at the hay as soon as Gavin got close enough to swing it around in front of him. I waited till he was on his second mouthful, then, just as he was finishing, got the rope onto him.

After that it was easy but we'd wasted another half an hour and it was getting seriously dark and seriously cold. I was shivering like crazy but there was nothing else for it but to go in again.

The blackness of the water made it look evil. I took half a biscuit of hay with me, to see if she was interested. Although her head wasn't far out of the water she wrenched a good bunch of it from my hand and munched it down. That was encouraging. But I had the feeling she was there for the night. I couldn't see any way to get her out. The hay should give her a bit of strength but I was worried she would get too tired to keep her head out of the water, and she'd drown.

I waded back to the bank. I started thinking almost longingly of the rifles in the ute. A swift flash in her brain, no time even to feel anything, and then the darkness. It would be kinder to finish her off, and most farmers would have been reaching for a gun by now. We'd done all we could. Sometime in the next twenty-four hours the mud was going to seep into her mouth as her head dropped, and her mouth would fill with water, and then her lungs, and she'd disappear forever. The rifle was the way to go.

Instead we made yet another trip to the house. Squelching into the ute we drove back and got the old table from the shearing shed kitchen. At the same time I filled a few five-gallon buckets with hot water.

When Gavin realised I was going into the lagoon again he suddenly starting bossing me around. I'd seen him do it with other people before, but never with me. It's true I was shivering uncontrollably. He told me to go in and dry off and change clothes. 'It's a waste of time,' I said. 'More laundry, and for no good reason.'

'You do it,' he said, using both his arms to push me away from the ute.

'But we've got to get back.'

'The cow can wait.'

Honestly, it was like having a mother again. But I did feel a bit better when I came back out dry and warmer.

I floated the table out to the cow and jammed it in the mud and got it under her head while Gavin shone a spotlight from the bank. It looked like it might work but I still didn't know if she'd die of hypothermia during the night. Poor thing. I gave her a hug then went and got the first bucket and poured that around her, to give her a few minutes warmth. Then backwards and forwards with the other two buckets.

I did the same routine with the buckets three more times during the night, without waking Gavin. Pulling on wet clothes is absolutely and totally my worst favourite thing in the world, but I knew if I wore dry stuff every time, I'd break all records for laundry.

I took her down a biscuit of hay each time, but I still didn't see a way to get her out. I tried to think laterally. Get a bulldozer and dig a trench to her? Get a front-end loader and lift her up in it? Wiggle my nose and say a magic spell?

The last time I went out, at three in the morning, under a clear cold sky, she was sinking, and not just literally. They say that three in the morning is when a lot of creatures, including humans, are at their lowest ebb. It's when hospitals have the most deaths. But there wasn't anything else I could do for her.

Or was there? I had set the alarm for six o'clock, because I thought our best chance would be at first light. Gavin, yawning and grumbling and about a quarter awake, came with me. I had a plan but it wasn't much of one. I chucked another biscuit of hay into the back of the ute, got in, started it up and drove forward, towards the first gate that would take us to the lagoon.

And suddenly, to Gavin's shock, I turned hard left. Because now I did have an idea. I don't know where it came from and even as we reached the road I was trying to figure out how it might work, but, totally stupid though it was, I sensed it might give us a chance.

Only ten minutes down the road were the Anlezarks. Jamie went to Wirrawee High School. Each morning he caught the same bus as Gavin and me. He was older than me. He was one of the best cricketers in the district. He had a girlfriend called Natalie. He had the personality of a cane toad out of mating season. And he had more drugs than the rest of Wirrawee put together.

Mr Anlezark just about swallowed his toothbrush when he opened the door and found it was me.

'Ellie, what's wrong?' he asked, but it was hard to understand him with his mouth full of Colgate.

'Is Jamie home?'

'Well, yes, but it's so . . . I think he's still in bed.'

'Do you mind if I see him? It's only for a second. Project for school. It's important, otherwise I wouldn't bother you at such an early time.'

I was already going up the stairs, hopeful that if I kept talking I wouldn't give him a chance to stop me.

Jamie's room smelt like he'd drenched it in cologne that he'd picked up for $1.99 a litre. I hadn't met Natalie but I don't think she had a lot of class.

If he hadn't been awake before I burst in he was wide awake a moment later.

'Ellie? What the hell is this?'

The shock sent his voice so high that it was like puberty had never happened.

I got down close to his ear, though it wasn't pleasant. I still hadn't had breakfast. I could feel my stomach going murky.

'Jamie, I want a truckload of those little pills you've been telling me about for so long.'

'Are you crazy?' His voice had gone hoarse and husky now. 'You come here at six thirty . . . my parents are right downstairs. What did you tell them?'

'Nothing to what I'll tell them if you don't give me a couple of dozen tabbies.'

'You are crazy. I don't even have anything. You are just plain crazy. Get the hell out of here.'

'Not without something very stimulating. Something wild.'

There was a knocking on the door. I heard Mrs Anlezark's nervous voice. 'Ellie! Are you OK? Can I help you?'

'I'll only be a couple of mo's, Mrs Anlezark. I just need a bit of help with something.'

Jamie got out of bed, kicking the doona aside, muttering and cursing and glaring, then stumbling over his cricket bag. He threw open his wardrobe and groped around at the back of the top shelf. He chucked a small plastic bag at me, but because it was so light I had to go halfway towards him to pick it up. There seemed to be about twenty green pills in it.

'Here. You owe me a thousand bucks. Now get out.'

I got out, feeling a laugh rising inside me. At six o'clock this morning, if anyone had told me I'd be inside Jamie Anlezark's bedroom . . .

I still don't know what Jamie's parents thought. I jumped down the stairs three at a time, yelled 'Thanks' to both of them as they stood in the kitchen door and was away before they could recover.

Gavin, still sitting in the ute, and getting cold, made a face at me. 'What?'

'You'll see.'

I tore back to the lagoon, hoping desperately that the cow wasn't under the water and blowing bubbles. Or worse, not blowing bubbles. It seemed to take an age for Gavin to get out of the ute and open each gate. At one point I blasted the horn to make him hurry, and of course he heard it in the clear morning air, and scowled at me. He recognised the sound all right.

There she was, tired eyes barely open, head half off

the kitchen table. She only had minutes left to go. I waded into the lagoon, giving a yell as the cold water bit into me again. I struggled out there to her. 'This is bloody crazy,' I thought, opening the little plastic bag. I tipped the tablets into my hand. There were only twelve. I got her mouth open and pushed them down her throat. She offered no resistance. 'Wish I'd asked him how long these take to work,' I thought. I offered her the biscuit of hay as well but she'd given up on food now. There was nothing more I could do in the lagoon itself. I backed away, watching with fascination and hope. Would anything happen?

My original plan had been to use the calf to motivate the cow, and I thought I should still do that. We got a lasso on him and dragged him around till he was as close as possible to his mum. I was still watching her to see if there was any reaction. I felt that something had to happen, sooner or later. Surely she couldn't swallow all that stuff and not be affected? Were cows so different to humans?

I turned away from her to get the other rope, to help drag her out. Gavin suddenly pulled at my arm. He pointed. There was the cow, shaking her head, then a moment later tossing her head backwards and forwards. She was certainly coming to life but she didn't look too happy. Maybe she was hallucinating little green men or little green bulls.

Now was our chance. I whacked the calf hard on the nose a couple of times. I'm not sure if any of the agriculture manuals would have advised this, but it was all I could think of. They probably wouldn't have advised using Ecstasy either.

Well, the calf played his part. He set up a wailing and

a hollering that would have put a baby with a burnt bum to shame. I looked around anxiously at the cow, just in time to see her rise up in a wild eruption out of the mud. She came floundering towards us, her white eyes looking murderous. Smelly bucket-loads of mud slid from her flanks, the water splashed around her, she mooed fit to burst, and I had the feeling she'd forgotten all the favours I'd done her during the night. Drugs or no drugs, she still wanted to look after her kid.

I grinned at Gavin. He was wide awake now. We had about two and a half seconds to get the lasso off the calf before we were butted into a weekend in late September. It was a close thing too, as the more desperately I tried to get it off the more I fumbled it. In the end I dragged it clear when she was two steps away. Gavin and I ran like hell, laughing hysterically. We slipped on the frosty grass, and rolled down the hill together, still laughing.

For the first time since the shootings I felt good. I had no idea what the long-term effects on the cow would be. Maybe I'd poisoned her so badly that she'd be dead by lunchtime. Maybe her calf would get a dose of Ecstasy for himself by feeding at her udder. Maybe when she eventually went to the Great Slaughterhouse in Stratton a hundred people would take a wild trip by eating steak and sausages carved from her side. But for the time being, a cow that should have been dead was alive. Alive and out of the swamp.

The shivers were getting worse, so we didn't spend much time on the cold ground. The cow was bucking around and looking nervous and more than half crazy. She was spooking her calf too. But she was eating from time to time, and the calf had managed to get one good long suck.

There was nothing more we could do for either of

them at the moment. I wouldn't dare tell a vet what I'd done as we'd have the inspectors on the doorstep in five minutes and be struck off for a hundred years. So we pushed the cow and calf back into the paddock, put the fence up again, and drove home in a hurry. The bus wasn't going to wait for us.

I didn't learn much in school that day. I reckon I fell asleep in half a dozen different lessons. And I only had half a dozen classes. Jess elbowed me awake a few times, then she gave up. At least Bronte lent me her History notes, and warned me about the Legal Studies test. That's what I call friendship.

CHAPTER 9

THE VERY NEXT day I saw another Liberation article in the paper. It was similar to the first one, only this time it was on the front page. Either this was a slow news day, which seemed quite likely, as there was also a story on the front page about Elvis Summers getting remarried, or else the group was becoming better known and starting to get serious attention.

A group calling itself Liberation has been credited with another successful cross-border raid.

It is believed the group rescued a man and a woman who were being held on suspicion of espionage. The names of the couple have been suppressed.

Sources close to Army Headquarters say they strongly discourage vigilante activities, but there had been grave fears for the safety of the couple.

The group is believed to operate in a number of

areas but a division based around Stratton or Wirrawee has been credited with the latest mission.

It was frustratingly lacking in details. I read it in the library at school. I'd cancelled Mum and Dad's subscription to the paper, as another small way to save money.

At lunchtime I went and found Homer. It was raining on and off and he was in a classroom at the end of the corridor, with Bronte and Jess, along with Sam Young, Shannon's twin, the comedian from our bus. I didn't want to mention the delicate subject of Liberation in public, so I just settled into the conversation, which was about the usual subjects: the war, the peace, the prospects for the future. And relationships.

Jess said slyly, 'I reckon Homer and Ellie'll get married and never leave the farm and just walk around all day chewing on bits of hay and talking about the weather.'

'Yeah right, Jess,' I said. But I knew I was a bit pink. 'Homer's only ambition in life is to find a bimbo, the blonder the better. Someone who'll bring him breakfast, lunch and dinner in bed.'

'And serve herself covered with trifle as the dessert,' Sam added.

I rolled my eyes at Bronte. She just grinned back.

'You guys know me so well,' Homer said, smirking away like he really thought it was going to happen.

'Whatever happened to Lee, Ellie?' Jess asked me.

Jess was always so, I don't know what the word is, forceful. You were never left wondering about her opinion. And she liked to know everything. She'd never even met Lee, as far as I knew, but she sounded like she and he were old buddies.

I shrugged. I didn't feel like telling them all the details of my love life. I didn't want to tell them about the flow of letters I got from Lee straight after the shootings, letters where he raved with such passion about what had happened that I started to worry he was cracking up. I didn't want to tell them about the way the letters had stopped suddenly and how I hadn't heard from him since. And most of all I didn't want to tell them about the nights I spent in bed on my own or with Gavin, dreaming of nights with Lee, longing to feel his hot hard body against me again.

So I just shrugged.

'Tell us about your love life, Jess,' Bronte said provocatively, like she was winding her up.

'Ah, wouldn't you like to know?'

I wasn't sure if I would actually, but it was good to have the spotlight off me again. The truth was, my mind went like a washing machine on spin cycle when I thought about Homer and Lee. Was it possible to like them both at the same time, to be attracted to both of them, even to be in love with both of them? And to have regular rage attacks towards Homer as well? Oh, and by the way, Jeremy Finley wasn't so bad. I didn't necessarily want to leave him to Jess.

'You know who really likes you?' Sam asked Jess.

'Well, pretty much everybody,' Jess said. 'But who in particular did you have in mind?'

'He's in our year. He's a townie. I reckon he's pretty gay myself, but the girls don't seem to think so.'

'Cal Graham?'

'He's not a townie,' Homer said.

'Someone in this room had a relationship with him,' Sam said.

Well, seeing that Bronte was new and it obviously wasn't Jess, that didn't leave many possibilities.

'Steve,' Homer guessed.

Sam just grinned.

I tried not to react. Seemed like it wasn't enough that Jess had my old black top, the one with the silver edging. She had to pick up my old boyfriend too. There was a pattern here.

I had been with Steve for a long time before the war. We'd kept away from each other since school started again. I don't know why. With some people it seemed like the stuff that had happened was too much to cope with. You couldn't talk about the war because it was too big, and you couldn't talk about trivial things because compared to the war they were too insignificant, so you were left with nothing.

But I liked Steve. I'll always like Steve. He was funny, nice, friendly to everyone, confident. He believed in himself and what he could achieve. And I didn't think I wanted him to be in a relationship with Jess. That's the thing about relationships, once you've been in one you think you have some kind of ownership of the person for the rest of your life.

Of course the other thing about Steve is that he's pretty immoral. He'd go with a vampire if he thought their blood groups matched.

It was a frustrating lunchtime because I wanted to ask Homer about Liberation but it was hard to get a chance. He looked tired and was yawning a lot. Well, I could relate to that. But as we headed off to class I said to him casually, 'I saw another Liberation article in the paper today.'

'Oh yeah? Scarlet Pimples I call them.'

'So what's your connection with them?'

'Connection? Who said I've got a connection?'

'No-one. But you gave me that article to read . . .'

'I just thought you might be interested.'

'Well, I am.'

'Well, good.'

'So you're not connected with them?'

'I've heard a few things,' he said cautiously.

'Homer! This is me you're talking to, remember?'

'Oh yeah! Isn't that funny? I could have sworn it was Kevin.'

'Thanks very much. So, what have you heard?'

'Ellie, don't you think you might have enough on your plate already? Sometimes it's a case of what you don't know can't hurt you.'

Ouch! Right on my sore spot. And I fired up. 'So you're going to decide what I should and shouldn't know? Anything else you want to decide while you're at it? You want to go through my wardrobe, or check what shampoo I'm using?'

'Yeah, thought I'd come over at the weekend. Whatever you shampooed with today smells a bit minty for my taste. Hey, that looks like Mrs Slatter. I think we're late. Ouch!'

If he'd ouched me I'd ouched him, with a good punch to the upper arm. I hoped he would feel it all the way through Maths and Chem. But I still didn't know any more about Liberation.

The next day there was a hearing about my guardianship. I had to go to the Courthouse. 'Be there at 10 am' the notice said. 'Be punctual. If you are running late you must ring the Clerk of the Court.'

It turned out everyone had been told the same thing,

so there were like forty cases all scheduled for the same time. It didn't take a genius to work out that they weren't going to hear forty cases simultaneously. I settled in for a long wait but then Fi's mum came out of a side door to tell me she'd fixed for me to go on early.

They only did it because Fi's mum had come from the city and they didn't want to keep her hanging around Wirrawee all day. Nothing like having powerful friends.

It was great to see her, just great. These days I was willing to take a bit of mothering wherever I could find it. A bit here, a bit there. Even if I'd blown her house to smithereens, even if she'd chopped our farm into five and given four of the parts away, I loved and admired her. She was one of the really important people of my childhood.

She went back in to get ready. I waited outside for Mr and Mrs Yannos, who were sure to be running late, no matter what the notice said. I got pretty anxious because I didn't think they'd impress the court if they weren't there when the hearing was called. As I waited it did strike me that the whole situation was kind of funny, in that whereas I had to go through all this legal stuff, no-one was a bit concerned about Gavin, who was much younger than me. Even his school was just taking it for granted that I was his 'parent'. They sent me notes and I signed his homework diary and consent forms and it didn't seem to bother anyone. I suppose that legally Gavin hardly existed: he was just part of the flotsam and jetsam of the war, a little boy with no connections, no records, no official identity.

I was a bit startled in the middle of all these thoughts to see Mr Sayle walking up the steps. He detoured around the smokers and came straight for me. He was very businesslike, giving me a pile of papers and explaining them so fast that I only understood about one word in every four.

At the end of that he looked around and said, 'Where are these people, the . . . ah, the ones you want as guardians?'

'They'll be here in a minute,' I said.

'They're not here yet?' He looked around as though they were probably standing near us and I just hadn't noticed them. Then he said, 'Look, Ellie, I have to say I don't think you're getting very good advice in all of this. What I want to suggest is that I take on the role of guardian to you. It makes perfect sense, when you think about it. If I'm the guardian as well as executor of the estate, it'd be easier to coordinate everything and to make sure the decisions are in accordance with your best interests.'

He had me in a corner and was talking to the bottom of my throat. I felt very uncomfortable.

'Uh, well, thanks a lot, Mr Sayle,' I mumbled. 'But I really don't think . . .'

'Look,' he said, 'I've got an application to the magistrate, in case you change your mind. All you have to do is sign it, and then when you get into court, explain that you'd prefer to have me do it. It's very simple, and the court will be happy either way. After all, at your age you don't need a guardian for emotional reasons. It's more for the business and financial matters.'

Showed how much he knew. Somehow I pirouetted out from under him and got into fresh air. He turned to face me and I said, a little desperately, 'No really, Mr Sayle, I'm happy to go with Mr and Mrs Yannos.'

'Ellie,' I heard from behind me. 'Sorry we're late.'

Mr and Mrs Yannos had arrived like the cavalry and saved me in the nick of time.

In the courtroom I sat next to Fi's mum, at the desk for the lawyers. They were just finishing a .05 case. The guy lost his licence for six months and copped a five hundred buck fine. The magistrate was surprisingly young, a woman who didn't look any more than thirty. I'd thought that all judges and magistrates were male, white, seventy years old, and talked like people out of the eighteenth century.

She looked at me over the top of her glasses. Again she surprised me, this time by talking about the death of my parents, as though she really cared. She was businesslike but she seemed nice.

'Ellie Linton,' she said. 'I've read the papers in this application. I am so sorry about the events that have led to your being here today. Your parents sound like fine and decent people. These murders were an affront to our society, and in particular a terrible affront to you. Now, I understand that you have asked for your neighbours, Mr and Mrs Nicholas Yannos, to become your guardians. Wouldn't you prefer to have one of your relatives take on this important job?'

Fi's mum nudged me to stand up. 'Go on, you can talk for yourself,' she whispered.

I faced the magistrate. 'I don't really have any close relatives,' I said. 'I mean, I've got aunts and uncles, but they live a long way off, and we've never had that much contact with them.'

'I see. And are Mr and Mrs Yannos here?'

They stood up too. She asked them, 'Are you willing to become legal guardians to Ellie?'

They nodded. They seemed a bit overwhelmed by the whole thing.

'You understand the ramifications of doing this? The officers of the court have explained them to you?'

They nodded again.

'Well, it seems like a very good solution. The references you have supplied are most impressive. Unless anyone else has an objection I propose to make the order.'

She looked around the courtroom for a moment. And blow me dead if Mr Sayle didn't stand up and clear his throat.

'Ah, Your Worship, if I may?'

'Mr Sayle?'

'Your Worship, I am the executor of the Linton estate and was a good friend to the deceased persons.'

Good friend! Not that I ever noticed. Anyway, good friends don't talk about 'the deceased persons'. That didn't sound too friendly.

'Yes, Mr Sayle?'

'In my opinion, given the complexities of the Lintons' farming operations, and the difficulties of having too many people involved in these matters, I want to ask the court to appoint me as guardian to Ellie. This would have the advantage of combining the financial decisions on running the property with the financial decisions on running the estate. It would mean that things can be managed with greater efficiency. The advantages of this may not be immediately obvious to Ellie, but the Lintons' business is a large one and is in a critical state financially. If there are different forces all, how can I put it, pulling in different directions, then that can hardly be in Ellie's best interests.'

The magistrate looked back at me. 'Ellie?'

'I hardly even know Mr Sayle,' I said. I was feeling majorly pissed off. 'I know Mr and Mrs Yannos really well. They've been my neighbours all my life. They've been so good to me, not just since my parents were killed, but for as long as I can remember. I trust them totally. I just think they'll be able to help me in a heap of different ways.'

Mr Sayle wasn't flustered. He turned back to the magistrate and launched into another of his long speeches. 'The fact is that Mr and Mrs Yannos are Ellie's neighbours, whether they are officially appointed her guardians or not.' He gave them a warm smile. 'I'm sure we can assume they'll continue to be her friends as well, and that they'll support her in many different ways. But at Ellie's age what she needs is not so much a guardian who will provide emotional support as a guardian who will take care of her legal and financial requirements.'

I started sweating, thinking about the bank loan Mr Yannos had guaranteed, because the bank had assumed he was my guardian. They'd never bothered to check. I'd thought at the time that it was a bit slack.

Fi's mum stood, in her usual graceful way. She reminded me of a swan slowly unfolding its wings. 'I suppose, Your Worship, we could say with equal confidence that Mr Sayle will continue to be executor of the estate, whether he is Ellie's guardian or not. Surely it is in Ellie's best interests to have as many people as possible on her side, rather than having everything rest on one person. And despite what Mr Sayle says, Ellie still needs someone in her life to give her support in all kinds of abstract ways, including emotional. For Mr and Mrs Yannos to take on this role in an official capacity helps to stabilise the whole situation.'

The magistrate looked down and made a few notes. Then she said, 'With someone of Ellie's age it's important that we take her wishes into account. On the other hand there are obvious advantages in having the executor take on the role of guardian. I can see the force of Mr Sayle's argument that Ellie's friends, like Mr and Mrs Yannos, will always be there for her. And really, we're only talking about a relatively short period of time, before she comes of age, in the legal sense.' She paused. I was doing some serious sweating now. I felt sorry for the next person who sat in this chair. She was going to get a wet bum.

'Excuse me?' I said.

'Yes, Ellie?'

'I had to get a loan from the bank to keep the farm going, and Mr Yannos personally guaranteed the loan. Will Mr Sayle be able to take over that guarantee and guarantee any future loans the property needs?'

'Well that's just it,' Mr Sayle said, standing up again. 'That's exactly the kind of problem I'm having. That loan was particularly ill-advised and in my view was not in the best interests of the estate. Ellie and Mr Yannos charged off to the bank and arranged it without reference to me. If I were Ellie's guardian this kind of thing simply wouldn't be allowed to happen.'

The magistrate glanced at her watch. 'Ellie, unless you have some very strong objection to Mr Sayle taking on this role in your life I propose to make an order appointing him as your guardian.'

'Oh I do,' I said. Tears started stinging my eyes. 'I don't mean this the wrong way but I really don't want him to do it.'

Fi's mother stood up again, quickly. 'This application

by Mr Sayle has been totally unexpected, Your Worship. Perhaps Ellie could have some more time to consider her position.'

The magistrate made another note while I waited. I hated the idea that a stranger could make a decision like this in ten minutes, and change my life.

She closed the folder and pushed it away.

'This is obviously more complicated than I first realised. I propose to adjourn the matter for two weeks and have another hearing on Thursday the third. I appreciate the need to have things clarified, but it's also important that we arrive at the best possible outcome. That is all. Clerk, call the next case, please.'

CHAPTER 10

'LEE!' GAVIN YELLED. He was off his stool and across the kitchen and into Lee's arms before I had time to put down the spatula and turn around from the stir-fry. Gavin always seemed to beat me to the hugs these days.

'Good timing,' I said. 'I'm doing Thai.'

'Yeah I know. I smelt it from the city.'

I met him halfway across the kitchen and we had our hug. He'd put on another inch or two, and he'd been tall before that. I felt off-balance. His intensity filled the room already. When I thought of Lee it was always images of the brilliant piano player, and the effective killer of enemy soldiers that came to mind. The pianist and the killer existed in him side by side.

I had no memory of his being at the funeral so as far as I was concerned I hadn't seen him for ages. Except in my dreams. And I wasn't sure if that counted.

'Better get back to the stir-fry,' I said. I needed an excuse and that lame effort was the best I could do. 'Have you eaten?'

'Only if you count a ham and tomato sandwich on the bus. Cost me seven bucks and tasted like a Chux. A very old Chux. The stir-fry is looking pretty good right now.'

I think he was nervous too.

'I'll do more noodles.'

I put some of the stir-fry aside for Gavin then chucked about a kilo of chillies in what was left. I knew how Lee liked his food, and I don't mind the odd sinus clean-out myself.

'So, where are your brothers and sisters?' I asked. 'Don't tell me you've brought them with you?'

'No, called in a few favours. A lot of favours actually. They're all at sleepovers for the weekend. Sorry I didn't ring but I couldn't confirm it till this morning, and then when I did ring I didn't get an answer. Guess you were at school.' He slumped down on a chair. Not the broken one.

'You guessed right.'

'Geez, Ellie, how are you doing all this? Running the farm, looking after Gavin, going to school? I know you're Superwoman but even she got knocked out by kryptonite. Or did she? Come to think of it I don't know much about Superwoman.'

'Neither do I,' I said, serving up the stir-fry. 'Gavin get over here and stuff this down your gob.'

'How's he been?' Lee said as Gavin slid into the seat beside him.

'Well, obviously better for you being here. Normally I have to tell him six times to come to the table.'

'Are you having fun with him?'

'Fun?' I looked at him in shock, the spatula in mid-air. 'What's fun?'

He laughed. 'Yeah, took me a while to figure that out too. But I finally got it with my brothers and sisters. I woke up one morning and thought "I'm not their father and I'm not their mother. I'm their brother and what's more, I'm a teenager. Why am I trying to be a parent?"' He grinned at me. 'I mean, of course we are like their parents. But we're kids ourselves. We've got to do both, be their parents for some stuff but at the same time, muck around with them. It makes it harder in some ways, but it's the way to go.'

I was eating slowly, listening to this. I realised almost at once how right he was. It had been the same in the later stages of the war. I'd lost my sense of humour, become tough and intolerant. I remember Fi telling me exactly that, one day up near Tailor's Stitch. Now here was another friend, pointing me in the same direction. I could see how I owed it to Gavin to fill about fifty different roles in his life. And those roles included being a teenage big sister who had fun with him once in a while.

Lee was gasping for breath. 'Wow, this is some stir-fry. Have you just brought in the chilli harvest? Look, I know this isn't a very good time to be talking about fun, with your parents being killed and all, but in the long run . . .'

Yes, he was right. But at the same time I started to feel incredibly depressed. I pushed the rest of my meal away.

He watched for a minute before saying anything. Gavin kept eating but he was watching me too, between mouthfuls. I put my hand over my face, with my elbow on the table.

'What's wrong?' Lee asked after a while. 'Too much chilli?'

'Nothing much. Just missing Mum and Dad. Oh, and wanting to be perfect. I think that's all.'

'Oh, that's all? I don't see the problem then.'

'Very funny.'

'You know the way life works?' he said. 'You're on this moving footway. It starts with everyone telling you that you've got to get to the end. There's a big pot of gold waiting, but if you don't get there you're a failure. So you try and try but you don't make it. So you feel bad. So you try even harder. You still don't make it. You feel worse. Some people try even harder after that. Some people give up and let themselves slide back to the start. So it goes on. That's it. That's life.

'Oh, and by the way, you're one of the ones who keeps trying harder.'

He leaned back. 'And you know the big joke?' He fixed his dark eyes on me. 'There's no pot of gold. Never was, never will be. It's just an illusion. They show you photos of film stars going to the Oscars and billionaires on their yachts to make you think that they've found the pot of gold, but if you talked to them they might tell you the truth. Or they might still be running along the moving footway themselves.'

'And then there's death.'

'Yes, sorry, left that bit out. You're right, that's the end of the walkway.'

I got up and filled a jug with water. I brought it back to the table and poured glasses for the three of us. He drank most of a glass without stopping. 'I'd forgotten how good rainwater tastes,' he said. 'The city stuff is terrible. It's got so much chlorine. Smells like a swimming pool.'

'Yeah, well this has got wrigglers. Always has.'

'Wrigglers I can live with.'

'I guess I worry that if I let myself off the hook, if I don't keep trying to be perfect, I'll get too slack,' I said. 'I use that to motivate me.'

'Ellie, trust me, you're never going to get slack. Anyway, you can aim high and get a glimpse of the end of the footway once in a while and be satisfied with that. Instead of trying to be perfect.'

I didn't say anything. I looked at the plates on the table and wondered if I had the energy to load the dishwasher. Then Lee got up and started clearing away. I've got to admit, that made me feel good. Gavin wasn't too strong on household chores.

'What have you got planned for tomorrow?' Lee asked.

'Saturday? Pick up sticks in Parklands so I can put the slasher into the baby broom. Prepare One Tree for a crop of lucerne. Clear more rocks in Nellie's. Check the cattle, of course. We've got thirty-six baby calves. That's not so bad, considering none of the cows exactly looked like they were lining up for Mother of the Year competitions.'

'Good on you.'

'Then there's the usual jobs. Cleaning. Laundry. Shopping. Cooking. I try to make a lot of stuff over the weekend and freeze it for during the week.'

'So how much of the stuff you've got lined up is urgent?'

'Oh well,' I said reluctantly. 'Checking the cattle. Doing the laundry. The shopping.'

'If I give you a hand with those, why don't you take the rest of the weekend off? Have a holiday?'

'Yeah!' Gavin cheered. 'A holiday!'

'This sounds like a conspiracy.'

Gavin made a face at me. 'What's that?'

I sighed, grabbed his notepad, which for the first time in about a month he had with him, wrote the word down for him, then struggled to explain what it meant. But I was too tired. Finally I said, 'Ask Uncle Lee.'

Gavin wouldn't go to bed and I didn't care much, seeing it was Friday night. So we watched TV and talked till quite late. To tell the truth I was getting nervous about where Lee planned to sleep. It had been so long since I'd seen him, and even longer since we'd had sex, and I had no idea where we'd parked our relationship. Although I'd been thinking about him so much recently, and with a lot of longing, I didn't want to jump straight back into bed with him. I was still too upset about my parents to have sex with my boyfriend, or ex-boyfriend, in their home, such a short time after they'd died.

I didn't really want to have sex with anyone anywhere. Maybe not for the rest of my life. I think that was one of the effects of the murders on me. I hadn't felt that way before.

At about eleven o'clock I got up and said, 'Well, better make you up a bed.'

Lee didn't move a muscle, just kept that poker face. 'I'll do it,' he said, getting up.

I put him in the spare room, said a quick safe goodnight, then headed back out through the TV room, where Gavin was gazing at re-runs of 'Touched by an Angel'. He looked up at me. 'Isn't Lee going to sleep in your bed?' he asked, with a cheeky grin.

'What? What did you say?'

I grabbed a cushion and attacked him, pounding him without mercy. Somehow he got out from under that and before I could turn round he jumped on my back and grabbed another cushion and laid into me. I raced around the room trying to throw him off. Eventually I went into a death roll on the old sofa and loosened his grip until I could break free. By then we were both panting and sneezing with the dust. Made me think I hadn't been doing enough house cleaning. But we were both armed with cushions and we closed in on each other, in a no-holds-barred fight-to-the-death world-championship-wrestling duel. God that little tyke was a fighter. I backed him into a corner but only by using my bigger size and strength. And even when he was stuck firmly in the corner he never let up. After a while I let him fight his way out again, and just then I got ambushed by Lee from behind, so from then on I didn't have a hope.

Later, in bed, I thought about how much fun it had been and realised that Lee was right. I couldn't be a parent to Gavin the whole time. I had to remember to be a kid sometimes too, for both our sakes.

Next day I chucked a load of laundry in the machine, while Gavin and Lee checked the cattle. Then we went into Wirrawee and did the shopping. For a start I had to stock up on chillies. And bloody expensive they were too. I didn't get any refrigerated or frozen stuff, because this was meant to be our holiday so I didn't want to go back home just to put groceries in the fridge.

Then we went to Juicy's, the new coffee shop in Barker Street, where Gavin ordered this revolting bowl of chocolate ice-cream, lime flavouring, nuts, wafers, banana, malt and cream. All it needed was tomato sauce. I sat looking at it as I drank my cafe latte, thinking, 'You know you've grown up when you realise that whatever looks good isn't necessarily good.' Then I said to the waitress, 'I'll have what he's having.'

We wandered down to Jubilee Park to have a look at

the market. Markets are kind of cool. I bought a candle for Lee and a balaclava for Gavin. Lee bought me a pair of uggies. I talked for quite a while to the girl who sold me the balaclava. She was into Taoism, which is a faith I'd never heard of, but it's all about how everything has its own nature and the more you try to interfere with stuff the more you mess it up. That's more or less what I thought she said, anyway. The bush and the ocean and everything from elephants to buttercups have their own inner rightness, but humans keep wanting to improve them, or change them into something that will be useful for the humans, but this isn't actually a great idea. And she talked about wu wei, the Chinese name for the idea that you let things follow their natural laws.

She said something which struck home with me. She said, 'It's only humans who believe in mistakes. Nature doesn't have any understanding of mistakes. If a branch falls from a tree, it doesn't mean the tree's made a mistake. Nature just reorganises itself around the fallen branch. So now it becomes a home for the insects that live on the ground. Its leaves rot down and make the soil richer. If the branch falls into a creek, fine, the water now flows in a different way.'

'Yeah, I guess that's true,' I said.

'So, life goes on. Things happen. If you let things happen, they do.'

'So,' I said, feeling myself go a bit red, 'if people you love die, or get killed, what does Taoism say about that? How are you meant to cope with that?'

I waited on her answer as though it would be very important.

'You do nothing,' she said. She shrugged. 'This has happened. It doesn't matter in the long run how they died. They've died, so your life reorganises itself. It will affect you in different ways. So, let it affect you. Feel what you feel, do what seems right to you. Don't imagine there is a right way to act or a wrong way. Just let your life continue according to its own inner nature.'

'OK,' I said.

I turned away to leave.

'Hey,' she said, 'good luck.'

'Bit of an angel encounter, that one,' I thought.

We went to a four o'clock movie, not a very Taoist one I'd say. But Gavin chose it. It amazed me that after all he'd seen in the war, all he'd experienced, he still liked violent movies, but they were always his first choice. He was still quite violent by nature, as he'd proved with the cushions last night – not that I could talk – but I don't think his violent behaviour came from the violent movies. The movies must have seemed a bit tame sometimes, compared to what he'd gone through.

It wasn't a bad film. The special effects were cool, and it had Jed Barrett, who I can look at for quite a long time without getting a headache.

It had been a good afternoon and it had been fun. We went to Macca's – sign of the times, Wirrawee had grown so much since the war that it now had a Macca's – then headed home.

That night in bed I was thinking about the way creeks and streams operate. They start off little, gurgling and bubbling and jumping over rocks and stuff, full of energy, going all over the place. Then they get older and bigger, become rivers, take a more definite course, stick to their path, know where they're going, get slower and wider. And eventually they reach the ocean and become part of this vast mysterious world of water that stretches away forever.

Yep, just like people.

My parents had joined the ocean. I was back up in the hills, bubbling around. What I'd seen and done in the war had made me grow up pretty fast, and what had happened since, even faster, but I was still a kid and I had a way to go yet before I became one of those slow old rivers just cruising along, not noticing too much and not bothering about the rocks and the rapids.

The next morning, as we walked through the paddocks checking the cattle, Gavin far in front on the left and Marmie far in front on the right, Lee began the big conversation. It had to happen sooner or later, I knew that, but I was not looking forward to it. He was nervous too. I still didn't know if he'd been expecting a weekend of wild sex but he would have been sadly disappointed so far. And he had to go back early in the morning, catching the school bus into Wirrawee and the bus to the city from there.

I don't know, I was probably doing him an injustice though. It wasn't fair to assume that he'd come all this way for selfish motives. I still had huge respect for Lee. He was a generous guy and I think his first, second and third reasons for visiting were to see how Gavin and I were going, and to help in any way he could.

His fourth reason could well have been to do with sex. But he had helped a lot.

Anyway, as we wandered up the hill, leaving the ute behind, watching the cattle totally engrossed by their breakfast sandwiches of hay, he said nervously, 'So, are you like, with anyone else? Anyone new?'

'No,' I said, then, after a pause, 'How about you?'

'No, no-one.'

'So we're both single, huh?'

'Desperate and dateless,' he said.

'Speak for yourself. Just dateless, thanks.'

'For a guy, we can't be one without the other.' But he grinned as he said it.

'Have you met anyone you've liked?' I asked.

'Oh yeah, you know how it is. You see someone from the bus window, or in the canteen queue at school, or a new girl comes into your class. But there's no-one who's totally grabbed me.'

I didn't say anything. I wasn't trying to be rude. I was just thinking about the Taoist girl yesterday, and how she'd talked about letting things follow their natural laws, not trying to force people or anything – relationships for that matter – into a different rhythm, or an artificial shape.

Lee said, 'So, are we still, like, together, or what? I'm a bit confused.' He said it gently but I could hear the tension in his voice.

I gulped. 'I wish I knew. To be honest I kind of thought it was over but when you walked into the kitchen the other night, I've got to admit, it felt pretty good to see you.'

He didn't say anything so I kept going. 'When you moved to the city – and you had to look after your brothers and sisters, and you sounded so stressed in those phone calls – it just seemed like we were going in majorly different directions. I got caught up in the wild lifestyle of Wirrawee, and you were drifting out of sight. Now . . . well, I've enjoyed this weekend a lot. But it doesn't mean I'm ready to jump straight back in. Can we just let things drift a little longer? Would that be OK?'

'We're pretty good together.'

It was unusual for Lee to press like this. Normally his pride wouldn't let him.

'Well, I guess. But we're young. And we're coping with a lot of stuff. God are we coping with a lot of stuff.'

'Has it struck you that we're both orphans?'

I had to blink back the tears then. We were sitting on an outcrop of rock, at the highest point in the paddock. Below us Gavin was using a stick like a golf club and trying to hit cattle dung up the hill towards us.

'Oh I hate that word,' I said, when I could trust myself to speak. 'I haven't let myself think that word.'

He put an arm around me. 'I've had longer to get used to it than you have.'

But I didn't want his arm around me and I shrugged it off.

'Orphans!' I said angrily. 'That sounds like Anne of Green Gables, and Little Orphan Annie. I can't think of myself like that. I can't think of you like that.'

But he seemed to want to rub it in.

'Gavin's an orphan too, as far as anyone knows. Three orphans in the one field. What are the odds on that?'

'Oh come on,' I said, standing up. 'I've had enough of this. Let's go home.'

When we got there, Homer was waiting. He'd rung the day before about coming over, staying the night, and catching the bus from my place with Gavin and Lee and me the next morning.

I told them that they could make lunch themselves, so they broke out the barbecue. I got some chops and sausages from the freezer. Our stocks were getting low. I realised that if I wanted more meat I'd soon have to kill a beast myself. I'd helped my father often enough but I didn't like the thought of doing it on my own. Plus all the butchering afterwards. It made me feel a bit sick. Maybe I'd have to come up with a different way of getting meat.

After I'd found them the Dickhead matches – a name which always made me smile – I sat and watched them cook, giving regular helpful advice which I feel they deeply appreciated. But I got their sudden and undivided attention when I said to Lee, 'Get Homer to tell you about Liberation.'

Two heads whipped around towards me, two sets of eyes gazed at me intently.

'What do you know about Liberation?' Lee asked. I was a bit shocked at their reaction. I was surprised that Lee had even heard of them.

'I know quite a lot,' I said. 'But not as much as Homer.'

It was a complete bluff, but I hoped it might get me somewhere. Unfortunately these two guys knew me too well.

'You don't know nuffin,' Homer said, turning back to the sausages.

I thought I might as well go for broke. 'They're a group from around here,' I said to Lee, but watching Homer for his reaction. 'Well, there's groups in different areas, but there's one based in Wirrawee. They sneak over the border and do stuff, rescue people.' I decided to push a bit harder. 'Homer's involved, but he doesn't want me to know about it, because he thinks I've got enough to worry about for the time being. You know Homer, always wanting to make my decisions for me.'

Homer had his back to me but he stabbed a sausage with a fork, so hard that it broke in two.

'So who else is in it?' Lee asked. He was watching me closely. Now he was off-balance. He wasn't sure what I really knew.

'Jeremy Finley,' I said. 'General Finley's son.' I was fairly sure of that one. 'And Jess, this girl who came here a few weeks back with Jeremy, and hit me with a whole lot of questions.' I asked Lee, 'Do you know her? Or Jeremy Finley?'

He shook his head. 'So, who else?'

I gave up at that point. 'I'll be honest. I don't know.' I said to Homer, 'So, how'd I do?'

'Why do you want to make your life more complicated than it is already?' he asked, putting the chops onto a plate.

I waved at Gavin to get his attention. When I was his age the smell of food was enough to bring me running, but not Gavin. This time he was absorbed in trying to teach Marmie to fetch a ball. I had to go and tap him on the shoulder. By the time I got back I had the distinct feeling that Lee and Homer had quickly agreed what they would tell me and what they wouldn't.

I settled into a chair opposite them. 'So, what am I going to be allowed to know?' I asked them, taking my first mouthful of food and smiling sweetly across the table.

Lee shrugged. 'Hey, don't look at me. I know bugger-all.'

'Bugger's a rude word,' Gavin chipped in.

'Yeah, like you really care,' I said. 'Eat your vegetables.'

'Look,' said Homer. 'It's true, I do know something about them. And I am just a little bit involved. But the deal is that none of us is allowed to talk about it to anyone not in the group, for obvious reasons. So the thing is, do you want to join the group? You say I'm always wanting to tell you how to live your life. Well, I don't know about that, but I did figure you wouldn't want to get into any heavy scenes while you're trying to cope with what happened to your parents, as well as run this place, and look after Gavin, and the whole thing.'

'Fair enough,' I said.

That rocked him, although he didn't like to have me see it. But I meant it. I understood the sense in what he was saying.

'I read the book, you know,' I told him.

'What book?'

'*The Scarlet Pimpernel*.'

'Oh, that one.'

'So what I want to know is, in the book, there's this guy who's like the idiot, the clown, and he turns out to be the genius who's the secret leader. Is that the way it is with your group?'

'It's not my group,' Homer complained.

'So you're not the leader?'

'An idiot who's really a genius? Does that sound like me?'

'Just give me a yes or no answer. Are you the leader? Are you Mr Pimpernel?'

'No I'm not.'

I believed him.

'OK, but is there a secret genius who's the leader?'

Homer considered. 'You could say that.'

And you're not going to say who it is, right?'

'Right.'

'Is it Jeremy? Jeremy Finley? I mean, he's the one who'd have access to the kind of military information you'd need.'

'Doesn't mean he's the leader.'

'No. But I think he is.'

CHAPTER 11

HOMER AND LEE were pretty boring that afternoon, both of them sleeping for a couple of hours after lunch. They weren't much help. I took Gavin off to do a bit of stick collecting in Parklands, but my heart wasn't in it. I did think a lot about this group though. Liberation. It was a cool idea. But I had very mixed feelings about getting involved in anything like that. Of course on the one hand I wanted to avenge my parents' death. Theirs, and Mrs Mackenzie's. My whole body burned with a primitive desire to take the guys who'd killed them in such a foul and filthy and cowardly way and tie them to a railway track and have a train approach them very very slowly before running over them a millimetre at a time. Or tie each of their arms and legs to a different tractor and have the tractors drive away in opposite directions. Like the nice old-fashioned method of drawing and quartering people with horses.

Oh yes, I was in a bloodthirsty mood that afternoon. A couple of times I smashed poor innocent sticks against tree trunks and broke them into matchsticks, just to express my frustration.

By the end of the day I could have throttled Gavin too, as he was in a really aggravating mood. I think having both Lee and Homer there stirred him up. He wouldn't lift a finger to help, and I had bitter thoughts about the promises he'd made: all the work he was going to do to keep the property in our hands.

Then I got home and found no-one had even started cooking dinner. By then I'd had enough: more than enough. I'd had enough with strawberries and whipped cream on top. I stood in the middle of the kitchen and screeched at Homer and Lee like I was a white cockatoo separated from the flock at sunset. Neither of them looked too bothered. When I'd finished, Homer said, 'But no-one's hungry, Ellie. We thought we'd have dinner in an hour or two.'

He was probably doing it to stir me and I was so tired that it actually worked. I stormed down the corridor to my bedroom, then had a shower, which cooled me off a bit. By the time I got back to the kitchen they'd put together a spinach and ricotta tortellini, and I've got to admit I've had worse.

We watched TV for a while. About the only thing we'd agreed on all day was that the stuff on TV since the war was absolute crap.

I went to bed about nine thirty and slept solidly.

The next morning Homer and Lee weren't there. It took me a while to realise. Half an hour before we had to leave I said to Gavin, 'You'd better go and wake Homer and Lee before they miss the bus.'

He came back and said, 'They're not there.'

I thought they must be in the bathroom.

With fifteen minutes to go I started to think it was a bit odd that I hadn't seen or heard anything of them.

I said to Gavin, 'Do the boys want any breakfast?'

Gavin was looking worried. He said anxiously, 'They're not there.'

I put down the knife I was using for the sandwiches and, feeling a little sick, went down the corridor to their room. Their beds had been slept in, but not for a while. They were cold.

'Where are they?' Gavin, behind me, asked.

I was fighting with panic, and a choking, slippery wrestle it was. Had they been abducted in the middle of the night by soldiers? Abducted and killed? I had a memory of my parents and the Websters and the McGills sitting around the barbecue one summer Sunday afternoon and Mr Webster telling the story of the Gurkhas in World War I. 'Gherkins', I thought he had said. I was only nine or ten. But the Gurkhas were from Nepal and they were the world's fiercest soldiers. With shining eyes Mr Webster described how one night the Gurkhas crept across no-man's-land into a tent filled with German troops, where they cut the throat of every second soldier. And they did it without waking the others.

That story had haunted me. What went through the minds of the men who'd died, as they died? But almost worse than that, what went through the minds of the others when they woke in the morning? Did they have minds left after that? Did they ever sleep again?

Sometimes the brain has to cope with events and thoughts so awful that it feels like it must explode: there is no other possibility. Like a balloon, like bubble gum, like a bloated cow.

I actually gripped both sides of my head with my

hands as I stared at the empty beds. It seemed like the only way to keep a massive blast from happening, deep in my brain. Through the window everything looked cold and grey, and the light was poor: it was not as though they would have set off for a run, or gone to check the cattle.

My head no longer felt like it might explode but my mind was completely out of synch. I had to try to get the bits back together, into the right pattern. To line them up again. I fought to do it. Homer and Lee could not have been abducted. I locked up every night. I was obsessed with doing it since the killing of my parents and Mrs Mac. The windows were secure. No-one had got in. The two boys had let themselves out, closing the door behind them . . . and taking the spare key from the hook in the pantry.

There had to be a reason. It wasn't to visit anyone. They wouldn't do that to me. And it sure as hell wasn't to check out the Wirrawee nightclubs. Think, Ellie, think. But in the back of my mind, and already forcing its way to the front, came the reason. It was just that I didn't want to recognise it. Those bloody Liberation people. It had to be that. I knew Homer was mixed up with them and now he'd taken Lee as well. And whatever they were doing, wherever they were, something had gone wrong. They had planned to be back by the time I woke up. That's why they took the key. They'd made it clear they would be on the school bus. They wouldn't have willingly left me in a situation of ignorance and raw terror.

Gavin watched me closely. He studied my face like he did when he was anxious, as though I were a map and he a geographer with a magnifying glass. He was trying to read every contour line, every creek and river, every hill and gully. He said to me, 'Where are they?'

'I don't know.'

'Yes you do.'

He said it so clearly, like he knew it for a fact. I was completely taken aback. But I couldn't lie to him, and right from the start, when we first met in Stratton, there'd been no point treating him like a little kid. So I said, pointing into the distance then putting my fists up, 'I think they might have gone across the border, to fight.'

He nodded, like he'd suspected that.

I went back to the kitchen, trying to think. Still trying to force my brain into logical patterns. My brain was resisting that strongly. It was telling me: 'Throw your hands in the air. Run crazily around the kitchen table. Smash all the plates on the dresser. Scream.'

I said to Gavin, 'Can you check the vehicles? See if they took any? I'll try to ring someone who might know where they are.'

I believed Jeremy Finley to be the leader of Liberation, the Scarlet Pimpernel himself in fact. But I didn't know how to contact him. Sure the phone system was working fairly well these days. But it wasn't working very well. In particular, Directory Enquiries was putting in a shocker. I'd almost given up ringing them. They sounded like they were staffed by a bunch of semi-literate alcoholics who saw telephones as Satanic devices.

But this time I had no choice. I dialled the number, and waited. And waited. At least before the war you got recorded music. I'd never appreciated it enough.

Gavin came back. 'The Yamaha and Homer's Honda are gone,' he said.

'The Yamaha?' I thought. 'Well thanks, Lee, thanks for asking me. Just feel free to help yourself.'

'Who are you ringing?' Gavin asked.

'Jeremy Finley.'

'Who?'

'You remember, he came here that Sunday night with Homer and two girls.'

'Why would he know where they were going?'

We could have had a three-hour conversation but suddenly an operator came on line. I was so not expecting a human voice that it took me a moment to realise. 'Uh, I'm wanting a number in Stratton.'

'What name?'

'Uh, Finley.'

'What initial?'

'Um, I don't know.' Damn. If Jeremy's mum had remarried, or gone back to using her maiden name, I was sunk.

'What address?'

'Well, I'm not sure actually.'

'I've got six Finleys in Stratton. I'd need more information.'

Click. The sound of a truck reversing. Beep, beep, beep.

I slammed the phone down.

I had a feeling Jess was involved in this too, like I'd said to Homer the night before, but there were two problems ringing her. One was that she had a common surname – Lewis – and it would mean another battle with Directory Enquiries, a battle I was most likely to lose.

The other was that I wasn't sure enough that she was involved. I could cause more problems than I solved by calling her.

In the middle of that I had a sudden image of Homer or Lee lying dead. I clutched my stomach and turned away from the phone. Gavin, looking frightened, took a couple of steps towards me. I realised that I couldn't give in to thoughts like that. Not yet anyway. I had to stay strong.

We'd missed the school bus. I briefly thought of going into school and finding Jess and sussing out what she knew, but it would take half the morning. Reluctantly I came to admit the obvious: that I would have to wait here and see what happened. I was in the role I hated most: helpless, ignorant, passive.

Furious with Homer, with Lee, with wars, with life, I went for a quick run round the cattle, to check on them and distribute a bit of hay. To be honest, if half the cattle had been down with bloat I don't think I would have noticed. But while I was doing that I did at least decide on a timetable. I would wait till lunchtime. If they didn't turn up I'd go into school and see if I could find out anything there. If that failed I'd have to go all the way to Stratton and track down Jeremy. At the very least Jess should be able to tell me how to get in touch with him. I was halfway certain that those two had something going between them.

Back at the house I literally walked around in circles. Well, in rectangles. I did laps around the house. After a while I thought there was a good chance Gavin and I would send each other crazy. I had to do something. But I couldn't think of a single thing that would not cause awful complications for the two boys if I guessed wrong. All I could do was curse them for not being more open with me the night before.

It was just after ten when I heard a low buzzing sound

like a very big and aggressive mosquito. It could have been a low-flying aircraft but I knew straight away it was a motorbike, our motorbike, the Yamaha. Except it was being ridden harder than I'd ever heard it ridden before. Dad would have chucked a fit.

I ran outside. Gavin bolted after me.

'What?' he said as we panted up the slope, where we'd get the first view of it. 'What? What?'

'The Yamaha.'

We saw it just a moment later. 'Lee,' Gavin said. He's got astonishingly sharp eyes, Gavin. We hurried down to the track, where we could cut him off. I couldn't tell whether he'd seen us or not, as he gave no sign, but at the last moment he hung out the back wheel and skidded to a halt.

The first thing I noticed was the rifle slung across his back. He switched off the ignition and sat there, slumped over the handlebars. It was as if switching off the ignition took all the energy he had. He glanced at me and I was shocked at how thin his face looked, at the way his eyes had become dark sockets. All in not much more than twelve hours. I was frightened to see him. It was as though he was about to tell me very bad news.

'They've got Homer,' he said quietly.

I was expecting the worst news, just from the look on his face, but I still wasn't sure when he said 'got'. What did 'got' mean? Dead? Was Homer dead? Or was it something else?

I couldn't speak, just watched him fearfully, waiting.

'They caught him. We were coming down opposite sides of a hill. They didn't even know I was there. But he was a bit further down than me. I think he might have walked right into a sentry. The first I realised was when

148

I heard a lot of yelling and a minute later there were torches everywhere and I saw two guys marching him into their camp.'

'Did they shoot him?' I asked, trembling, holding my stomach.

'Not while I was there. I couldn't figure out what to do. I couldn't attack the camp on my own. I waited quite a while, looking for a chance to get in, but the place was swarming. Then soldiers started coming out and searching the bush, to see if there were any more Homers I guess. At that point I thought the best I could do was come here and get help.'

I shook my head and ran my fingers through my hair. 'You better tell me what the hell this is all about,' I said. 'In fact you better come back to the house and get something to eat.'

'No,' he said. 'There isn't time. We've got to get back there.'

'If you pass out through hunger and exhaustion it's going to get us nowhere at all,' I said.

Gavin and I both jammed ourselves onto the back of the bike and got a lift to the house. In the kitchen I gave him my lunch, and then threw a couple more sandwiches together – the fastest, sloppiest sandwiches in the history of catering. I didn't know if Lee would be too upset to eat, but he wolfed them down, at the same time trying to tell us the story.

'It's what you'd expect, one of these terrorist camps. The kind of place the people who killed your mum and dad would have come from. Homer and his Liberation are sure they're holding a prisoner there, a man named Nick Greene, who got kidnapped a month or so ago.'

'Who is he?'

'I don't know a can of beans about him.'

'Go on.'

'Well, we had some pretty good information. We had a map showing the hut where Nick Greene's kept, supposedly. Liberation had worked out a plan. Very low-key. Pairs work best, according to them. They gave us stun-guns for the sentries. We were going to come in at 5 am, on either side of the hut, and try to get him out through one of the windows. But of course at the end of the day you've got to make your decisions according to what you find. Anyway, we didn't get very far, and I left my stun-gun in the bush somewhere.'

'So what are we going to do?'

'I'm sure they put him in the same hut we thought Nick Greene was in.' He shook his head. 'We've got to get back there.'

I was as anxious as he was to get going. But at the same time it seemed like we were heading into a frightening situation, in broad daylight, with no plans at all. I was trying to stay calm but it was hard when I was torn between wanting to rush in to save Homer and the feeling that if we didn't think it through we'd all get killed.

'So they never knew you were there?' I asked.

'I'm sure they didn't.'

'That's one thing we've got going for us then.'

He stuffed the last bit of sandwich in his mouth and stood up. 'Come on, Ellie, we've got to go.'

'Wait. Wait.' I tried so hard to think. 'What about the other members of Liberation? Would they help?'

'I don't think there's time to get them. And I only know a couple of them. Homer's the one who's right into it. I'm not officially a member yet. This is the first time I've been on one of these raids.'

'So who is the boss? Maybe we should at least contact him?'

'Can you believe Homer wouldn't tell me? I was a bit annoyed actually. Like he couldn't trust me. But he said there was a good reason. I thought for a while that it might be him, like you said last night.'

'It's still possible I guess. How many people do you reckon are in the camp?'

'Liberation thought it was around twenty.'

'Could we get the four wheel drive close to the camp?'

Lee wiped a tired hand across his forehead. He was having trouble thinking.

'Not really. No, no. It's rough country, just over the border. Not all that far from here, a bit over an hour. Maybe I should have come back earlier.'

'What about the four wheel motorbike? Could we take that?'

'Yeah, probably be OK.'

'All right.'

I'd thought of something. It wasn't much of a plan; in fact it was barely half a plan, a quarter of a plan, but it might help a bit.

'We're going to have to take Gavin.'

'What? Are you crazy?'

'We'll need him.'

I ran out to the machinery shed, Gavin so hot on my heels that he really was like a shadow. I filled four drums with petrol, spilling litres of the stuff in my rush, then loaded them on the Polaris and tied them down. Then I went back into the house and got our .222, its sling, and the ammo.

We ran to the motorbikes. Gavin didn't even ask if he was coming, just jumped on behind me. Lee shook his head at the sight. I didn't blame him. But apart from the fact that we were going to need Gavin I couldn't help thinking that there was a case for taking him anyway. How cruel would it have been to leave him behind? At the farm on his own, going utterly mad with fear, not knowing if he was ever going to see me or Homer or Lee again? After all, as far as I knew, he had no-one else in the world. It might almost be kinder to let him die with us than to leave him alive in a world of loneliness.

CHAPTER 12

IT WAS PAST ten thirty when we got away. God, how could
a week start this badly? A few hours ago I'd been thinking about catching the bus, fattening the calves, why the
pressure pump was coming on more often than it
should, how much of the Legal Studies assignment I
could get done at lunchtime, whether I was still in love
with Lee, if we were going to run out of milk for breakfast . . . Now we raced across paddocks, past the lagoon,
heading for the bush and on into the hills, towards the
border, not knowing whether Homer was alive or dead,
not knowing whether we'd still be alive at the end of the
day.

Lee didn't spare the horses. He seemed to remember
the way pretty clearly. Good going, since the first time
he'd come up here was at night. At least the trip home
had been in daylight.

Once we got off my place we started climbing. I
didn't know this area nearly as well as I knew the
Razor's Edge, and Mount Wombegonoo, which were in

the opposite direction. It just wasn't as nice, wasn't as interesting, so I hadn't been here often. Scrub that was green with the winter rain, quite a few patches that had been logged, a mob of about twenty kangaroos thumping away at three-quarter speed, a fox pawing at something in the grass then bolting when he realised two motor-bikes were upon him.

We were on an old logging track that I had a feeling would peter out eventually. The problem was that it hadn't been maintained in a long time and there were fallen trees across it every few hundred metres.

For the two-wheeler this wasn't so bad, as Lee could usually detour round them through the scrub, even if it meant walking the bike at times, half lifting it at other times. For the four-wheeler it was a different matter. To detour into the bush I had to get a clear path, and sometimes that meant long, difficult treks. The grass was so high in many places that I couldn't tell whether it was clear or not. I'd charge through the undergrowth, hit another fallen tree (usually part of the one blocking the road) and have to reverse and try another route. One of the cans of fuel was leaking I think, so there were constant petrol fumes that gave me a bit of a headache.

We had three ways to get the four-wheeler past a fallen tree. One was to detour, one was to push the tree off the road, the other was to ride right over the top of it. The trunks were wet and slimy though, and they kept slipping out of our hands when we lifted them, and when I tried to ride over them the big fat wheels tended to slide all the way down the trunks and branches.

Before long my arms were aching. I was tiring fast, and we seemed to be taking forever to reach the border.

Lee offered to swap but I didn't think it was fair: he was the one who'd been up all night.

Then we got a good run of nearly a kilometre and suddenly we were there.

I'd never actually seen the border before. At this stage it was fairly rough. Apparently the highways and other roads were different – it was well marked, as you'd expect. But here it was pretty casual. Our track had almost faded away and was getting hard to follow. But a couple of strands of barbed wire, a splash of paint on trees either side of the path, and we were about to enter the occupied zone.

Apart from a trip to New Zealand during the war, this was the first time I'd left my own country. Except it was still hard for me to think of it as leaving my own country.

Gavin held up the bottom strand of wire and we rolled the bikes through. I had a quick whispered discussion with Lee.

'How far from here?'

'Not far at all. If we take the bikes another five minutes, then we better walk.'

'It'll be hard with the petrol.'

'Well, the walk's not much more than ten, fifteen minutes.'

'Twenty with the drums,' I thought.

We got going. Searching my mind, trying to find something that would help me feel better, trying to think of some advantage we might have, all I could come up with was that they mightn't know of Lee's existence. If they'd been searching the bush they should have given up by now. It wasn't much to pin our hopes on, but it would have to do.

The track became little more than a walking path, covered by thick green grass. It sure wasn't used very much. Time and time again the four-wheeler barely squeezed between the saplings. I had to keep ducking to avoid low branches, and I could feel Gavin behind me doing some fast swerving as several branches nearly wiped him out.

Lee glided to a halt under a big old gum tree and got off the Yamaha. He walked it into the bush and hid it. I got the drums off the back of the Polaris, then took it down the track another thirty metres and pushed it behind a tree. Without being told, Gavin covered it with bracken and branches.

We slung the rifles over our backs. Lee picked up two drums and Gavin and I got one each. I didn't know how long Gavin would last with his but every bit helped. I glanced at him as we set off. He looked calm but how could any of us be calm, walking into a gully full of killers? I'd rather be getting a family of snakes out of the woodheap.

For the first few minutes we took no great care but then Lee signalled with a finger to his lips that we needed to get quiet. Gavin was falling behind but when I tried to take his drum he snarled at me and I snatched my hand back. I counted my fingers quickly, and he smiled. I felt proud of that – getting a smile out of Gavin was hard work sometimes.

We side-slid down a gully into the bed of an old creek. A little water was running along it. That was good as it helped wash away any noise we made. My arms felt like they were going to drop off. I couldn't imagine how Gavin was still carrying his drum. Lee, in front, looked as steady and calm as ever. I think he had the leaking can though, as the smell of petrol kept wafting back over me.

The further we went, the slower Lee went. Soon he was stopping every five or ten metres to take a good look ahead. I realised in the middle of this just how quickly and easily I had slipped back into my wartime role. It was like the worries of my parents' deaths and the financial hassles with the farm, even the really important things like the Legal Studies assignment I was planning to do this same lunchtime, all of it had dropped away. I was back with Lee, on our way to meet Homer, we were out there in the bush against a dangerous enemy, and in a weird sort of way it was comfortable. All my senses were functioning at maximum revs. I was wide awake. Somewhere along the way, during the last year or so, I'd become good at this stuff. Maybe I should join the Army.

While I was congratulating myself on my brilliant military skills I nearly ran into Lee's back. He was behind a tree and he looked around and frowned when I bumped his petrol can. 'How about we leave the fuel here and see if we can get a look at the set-up?' he whispered.

'OK.'

I pointed to the drums, made a 'stop' gesture at Gavin, and mouthed, 'You stay here, look after the petrol,' and he nodded calmly. 'What does he do with his fear?' I asked myself. Occasionally it showed, but not often.

I knew he would be safe. He mucked around all the time when there was no pressure on, but he wouldn't do anything stupid in a situation like this. And he'd be happy now that he had something important to do.

Lee and I left the creek and, unslinging our rifles, went a bit higher. I could see that the gully was opening out ahead. We moved carefully through the bush. Lee led me about three-quarters of the way up the ridge. It was steep country but quite bare. I was trying to stay calm and focused but I couldn't help thinking that it was rare for us to be doing anything like this in broad daylight. Pretty dangerous.

We stopped about a thousand times. If sentries had caught Homer, we had to assume they would be out here somewhere. And probably more of them than before, now that they'd been spooked by Homer's arrival. On the other hand he could have just walked into a couple of blokes coming back from a party in the nearest town. We didn't know, but we always had to assume the worst.

At last I caught a glimpse of movement. I grabbed Lee from behind. He just nodded, to show he'd seen it too. We crouched slowly and shuffled into the rocks a bit further. I got up higher and found a friendly boulder, and from behind it realised I was looking down on the whole camp.

It was quite a set-up. There were four buildings that I could see, prefab places that looked like the demountable classrooms we had at school. They hadn't made much effort to camouflage them. I could see only six soldiers, who were in a mixture of uniforms and T-shirts and jeans. But two of the soldiers were definitely on guard, outside a yellow building. Of the others, one was crouched in front of another building, having a smoke, two, both carrying rifles, were talking to each other at the side of the clearing, and the last was walking away into the bush. Luckily on the other side of the clearing. He too carried his rifle.

I pointed to the building that was guarded and Lee nodded. So that was where Homer and possibly Nick

Greene were held. I assumed one of them at least was still alive, or there wouldn't be any need for guards. So that was the good news.

Now that we were here, looking at the reality of it, my confidence started fading. We couldn't just shoot these people out of hand. That'd be murder, wouldn't it? Officially we weren't at war with them anymore. And anyway, if we did start shooting we'd probably get killed. If there were twenty of them we were way outnumbered.

I slithered back a little and Lee joined me. 'What do you think?' I asked him.

'It's hard to say. Half of them could be out in the bush. But they're not very organised. They looked like a mess this morning. Torches rushing around everywhere. Half a dozen guys with rifles could have picked them off easily.' He looked at me then added, 'Where do you want to set off the petrol?'

'Over that way.' I nodded to the other end, away from where Gavin was waiting. 'Unless . . .'

'Unless what?'

I'd been planning to detonate the petrol some distance off, to start a diversion. But now, looking at the landscape, I had a different idea.

It would be wild and it would be risky, but if it came off it could just reduce the odds a bit.

CHAPTER 13

IT TOOK FOREVER to get organised. We had to be so careful. On the one hand there was a sense of urgency, because every time I looked at the campsite I felt they were getting busier. In particular there was more and more movement around the yellow building where we assumed Homer and the Greene guy were held. I couldn't work out what was going on, but I was getting bad vibes. As soldiers went in and out I imagined, or sensed, that they were acting cocky and aggressive. Kind of high-powered. Around the rest of the camp they seemed pretty lazy.

Then at about two o'clock a vehicle came in and parked quite close to the building. I had the feeling that it was going to be involved with Homer and Nick Greene in some way. My hunch was that it was going to take at least one of them away. I didn't have any evidence for that. Just the way it was placed I guess, and the way the driver, when he got out, talked to a couple of soldiers, with a lot of gesturing at the demountable.

The ute was a funny little green four wheel drive, a

Suzuki, with a tray back. For a moment I got the sick idea that maybe it was there to take away a couple of bodies but I shook my head fast to get rid of that one. I couldn't let myself think in those terms.

The car's arrival showed at least one thing though, that there must be a driveable track going out to the north-west. I didn't know if that information would be any use to us but I filed it in the back of my mind.

We spent nearly two hours watching to see what they were doing in the way of sentries. Boy, did that bring back memories of the war. Already, in the months since it had finished, I'd more or less forgotten these long, boring but tense periods of time. They were boring because you couldn't move, you just stayed hidden in your spot, watching and listening and getting thirsty and hungry, and they were tense because your life was on the line and at any moment there could be a disaster. I think only people who have been there can understand what it's like. From a distance I suppose war can seem exciting, but for every five minutes of wild head-spinning, gut-churning, nerve-charging action there's a hundred hours of hard slogging and tedious work.

Anyway, as far as I could tell there was no real system of sentries. Instead there seemed to be guys out in the bush wandering around with their rifles, each with his own area to cover. Some were dangerous and some were slack. For example, some came into the campsite to talk to their mates and have a smoke, until the guy in charge pointed them back into the bush. But there were times when a whole large area would be unpatrolled for more than twenty minutes, even half an hour. It wasn't much of a window of opportunity. But it was all we had.

At last I signalled to Lee that we should sneak out.

It was hard to move for the first few minutes – I was so sore and cramped from being in the one spot. But I knew we couldn't leave Gavin any longer.

When we got to the creek bed I couldn't see him for a minute but then he dropped from a branch right above my head. Gave me a hell of a shock. No matter how long I was caught up in this fighting stuff I seemed to have trouble remembering a few basic rules, one of which was that you need to look above the level of your own eyes. I wished I could remember it. My chances of staying alive would increase quite a bit if I did.

I explained to the boys what I had in mind. They looked doubtful but I guess neither of them had any better ideas, because they didn't say anything.

It meant using Gavin, which I didn't like as a matter of principle, but it's funny how when you're desperate and everything's on the line principles can fade fast from your memory. Of course he was happy to be involved, even if he wasn't confident about my plan. I think he was too lonely and even scared to be on his own for hours more. He figured that being in the attack had to be better than spending more time alone. I wasn't so sure I agreed, but we were fresh out of choices.

We had to do two trips with the drums. We left the leaking one till last, to cut the smell factor down. They really were too heavy for Gavin, and the ground was getting steeper, so Lee and I took one each.

It was an excruciating little journey. The trouble was, we couldn't just move on a hundred metres, have a look round, and move on again. We had to go from one hiding place to another. Gavin was quite useful, because we could send him ahead to check that the way was clear. It was his job to find each new hiding place. And in the bush, in daylight, there aren't actually a lot of hiding places for three people and two drums of petrol.

He did a pretty good job though. A couple of times he had us in situations where we really didn't have enough cover. One was a hollow in the ground where we were expected to lie down and somehow be out of sight, and the other was a hollow tree that barely had enough room for him, let alone us two as well. But I think we were able to convey to him that we didn't appreciate being turned into easy targets, and he soon got the message.

A hundred metres from the point I wanted to reach we holed up between a couple of grass trees. They were a bit prickly, but it was a good spot to wait. From there Lee could begin his journey to the other side of the gully, taking the drums, while Gavin and I went back to the gully to get the other two.

I had to take a short rest back there. I seemed to have no energy left. I wanted to get to Homer as soon as possible but I'd had no food, no water, and we'd been on the go all day. Gavin beckoned me down the creek bed a bit further and showed me a pool the size of a table. The water seemed clear enough and I drank it like a dog, head down and bum up, lapping away till I could feel it washing against my insides.

If the first trip had been tough the second was a nightmare. I knew it would be of course. Maybe that's why I felt so stuffed before we started. But even so. Again I got Gavin to range on ahead but this time I had to carry both the drums, with a rifle across my back that got heavier with each step. At least one of the drums felt only half full now. I wondered if Lee had taken both his drums together, like he'd planned, or whether he'd given up and done them one by one.

And then suddenly we were in trouble. I'd just joined Gavin between a couple of smallish boulders, neither of which offered much cover. I could see the problem though. There wasn't anywhere else for quite a way. But just as I got to him I heard footsteps coming towards us, at a slightly higher level.

They sounded like they were about fifty metres away. I tapped Gavin on the shoulder and gestured to him to be quiet. He looked up at me, anxiously, but with an expression of . . . I don't know what exactly, but he didn't take his eyes off me for the next few minutes. The steps got slowly closer and closer. I was sweating, feeling like a trapped fox, about to gnaw my leg off so I could escape. I knew there was no-one to defend us here. International law didn't stretch this far into the bush.

I shuffled around to get my rifle off my back. God, if I had to fire it here, there would be hell to pay. I'd probably be signing the death warrants of Homer and the Greene guy. And probably Lee's as well. But what else could I do? If he found us, if we let him capture us, that'd probably result in death warrants all round.

I had to manoeuvre the rifle around Gavin's head. There wasn't much room. The steps were so close and somehow the sounds were getting magnified in my head. I shifted my position slightly. I couldn't work the bolt on the rifle as it would make too much noise. Still, I'd have a moment. He'd be so shocked that he'd take a second or two to react, surely?

He was right at the rocks. He stopped. It was like he knew we were there, just a metre away now. He'd lean forward, turn his head slightly to the right and see us. That'd be the end. I could imagine it so clearly. I even knew what his face would look like. His shocked hard face, the face of a killer. I raised the rifle another few inches. What was he doing? Why the delay? Was he trying to torture us? I heard a funny noise. A gushing of water, quite a strong stream. A pungent smell drifted into the space between the rocks. At the same time a bubbling darkish pool started to spread towards Gavin's feet.

Any other time I might have got the giggles. My eyes locked on to Gavin's. Luckily we were both too scared to laugh. Then I started to feel revolted by the smell. Working on a farm, you see everything, you smell everything, you get used to anything, but somehow this really made me feel disgusted.

Maybe it wiped out the smell of the petrol for him though. Maybe he didn't have much sense of smell. Who knows? They say kids have a stronger sense of smell than adults.

The gushing stopped. I distinctly heard his zipper go up. That's how close he was. Then the footsteps started again and he went on his way.

Gavin, with a mixture of joke disgust and real disgust, showed me how the urine had reached his shoe and wet the side of it. I made a face then put my finger to my lips. We still weren't safe from this guy, not by a big margin.

But he didn't come back. After about fifteen minutes we crawled out, looking around like wombats sniffing the evening air, and set off again. I hoped Lee wasn't getting too worried. We hadn't worked out what to do if he got no signal from me. We should have. We already had enough problems.

It was another fifteen minutes before we got to the grass trees. And as we got the pair of drums into place, we started to lose control of the situation. It was like we'd triggered trouble. We hadn't of course, it was just coincidence, but I've never been too sure about this coincidence thing. My friend Robyn used to have some joke about coincidence being God's way of telling you to wake up. Except I don't think Robyn saw it as a joke. She was pretty religious. Maybe it wasn't a joke.

In this case though, it was more likely to be the devil telling us to wake up. Because suddenly it looked like they were going to do something with Homer and the other guy. The man in charge strode out of one hut, yelled a few orders, and the next minute half a dozen soldiers had lined up in a little squad in the middle of the clearing. They did it pretty efficiently too. I wasn't wildly happy about that. I'd almost been forgetting that they were in some way members of a military force. I'd been trying to convince myself that they were slack but they didn't look slack while this guy was in charge.

They had their rifles too. I was even less happy about that.

The way they kept looking at the hut where we thought Homer was held made me certain this activity was aimed at him: him, Nick Greene, or both. Then the boss started in on a speech, pointing at the yellow hut from time to time. The vibe was not good. Things were getting scary. I had a sour taste in my mouth, a sour smell in my nostrils.

At this point I decided we'd better go into action quick, even though I felt far from ready. I hoped the man in charge was making a long speech. I waved a quick goodbye to Gavin and started working my way around towards the back of Homer's building. 'This could get ugly,' I thought as I went. 'We're relying too much on luck here.'

A couple of times I had no cover at all and had to

dash across open ground: fifteen, twenty metres. In a way the group of soldiers on the other side, even if they'd forced me to move too early, were doing me a favour. It was like the parade ground had soaked up seven people. It had become the centre of gravity for this little area – all the energy was focused on it – and that somehow gave me more freedom to operate around the boundaries of the campsite.

I didn't know how long this mob had been camped there but it was quite a while, because they'd cleaned out all the sticks and bark for a long distance around. That would have been for their cooking fires. I knew what it was like. The first week it's so easy – you just grab kindling with one hand and firewood with the other and you hardly have to move from where you're sitting. The second week you find yourself walking fifty metres to get it. A week or two later you're scouring the bush at such a distance that by the time you get back the fire's gone out.

So yes, these guys had been here months I'd say. That was great for us because it meant we could sneak around more easily, making very little noise. And at the back of the yellow demountable the ground was so bare – well, except for a few rocks – that it was like walking on the asphalt playground at school.

All the same, I was pretty happy to arrive at the twisted old gum tree behind the hut, which Lee and I had agreed was my target. I wished I could have leaned against it for a moment to get my breath back, slow my breathing, and thank my lucky stars. No hope of that though. I picked up a rock, ready to lob it through the one little window in the rear wall of the demountable. I signalled to Gavin, then to Lee, with a quick wave. The idea was that they would be watching for the signal. I just hoped with ginormously great fervour that they were doing exactly that.

Everything seemed to stop for the next minute. My heart included. I could hear the voice of the commanding officer guy still, but I didn't see anyone. The breeze stopped, the leaves on the trees were still, the sun hung frozen in the cold sky. Then it began. I saw Gavin's side first. A flash of fire through the bushes, then a second flash. I don't know how he got them so close together. I grabbed a quick look at Lee's side. Yes, same thing there.

I couldn't stand around waiting for the full effect. I had to move, and now. I moved.

There was a whoosh from up on Gavin's hill and the first yell from the other side of the building. I chucked the rock straight through the window. It made some noise but not enough to be heard over the noise from the petrol drums. I grabbed the windowsill, hauled myself up, feeling the broken glass splinter my hands, and called, 'Homer, Homer, quick.'

It was a huge relief to hear his voice. 'No good, Ellie, Nick's too weak to get out the window.'

Oh shit. I'd never thought of that. Oh shit. Now what? I couldn't believe it. I looked around, desperate. Nothing. But at the front of the building was that funny little Suzuki-type vehicle. Well, if I couldn't use that in some way, we were sunk. We were dead. Half unconsciously I heard the roar of flames from the hillsides and even the 'bong, bong' noise of one of the drums as it bounced down to the bottom of the slope. I couldn't have much time before they realised it was all just a big distraction from the main event. I was the main event and I didn't want to be.

I ran to the car. Thank God the keys were in it. What was I to do? I yelled through the wall: 'Stand back, Homer, I'm going to ram it.' He shouted something but I couldn't hear. I was already racing back to the car. I started it, swung it around, reversed a bit, then drove hard at the wall. It felt weird. I was only in first gear but I was going, I don't know, between twenty and thirty maybe. The building gave a kind of lurch. The car bounced off the wall, and came to rest parallel to the hut.

I'd managed to open a split right down the wall. It didn't look nearly enough for a person to get through. I jumped out and ran to it. I could see Homer's dark skin through the gap. From the other side of the building the shooting started. If I'd been scared before I was petrified now. It reminded me too strongly of the shots I'd heard not long ago, the shots that killed my parents. I got the shakes. I glanced into the back of the Suzuki. Just the usual junk you'd find in any four wheel drive. A length of chain. Could I do something with that? My hands seemed like they wouldn't pick up anything. I had two goes before I could grab it. I dragged it out. I dropped the big link at one end, over the towbar, and carried the rest of the chain to the split. I was trying to calm myself. I know that the more you rush the more mistakes you make, but sometimes it's just too hard to stay steady. I yelled to Homer, 'Can you put this over something?' and shoved the other end of the chain at him.

He yelled back, 'Yeah, the tap.'

'The tap?' I thought. 'God, I don't know whether that'll be strong enough to hold it.'

But there was no time for a debate. However there

had to be time to wait till he did it. It would be hopeless if I took off in the car and he hadn't secured the chain.

That was the longest wait of my life. It had to be at least fifteen seconds. Maybe even twenty. Then I heard Homer: 'Go! Go!'

I sprinted to the driver's seat, threw myself in, turned the wheel hard, and tried to find the restraint to go forward slowly, not to take off at fifty k's an hour. I compromised. Probably got up to twenty pretty quickly. In my mirror I could see the split widening, opening, but at the same time there was a sudden mangling and twisting of the pipe going up the outside wall and into the demountable. It twisted and writhed like a snake on an electric fence. Then a jet of water shot up. I assume it was gravity fed, but it must have come from a high position to get pressure like that. It was stronger than we got at home. It was stronger than the fountain at the Stratton Mall. Stronger than a squeezed pimple.

I stopped as the roof of the building started to fold inwards and upwards at the same time. Lucky these demountables were made from recycled aluminium drink cans. I jumped out of the driver's seat then jumped straight back in when I saw a man staggering through the crack. I was hoping they'd only need me for driving. I glimpsed Homer's face in the darkness behind him. I remembered the chain, and got out again. I raced around to the rear and yanked it off the towbar. Now Homer was scraping out through the wall too and suddenly both of them were hurrying towards the little four wheel drive. The other guy looked pretty weak and skinny though, and Homer had to help him. The Suzuki was a two door with just a front seat. Luckily it was a bench seat.

It was so hard to hold the car there as Nick Greene started getting in. All my instincts screamed at me: 'Hit it! Take off! Get out of here.' I felt the Suzuki creeping forward as though it had a mind of its own, even if my foot was on the accelerator. Nick was in now and crowding close to me. He smelt terrible. Absolutely terrible. Overpoweringly foully awful. I tried not to show how disgusted I felt. Homer was half in the car and that was enough for me. I took off.

'Jesus,' I heard Homer yell, but I didn't care. He could look after himself. He was the one who'd been stupid enough to get caught in the first place.

I swung the little car round in a turn so tight that two wheels left the ground. I felt us rocking wildly. Nick clutched my arm, which didn't help. We landed on the ground again and finished the tight skidding turn. Now I was heading more or less in the direction I wanted to go. The car was still rocking from the violence of the turn but I hit the accelerator anyway. Out of the corner of my eye I realised Homer was still not completely inside. Maybe I had been a bit hard on him. Then I stopped thinking about him as I heard a bang from the back and felt the little car go up and down. I glanced in the mirror and nearly let go of the wheel in horror. A soldier had just jumped on the tray. I'll never forget that face in the mirror. I've never seen anything so ugly and frightening. I don't know where he'd come from. I thought they were all around the other side, dealing with the rolling drums and the fires we'd started. This guy had a rifle and he was already raising it. He had amazing balance. His feet were well apart, but the way we were rocking wasn't helping him.

We were sitting targets, literally. For the soldier, it'd

be easier than shooting those little tin ducks at the Show.

I did the obvious thing and slammed on the brakes. What happened next was maybe the most amazing thing I'd seen since the war started. He fell forward, crash-landing on the tray, and shot himself. I didn't realise for a few moments. I heard the rifle go off, and I shrunk down in the seat as though that would some- how protect me. Then I heard a wild, horrible scream from the back. I realised it was him. I pressed down hard on the accelerator. The Suzuki took off like a rabbit from a Rottweiler and aimed at the faint track I could see ahead. It wasn't really a track, but I could just follow the wheel marks from where the Suzuki had driven in.

At the same time I wanted to see whatever was hap- pening behind us, but it was difficult to do that and drive. In the wing mirror I did see the lines of fire burn- ing quite strongly down one side of the gully. I couldn't see the other side. I just had to hope Lee and Gavin had gotten out of there, but men were running up and down the hill with buckets of water. In the rear vision mirror I got a glimpse of at least three soldiers coming after us. It seemed like it had taken them that long to realise any- thing was happening on this side of the building. One of them had just fired – he was still on one knee and I saw him take his eye away to have a look at the result. I even saw the little puff of smoke drifting upwards. I hadn't been aware of any shots. I also had a glimpse of the arm of the man on the back tray of the Suzuki. He was waving to his mates, a weak little salute. It struck me that in a way he was now on our side. They'd be reluctant to shoot if they thought they'd hit him. He was our accidental human shield.

It was time for some creative driving. There was so little room to zigzag but I had no choice. I ran the four wheel drive up the side of the gully to the left then swung it back to the right. There was a scream from the back. I hoped he wasn't the kind of person who got seasick. I swerved around a huge log and went up the left-hand side again, but not as far. Everything depended on my being unpredictable. Nick was falling against me and I had to shove him off. The screaming from the back was louder than the car, louder than my heartbeat even. I actually saw a branch shot from a tree to my left, about a metre away. It wasn't a big branch, but it was just above the height of the vehicle, and it was unnerving to see the explosion of splinters and dust as it started to fall. I swung the wheel hard to the right and down the hill we went again, almost straight down. Up the other side and we hit a rock that I hadn't seen. We hit it so hard it jarred the steering wheel out of my hands.

I grabbed the wheel again and spun it round. I could see the end of the gully now. There was a clear track for fifty metres and I zigzagged along that. I was hoping for an intersection with the track Lee and I had followed on our motorbikes earlier. Trouble was, it had been a dying track. It had been fading quite some way back. But I saw a gap in the trees that could have led to it, so I raced straight for it, for the dark patch. We went flat out, maybe fifty, sixty k's an hour, and then yes, onto a corrugated old logging road, and we were in the bush.

I felt good.

The good feelings lasted all of twenty seconds, till the road ran out again. We were suddenly facing a wall of new growth timber.

I hit the brakes. I said to Nick, 'Can you walk for a bit?'

'I think so,' he said. He had a nice voice. I left him to think about that while I jumped out. It was good to get away from the smell.

I took a look at the guy in the tray. One look was enough. He was in serious trouble. Blood was smeared everywhere. It was bright red and it was literally smeared, like someone had taken a rough old paintbrush and pushed it around on the aluminium tray. His face was completely drained of colour. His eyes were closed. I thought he was dying, or already dead. I took his rifle and chucked it across to Homer.

'Maybe we should try to stay with the vehicle,' he said, ripping an ammunition pouch from the man's belt.

I knew what he meant. If we could drive further we would have a better chance.

'There's a gap,' he said, nodding at the trees up higher. 'Might be a track.'

I hesitated. 'All right,' I said. Making a face I dropped the back of the tray and pulled the bloke out by his feet and let him fall to the ground. He made a kind of groaning noise as he fell, so he wasn't dead, but I think he was pretty deeply unconscious. As he rolled a couple of metres down the track I caught a glimpse of some dark and light brown intestines or organs coming out through a hole in his stomach. I felt as though my own intestines were about to come out, through my mouth. My stomach rolled over like a heavy gym mat.

I threw myself into the driver's seat again and drove up to the gap, through the grass. It seemed like a long trip, and a rough and wild one. There were all kinds of hazards in the grass: logs, rocks, holes. It was like driving over twenty speed bumps every hundred metres, and doing it way too fast. As I got close to the gap in the trees Homer yelled out. His voice was muffled for a moment because he was turned right around, looking through the window behind us, but then as he swung back in my direction I got the full force of his voice. 'There they are, just down the hill. They're firing already – shit!'

The engine had stopped dead. Just when the gap was getting so close. Another thirty metres and we'd have been in the cover of the bush. I'd never had an engine cut out like that before. I realised it had to be a bullet through the motor. Nothing could be done about that. I threw open the door and piled out, trusting that Homer and Nick Greene were doing the same on their side. Putting my head down I started the sprint for the trees but realised even as I took my first step that I couldn't desert Nick, much as I was tempted to. I went round to him. Homer was already helping him, with an arm round his shoulders. He's a big boy, Homer, but he can be gentle when he wants to, which is about once every three years.

The bullets were whining past, mostly to our left, I think. Nick was panting, trying to walk and not doing too well. I think it was fear as much as physical weakness. I grabbed him around the waist and we half carried him. We got fifteen excruciating metres, then twenty. You could hear the bullets moving in as the soldiers adjusted their aim. Then one twanged by me so close I actually felt the heat from it on my cheek. I put my spare hand up to my face, expecting to feel a burn. Nick twitched and half staggered forward and I was sure he'd been hit. We were into the shadow of the trees. A bullet thwacked a trunk ahead of me and the whole tree trembled. We dragged Nick those last couple of metres. We were in cover. Very temporary cover unfortunately. But we'd bought a minute or so. I turned at once to Nick. I grabbed him by the shoulders, almost shook him.

'Are you OK?'

He nodded and gulped. His Adam's apple was jumping like a lamb on a spring evening. I still wasn't convinced. 'You didn't get hit?'

'No, no.'

'Well,' I thought, 'he ought to know.'

There was no time to carry out a medical examination. We had to turn our attention to other matters. Namely, how to outrun fit strong soldiers when we were half exhausted and one of us could barely walk. Homer did have the rifle I'd thrown at him. I'd left mine in the cabin of the Suzuki. We took a few steps forward but I knew we couldn't outrun them. The only options were to hide or fight. I said to Homer, 'Cover me,' and started back towards the four wheel drive.

'What?' he said.

But I didn't have time for a conversation. I was almost out of the protection of the trees already. I knew I had at least a few seconds free time before they'd react. The last thing they'd expect would be that one of us would come back. A glance downhill showed me I'd got that right. They were spread out across the slope, heads down, ploughing their way towards us. They hadn't even seen me yet. I was actually at the car and grabbing the rifle before the inevitable shout told me I was in trouble.

Homer must have been waiting for it too because the first shot came from him. That sent them all diving into the grass. I flattened out, staying at about snake level as I slithered back. Later I realised that they wouldn't have been able to see me when I got down low like that, because of the way the hill sloped. Wish I'd known that at the time. Instead I was shaking so hard I needed a straitjacket to hold me together. Apart from anything else I was worried about Homer shooting me by mistake.

We were on quite a well-defined track. It was fairly open bush, which was not good for us, but had under-growth a metre high, which wasn't bad. There was a lot of that thin sticky grass though, the stuff the old people call 'wait-a-while', because once you got caught in it you had to wait a while to get free again. That was more bad news. With no particular plan we ran along the track. I was looking for a place where we could either hide or make a stand. Nick was on his own and falling back so fast that after fifty metres he was twenty-five metres behind. So that was hopeless. We had only seconds left. And if we dived off the track looking for a place to hide, we would leave tracks so obvious that we might as well have driven a tractor through.

That's when I heard a faint buzzing. It was coming from the other side, the opposite direction to the sol-diers. For a moment I thought, 'Sheez, we're really in trouble now.' Then I realised it could only be one thing. I called to Nick, 'Quick, get round this bend.'

It gave him a bit of motivation I guess, to have a tar-get that he could achieve. As we got to the curve I heard the shouts of the soldiers behind us. Hiding was no longer an option. We would have to stand and fight and hope that those buzzing noises were coming in our direction, and that Lee and Gavin were responsible for them. If not, we were all done for. Our lives hung by a line as thin as a single horsehair.

I pushed Nick towards a rock and told him, 'Stay behind there.'

Homer and I went back a little way towards the bend. He took the right-hand side and I took the left. There were enough rocks for both of us to get some cover, but not much. I cocked one ear for the buzzing noise at the same time as I cocked the rifle. The noise seemed to be going away. I felt sick but I had to block out the fear and do whatever I could do. Whatever I was capable of doing. I lined up one of the first soldiers in my sights but hesitated, trying to get a good target. Again Homer fired first. He missed I think, but it sure had an effect on them. They went to ground. Bodies rolled in all directions and came up firing. I'd been underestimating these guys. They were real soldiers.

I cowered behind the rock. I think they were firing on automatic, because the bullets sprayed everywhere. But it didn't make any difference: if the air's full of bullets it's full of bullets. They flew past me. It was like the twanging of lots of rubber bands, like when we fired letters to each other in class – or when the boys fired pellets. I saw clods of dirt exploding on the track as bullets hit them, chips in the rocks as bullets hit them and whined away. I hoped Nick had his head down.

I got off a few shots but I know I didn't hit anyone. It was too difficult to take aim when they were keeping up such a barrage. Even worse was that they were advancing under cover of the fire. I listened desperately for the motorbikes. They didn't seem to be getting closer but the good news was that they didn't seem to be getting further away. Then suddenly the putt-putt of the engines came clear and undiluted from right behind us. I spun round, full of hope, but prepared to be disappointed. If it wasn't Lee and Gavin we were dead. But there they were, in the distance, at the next corner. Lee was on the four-wheeler and Gavin on the Yamaha. Lee was on one side of the track and Gavin on the other. Gavin was standing astride the bike, which was really too big for him, and both of them were trying to suss out the situation, poised to turn and take off at a moment's notice.

It was time for us to beat an orderly retreat, as General Finley would have said, or to get the hell out of there, as I would have said.

'Ready to go?' I yelled at Homer.

'Oh yeah, might as well,' he answered. 'Nothing better to do.'

Typical.

We both fired a volley of shots then started wriggling back. When we thought it was safe we got up and ran. There was no danger here from direct shots but there was a danger from ricochets. We had to take that risk. As soon as they realised we were gone they'd be after us like foxes in a chook shed.

At the same time I waved urgently to Lee. He revved up the bike and charged forward. He couldn't see what was ahead, so he had no idea of what he was getting into. But the only way we could get out of there was to put Nick on the four-wheeler.

We met at Nick's rock. We were in an elbow of the track, just out of the line of fire, but we wouldn't be safe for long. Nick picked himself up and Homer helped him out. Lee swung the bike around in a tight little turn that basically only involved the rear wheels. While he was doing that I went out wider, in a low crouch, then lay flat and kept firing down the track, pretty much anywhere, trying to hold them back a bit. Half a dozen times I saw soldiers in the scrub, heading my way, but not so as I could get a shot at them. They kept firing but like me, at random, as they worked towards us, trying for better positions.

Nick, looking pretty damn anxious, got on the bike. It took him three goes. When he was at last sitting behind Lee, Homer and I climbed onto the running boards. Two soldiers appeared, much closer, one on each side of the track. I realised they'd been more organised than I'd thought, those last couple of minutes. They'd been doing one of those military thingies where two of them go a few metres then crouch and call the next two through while they cover them. I yelled at Lee, 'Get a move on.' I tried to aim and fire and keep my balance all at the same time, but there was never much hope of that. 'Zigzag,' I yelled at Lee, and after that it was all I could do to stay on. Lee was a born zigzagger.

As we took the corner and reached Gavin he was already swinging the Yammy around. He followed us. Around the next bend we did a quick reorganisation. I took the bike off Gavin – although he wasn't too keen to give it up – and put him on the back of the four-wheeler with Nick and Lee. It was quite a crowd but there was room for them all. I took Homer on the Yamaha and away we went.

CHAPTER 14

IT WAS A long tough ride home. A number of times I made them stop so we could disguise our tracks. I couldn't afford to have clear motorbike tyre marks leading straight to my place. We did a few different things. Went on some major detours through kilometres of bush that was just scrubby stuff, no good to anyone. Went down a nice wide section of a creek for quite a way and left it again over an area of rocks that wouldn't show any marks once the tyre tracks had dried out. Mostly though we just got off from time to time and went back and used branches to smooth out the dirt where our marks were too obvious.

It was difficult, because the four-wheeler, with its wide tyres, ploughed up the ground pretty badly. It was also difficult because everyone was so tired. Nick, poor bugger, couldn't do a thing. I don't know what he'd been through but it was worse than a birthday party. Lee got progressively more wrecked – this was his second long return trip on the bikes. Homer didn't have much energy left after the stress of being locked up, thinking he was about to be executed at any moment. Gavin, despite his age, kept going pretty well. But to be honest I had to do most of the work.

The last hour or so we reached new depths of tiredness. None of us was any good by then. There were moments when the noise from the Yamaha seemed far far away, and more like the rumble of surf than the mumble of a motorbike. At those moments I had to make a huge effort to wake up. I remembered asking my father years ago if you could fall asleep on motorbikes. It seemed an amazing idea to me. It should be impossible, to sleep when you're sitting on a motorbike that might be going at a hundred k's an hour, and you're getting the full blast of air in your face. It was against all the laws of sleep, surely? But my father said, 'You can fall asleep anywhere,' and told me a story about how he'd been harvesting day and night and then gone to play cricket for Wirrawee on Saturday and fallen asleep while he was fielding at fine deeper legside, or somewhere like that.

Homer was definitely falling asleep against my back. I gave him the big elbow shove, nearly knocking him off the bike, and said, 'Come on, wake up, you're not allowed to go to sleep. You've got to keep me awake.'

He retaliated by launching into his full repertoire of the songs that he knew irritated me the most. But there was nothing else for it. If I was going to stay awake I had to join in. There were even occasional bursts from the other bike too.

This is the song that never ends,
It just goes on and on my friends,

Some people started singing it,
Not knowing what it was,
And now they keep on singing it,
Forever just because
This is the song that never ends . . .

A million green bottles,
Sitting on the wall.
And if one green bottle
Should accidentally fall,
There'd be nine hundred and ninety-nine thousand, nine
    hundred and ninety-nine green bottles,
Sitting on the wall.

This was not much good to Gavin. At one stage Lee had to stop and move Gavin to a position between Nick and him, because they were worried he would fall asleep and disappear off the back of the bike. He looked quite comfortable wedged between the two older guys though.

We set off again, with another burst of awful music. The only other song Homer knew required a bit more imagination. You had to make up verses using people's names.

In the store, in the store:
There was Ellie, Ellie,
getting pretty smelly,
in the Quartermaster's store.
My eyes are dim, I cannot see,
I have not brought my specs with me,
I have not brought my spectacles with me.

There was Lee, Lee,
he'd gone for a pee,
in the Quartermaster's store.
My eyes are dim, I cannot see,
I have not brought my specs with me,
I have not brought my spectacles with me.

Oh we were regular karaoke machines that evening. But I'd better not mention what we rhymed Homer with. It wasn't a true rhyme anyway.

It was really dark by the time we got home. The answering machine was full: mainly with worried messages from Homer's mum and dad. He was meant to have been home after school and when they couldn't get any answer at my place they started getting panicky. And there were a couple from Jeremy Finley and from Jess. I was sure one of them was the leader of Liberation and their carefully worded messages didn't do anything to change my mind.

Homer rang his parents straight away and told them I'd had a cow stuck in the lagoon and it had taken all that time to get her out, which was true enough, just a couple of weeks out of date. Then he rang Jeremy and told him in fairly guarded language what had happened. Nick was keen to get to a phone too, but I persuaded him to have something to eat first. I thought he was going to pass out at any moment and I didn't want him fainting on the phone. We were all desperately hungry. We sat at the kitchen table hoeing into minestrone that I'd made at the weekend. The only way I'd been able to manage the food side of life was to get in the habit of making a whole lot of stuff at weekends and freezing it. As I took the minestrone out of the microwave I thought ruefully that this weekend's work hadn't lasted long. Thanks to Lee's bad influence, the minestrone was all I'd done.

I asked Nick, 'Have you been a prisoner since the war ended?'

He did seem a nice guy. He was very tall and serious looking, but why wouldn't you be serious after what he'd been through?

'No,' he said. 'Just the last seven weeks.'

He didn't talk much at first but with each spoonful of minestrone he seemed to get strength back. Good advertisement for my soup. I hoped Gavin was paying close attention. He'd never been crazy about my minestrone. But Gavin looked like he could hardly get the spoon to his mouth. He was a fair bet to fall asleep by the halfway mark.

'So how'd it happen?' I asked Nick.

'I'm a member of Cross-Country.'

'Oh, OK.'

I could kind of guess the rest, although Nick told me anyway. Cross-Country was an organisation of people who believed that the best hope for the future lay in reconciliation, trying to build bridges between the two countries, trying to understand each other's cultures, that sort of stuff. They had friends and enemies on both sides of the border. I knew quite a few people who thought they were disloyal, or to put it a bit stronger, traitors. To be honest, I wasn't too keen on them myself.

Nick's particular group had gone over there, legally, to give advice on agriculture. Even though the peace settlement meant that ninety per cent of the best country was in enemy hands, they were making a mess of it, because they didn't know anything about local conditions.

'I'm an agricultural economist,' Nick explained, 'and I was going round the place giving advice on cereal crops. It seemed to go well at first. Then, I don't know, I felt that they were getting more hostile. There was a different mood. My interpreter disappeared one night, just wasn't there suddenly, and late the following morning these guys turned up at my hotel and said they were taking me to meet a group of farmers. The atmosphere wasn't good, I'd have to say, but I didn't feel I had much choice. Well, as you can imagine, I never got to meet the group of farmers. I got in the car, and no sooner were we out of town than they pulled guns on me and took me to this camp, not the one where you found me. Originally it was down by the river, in quite a nice open area, but then they moved into the bush. We've been there ever since.'

'Why'd they kidnap you anyway?' Lee asked.

'They said I'd been preaching Christianity.'

'And had you?' I asked.

He looked a bit disconcerted by that. I suppose I did ask it aggressively, but I've never been a big fan of the idea that you can go in and superimpose your idea of the true religion on top of other people's idea of the true religion. After all, your idea of the true religion seems to depend entirely on which family and which country you're born into.

Robyn was heavily into Christianity but she'd never have done that kind of stuff.

Nick went a bit red and tried to look straight at me.

'Not really,' he said. 'If people asked me, I gave out some literature. That was all.'

I wasn't too sure that I believed him.

'You want to make those phone calls now?' I asked him, as Homer came back into the room.

'Oh yes, thanks very much.'

He was on the phone a long time. It was terrible of me but I couldn't help thinking ruefully of my telephone bill. Now that I had to pay stuff like that myself, I'd taken a slightly better attitude to wasting money. It still seemed to pour out the door and windows anyway. Even all the fuel we'd used on this raid – the four drums we'd exploded, along with the amount the bikes had used – it was all money, and I didn't like my chances of Liberation or anyone else offering to reimburse me.

Half an hour later I felt really guilty for thinking that. I was on the way back from putting Gavin to bed and I heard Nick crying on the phone. It made me sympathise a lot more with what he'd been through.

Homer had gone home, borrowing my Yamaha. He was still trying to work out how to explain to his parents the complete loss of his motorbike. Lee was waiting to get to the phone, to check that his brothers and sisters were OK. My energy levels were like my bank statements, in the red. Feeling depressed I went to bed.

I slept for eleven hours. Another missed school bus, another missed school day. I took another hour to get out of bed. I was still so exhausted I could hardly walk in a straight line. I don't think it was physical tiredness so much as the aftershock of yesterday's danger and excitement. At least I managed to reach the kitchen OK. I sat waiting for the electric jug to boil, thinking of the cattle and how hungry they'd be, trying to motivate myself to get out and deliver their hay.

A scrunch of gravel outside did wake me up. It was the scrunch of car wheels.

My first reaction was fear. Could this be a reprisal already? Who'd be visiting at this time on a school day?

I peeped through the kitchen window, but there was only an old Falcon. A man and a woman were getting out. They were both tall and stringy. I realised then who they were.

I went out, wincing as the cold air hit me. 'Hi,' the woman said, holding out her hand and giving me the chance to inspect every tooth in her mouth. 'You must be Ellie.' She took a deep breath. 'Thank you. Thank you. We're so grateful that you answered God's call and brought Nick back to us.'

'So you're Nick's parents?'

The man had been busy locking the car but now, as she nodded, he came over too and shook my hand. 'We owe you a lot,' he said.

I was deeply embarrassed. This kind of stuff had never happened during the war. In those days it was all survival. There wasn't time for anything else.

'Well,' I said weakly, wondering why he'd locked his car, and still trying to function properly, 'would you like a coffee? I don't know whether Nick's even up yet. We were all pretty flattened when we got back last night.'

But Nick came into the kitchen at a half-run so I guess he'd seen them from his window. I figured this was an absolutely excellent time for me to feed the cattle so I did a quick change and headed out the door.

It was good to get back to the natural rhythms of life. I don't know what it is about cattle. They're so different to sheep. The original beasts Dad bought had been in such poor condition and now they were fattening up nicely, putting on some serious kilos.

I'd gotten to know them well. They were a motley crew. There were quite a few escapees among them, two especially. They were both on the small side but they kept pulling off escapes that would have made a World War II prisoner proud. They could have taught Nick a thing or two. It didn't matter how many times I improved the fences, they kept getting out. Usually leaving their calves on the other side of course, which wasn't very considerate of them. Sometimes they took one with them. I'd get rid of both cows in the first draft I sold, just as someone had gotten rid of them to us. They were too much trouble.

Then there were the ones with poor forequarters or the ones whose back lines were out, or the ones who rejected their babies or were too aggressive towards Gavin or me. In my mind they all got pink slips. I had to build up some decent bloodlines again, as soon as possible. We used to have a reputation for that. I was a bit embarrassed that these beasts would be sold with our name on them.

Still, for all their faults you always end up feeling affectionate towards them sooner or later. As with any mob there were characters. We'd given nicknames to a lot of them, and some of those were for obvious reasons: Dribbles, Patches, Fatso, Sticky-Beak, Big Tits. Big Tits was Gavin's choice, needless to say.

Some of them weren't so obvious. Phar Lap got her name because she could out-gallop the others. If you turned up with hay at a time when they didn't expect it she was the first one there. Casanova, because even though he was a steer he was always on the back of other steers. Winfield, because he blew great clouds of steam on cold mornings.

OK, they were pretty dumb names, but you've got to do something to entertain yourself when you're out in the paddocks on those same cold mornings.

By the time I got back to the house everyone was up

and about. Nick was waiting to say goodbye so I got that over and done with. He said some pretty sickly things, but he couldn't help that – I'd probably have done the same if I'd been in the hands of guerillas all that time, not knowing whether I was going to live or die.

To tell the truth I was proud of how we'd managed it. I mean, just over twenty-four hours ago I'd been getting ready for another boring week at school. But I was feeling a little inner glow at the fact that I could still do it, that I still had it. Whatever 'it' was. I even thought that if the farm failed – and there was every chance it would – I could look at a career in the military. Didn't know what I'd do about Gavin in that situation.

With Nick and his folks out of the way I could at least sit down in the kitchen, build up the fire, and relax with Lee and Gavin. Lee had negotiated by phone with the people looking after his brothers and sisters, and he was staying another two nights. Gavin was delighted about this. I was happy but wary.

Homer turned up just before lunch. Trust him. He could smell food from ten k's, and that was on a still day.

I just chucked bread and marg and stuff at them and told them to make their own sangers, but it did give me the chance to hear what had happened to him.

'Yeah, it was pretty embarrassing really,' he said. 'I was sneaking down the hill and the next thing there's a rifle jabbed in my back and a voice telling me to drop my gun.'

'How did that happen?' I asked.

He looked disgusted and embarrassed and amused, all at once.

'He was taking a toilet stop in the darkness, in the bushes to my right, sitting there quiet as a mouse, as you do, when I came sneaking past, quiet as another mouse.'

We all laughed. 'You should have smelt him,' Gavin said.

'Yeah, well, I did a moment later. A moment too late.'

'These guys have a bit of a toilet problem I think. They're always doing it. Gavin and I almost got caught by one of them taking a leak.'

Gavin held his nose. 'Yeah, they stink,' he said.

'So what is it with Liberation?' I asked. I hate not to be part of a secret or a mystery. Homer knew that, and it maddened me to have to ask him straight out, because it guaranteed he'd enjoy telling me as little as possible.

'Hey, I told you, it's all secret.'

'Don't we get automatic membership for saving your ass?'

'Do you want to join?'

'I don't know.' I sat back and considered.

Gavin piped up: 'I want to join.'

'Look,' Homer said, 'it's not like the Secret Seven or the Famous Five. We're not some club with passwords and secret handshakes.'

'Oh. Well, in that case I don't want to join,' I said.

'But seriously . . . ?' he asked.

'I'll be totally honest with you,' I said slowly. 'Yesterday was frightening. Trying to get that hole to open up in the demountable, thinking that at any moment these guys would pop around the side and start shooting, yeah, on the terror scale that was right up there with the best of them.'

'But . . .' Homer said, staring at me, knowing there was more to come.

'OK, yes, there is a but.'

'And I bet I know what it is,' Homer said.

'It was bloody exciting,' I said slowly.

'Exactly,' Homer said, leaning back in his chair.

'I know what you mean,' Lee said. He leaned back too, and folded his arms.

'So are we turning into thrill junkies?' I asked. 'Do we have to put our lives on the line every few days just to get a bit of satisfaction in life?'

Homer shrugged. 'Why are you acting so surprised? Didn't you know that already?'

'No, I didn't as a matter of fact.'

'Think back to before the war,' he said. 'If you can remember that far back. The way Sam Young jumped on the bull in the stockyard? Or Jamie Anlezark and Melissa Carpenter surfing on the cattle trucks as they came into the saleyard. Or you and me playing polo on the motorbikes? Without helmets? How many times did we come off? How come we didn't kill ourselves sixteen times over? What about that time you knocked yourself out on the rock? I thought you were dead then.'

I shuddered. 'Don't remind me. And we agreed not to tell my parents, because we thought we'd get in so much trouble.'

Homer went on: 'Why do you think people went canyoning before the war? Parachuting? Bungy jumping?'

'OK, wise guy, you tell me why.'

'It's because the only real enemy humans have is death. Every other enemy, like a kid who slags you off at school, or a cop who pulls you over, you think they're enemies, but they're not really. They're just, I don't know, irritations. But death, that's the serious one, because you know he'll win eventually. And that makes you, like, you've got to try to beat him. The bigger the challenge, the harder you try. That's true of anything. In a way our enemies aren't these soldiers themselves, our enemy is death, and the soldiers are just his little local representatives.'

'Yeah,' Lee said. 'You know fun parks, all those rides. People think they're spitting right in the face of death when they go on those things. They're not of course, but they think they are.'

'So you're saying that we've got to do this? To prove we're immortal?'

'Well, it's not that simple. It started off that we had to do it. But even though we were so scared and sick and confused, right from that first day I can remember something else: just a little tingle of I don't know what . . . "We're on our own and this is a massive adventure". Something like that.'

'And then it did become a bit of the death-defying stuff,' Lee said. 'Along with a lot of other things.'

'Yeah, I admit I was aware of that at times,' I said. 'At Cobbler's especially. And the airfield. But ninety-nine per cent of the time I was like "I hate this, get me out of here, I want to go home to Mummy and Daddy".'

Through the window I could see Gavin, who'd given up on this discussion and gone out to the courtyard. He was up on the high wall doing the tightrope walk to the other end. Just like I'd done when I was his age.

'Oh sure,' Lee said, 'we were all "Help, I want out", most of the time. But you can't just choose that out of the war and say it's the whole story. People are always doing that. They announce that teenagers do drugs because they're bored. Or because of peer-group pressure. Or because, I don't know, because they get coded messages when they read a magazine in reverse or something. Well, here's a bit of Asian wisdom for you. It takes many ropes to make a fishing net. And what's more, if one rope's missing, you don't get no fish.'

'So one of our ropes is that we love danger and we want to defy death?' I asked.

'Yeah, I think so,' Homer said.

'Hmm, one time I would have laughed at all this. But now . . . I don't know. Yesterday I was more aware of this stuff than I was before. I knew I was on a high at the same time as I wanted Superman to fly in and do the job for me.'

'So do you want to join Liberation?' Homer asked.

'But why do you need Liberation? Why can't the Army or someone do it? What do they do exactly?'

Homer shrugged. 'That's easy. There's no way official Army units or people can go over the border for this stuff. If they were caught and interrogated and it turned out they were in the Army, it'd be a disaster. It'd be obvious the government had condoned it. It'd mean another war. But there are a lot of occasions when people are needed to go over the border, like to get Nick Greene, nice geek, I mean guy, that he is. So there's actually quite a bit of unofficial encouragement for groups like ours. It's my guess that we're getting information from the Army about what's needed and where to go and how to find people.'

'I can guess where that would come from,' I said, thinking of Jeremy Finley. I could imagine a line stretching right across the Tasman, from the Australian military to General Finley in New Zealand, and the line coming all the way back across the water to Stratton or Wirrawee.

Ignoring me, Homer went on: 'For example, we even knew what hut Nick was in. Usually Liberation's intelligence is pretty good, although sometimes they make mistakes, or of course things can change between their getting information and us arriving on the scene. I think a lot of it comes from paying people on their side. It all seems pretty corrupt.' He shrugged. 'Anyway, I'm just repeating what I've been told really. I've only done two of these raids. And the first one was easy. Four of us went and it was tame. See, the thing is, their Army's kind of slack. That group holding Nick seemed a cut above the average.'

'They weren't bad,' I said, remembering how quickly they'd fallen in when their boss yelled at them. 'But why do they get young people to do this stuff?'

'Why not? Plenty of people our age have been involved in wars over the years. But in fact I think most of the other Liberation groups are older people. There are at least five groups in other districts. We're known by different colours, like Green, Purple. We're Scarlet, just as a joke, after the book. And our head honcho, the Scarlet Pimple, happens to be a teenager who happens to be in a unique situation to do it. Also, don't forget what our little group achieved during the war. We did get kind of famous for five minutes, remember. In fact nearly ten minutes. We basically did a better job than any other group operating behind the lines.

'There's quite a few people in the Army who'll tell you that teenagers are especially good for this stuff, because we think more flexibly. We're faster on our feet. It makes sense. I mean the older you get the more likely you are to be locked into certain ways of doing things, certain patterns of thinking.'

'God, I hope the day never comes when I'm like that,' I said.

'You already are, the way you're looking after Gavin,' Lee said.

I thought that was a cheap shot, even though I knew what he meant. I filed it away for future reference.

'I mean, don't underestimate yourself,' Homer said. He was starting to sound like a school counsellor. He sure had changed since the war started. 'We developed skills doing that guerilla stuff, and we became really good at it. The way you got Nick and me out of there, and that thing with rolling the drums down the hill, and the way you and Lee and Gavin worked together, that was classy. You wouldn't have been able to do all that a couple of years ago. Anyway, to cut a long story short, Liberation'd be rapt if you joined. They'd be over the moon.'

'Even Jess?' I asked.

'Oh yeah, Jess, once you get to know her –'

He stopped, realising he'd been sucked in. Now I knew the name of at least one other member of Liberation.

'Very funny,' he said. He was furious.

'I'd hate to see you under interrogation,' I said cruelly. 'You'd give them everyone's names in five minutes.'

There was a yell of pain from outside. Gavin had fallen off the wall.

CHAPTER 15

IT WAS LEE'S last night, definitely his last night. As he said, 'No matter what happens, I'm out of here tomorrow morning. Come floods, bushfires, locusts or Jehovah's Witnesses, I'm going home.'

As I served up yet another stir-fry from my very limited repertoire I felt that there was a bit of tension in the air. We hadn't discussed our relationship again since the day in the paddock. As far as I was concerned we didn't have a relationship. Well, not counting friendship. But we'd never officially put it to rest and I suppose there was almost a feeling that it was dormant, not dead, that it could be revived given the right conditions. Like, for example, if we were the last two people left in the world.

Maybe Gavin felt it too. Or maybe he was upset that Lee was going home. Maybe he was just tired. Anyway, he was terrible that night. He actually picked up a handful of food and chucked it at me when I told him to hurry up and eat his meal. Both Lee and I stared at him in shock. But he just looked sulky and angry. I didn't have the energy to deal with this. I sat down opposite him and said, 'What did you do that for?'

He wouldn't answer. He dropped his head, and of course it's hard to talk to a deaf kid when he won't look up. It must be one of the great things about being deaf. You can sulk so spectacularly.

'Oh God,' I said to Lee. 'You do something. I'm not in the mood.'

'What do you want me to do?'

'Well, what do you do with your brothers and sisters when they carry on like this?'

He considered for a moment. 'If it's Pang, I'd ban her from the computer for a week. If it's Phillip, I'd send him to his room. Paul, I'd yell at him and chase him around the house wishing I had an AK-47. If it's Intira, she's so good this would never happen.'

'Great. And you're the one who tells me I'm too boring and inflexible when it comes to Gavin.'

'I didn't say I was any different.'

I laughed. 'But we shouldn't have to be doing this. We're too young. Our biggest worries should be homework and parties and dating.' I blushed when that word slipped out, and hurried on. 'A bit of babysitting, OK, fine, but not 24/7.'

'I guess I'm getting used to it,' he said. 'I hated it so much at first. But you look at those photos from Africa and the one thing you always notice is kids looking after their sisters and brothers. I mean, four-year-olds carrying babies, five-year-olds with three smaller kids trailing after them. So in a sense we had it good for a long time.'

'Oh yeah. I suppose. But it doesn't actually help much when I have to turn down a cappuccino with friends from school because I've got to come home and look after Gavin. Or I have to quit a party early. I can't leave him here on his own because I'm so scared that the soldiers might come back.'

'I've got good neighbours. They help out. But I don't like to keep asking them.'

'Yeah, Homer and his mum and dad are good. And the Sandersons, but Gavin doesn't like them much for some reason.' I sighed. 'I guess I shouldn't whinge. I've only got Gavin to look after; you've got four.'

'Yes and no. You really can't compare, because everyone's different and the circumstances are different.' He paused. 'I mean, what's the real story with Gavin? Are there any good things about having him here?'

I opened my mouth to answer and as I did I glanced across the table. Gavin had lifted his head again and was watching me like a sheepdog with a mob in a corner of the paddock. You could never tell how much of a conversation Gavin was following – usually with long conversations he didn't bother trying after a few minutes – and I didn't know how long he'd been tuned in to this one, but he'd certainly understood Lee's last question. I said, 'Oh yeah.' I grinned across at Gavin. 'He's only smashed up the motorbike three times.'

I knew it was wrong as soon as it was out of my mouth. Gavin pushed back his chair. It fell with a clatter onto the old stone floor. He yelled at me, 'I hate you,' and ran down the corridor. A moment later I heard his bedroom door slam so hard that dead moths fell off the light shade in the kitchen.

Lee looked at me and started to say something but when he saw my expression he changed his mind and cleared away the dishes instead.

I'd been psyching up for the last big talk of this visit from Lee. At first I didn't want it and then I thought perhaps I did, but whatever, I'd been all tense and now that tension was draining away into nothing. It was like getting all passionate with a guy – and that guy could even have been Lee – and then having to stop just as this amazing feeling is spreading right through you. And part of you has been saying all along 'Bad idea, shouldn't be doing this,' but another part is ready to throw everything to the four winds and go for it. As I realised that Gavin had sabotaged any chance of Lee and I talking things through I started to feel flat and depressed. The conversation with Lee got more and more lame. When we were down to a word a minute I chucked some scraps in a bowl for Marmie and went to bed.

Gavin's door was still shut and I think his light was off. I didn't bother reading for a while, like I normally do, just turned my light off and lay there feeling defeated by everything. The farm would go broke, I would fail school, Lee was going back to the city leaving me alone again. I couldn't even do a good job of looking after Gavin.

My door suddenly creaked open and I looked up. My first thought was that it might be Lee. I think I wanted it to be Lee. But in the dim light that came down the corridor from the kitchen I saw a smaller figure. Amazing how someone who was deaf could move so quietly, but Gavin had always had that skill.

I moved over. He burrowed in beside me. After a minute he put out his hand into the cold air and turned on my bedside lamp. Seemed like I was going to have a conversation after all, even if it wasn't with Lee. I looked at him and waited. His right eye had always drooped a little but now both eyes were half closed. I couldn't tell if it was because he was sleepy or because he'd been crying. Gavin crying: that was an entry for the Guinness Book. But when I looked closely I thought it was more that his eyes were adjusting to the light of the lamp.

He didn't say anything. But he'd turned on the lamp. Seemed like I was being given an opportunity to make up for my unfortunate comment in the kitchen. I didn't know what to say though. It was always so difficult with Gavin. His life was built on no foundations. He stood on a flimsy structure of balsa wood and paper, trying to get as high off the ground as everyone else. Any time you wanted to knock him down you blew on the paper and he crashed all the way to the ground.

'Why'd you chuck the food at me?' I asked.

He shrugged. His face started to darken, to close over. He thought he was in for nothing but a nagging.

'It was a pretty good throw,' I said, teasing him.

He almost smiled.

'You're getting a bit of muscle.'

No reaction.

'You are quite handy to have around.'

No reaction.

'You're good with the stock.'

He frowned. 'What?'

'The stock. The cattle.'

'Oh.'

'You're a good fighter. Brave.'

No expression.

'Not bad on a motorbike. Bit dangerous sometimes.'

'You can't talk.'

'Oh! Excuse me!'

Period of silence. During it I heard something Gavin couldn't hear. Lee's footsteps coming softly along the corridor. My bedroom was at the end of the corridor. Already he had passed the other rooms.

I said to Gavin, 'Are you sad about Lee going?'

He shrugged. Trust Gavin not to admit to anything like feelings or emotions.

'I'm sorry I didn't say the truth in the kitchen,' I said.

Lee's footsteps stopped outside my door.

'What truth?' Gavin asked.

There was a light knock on the door and the handle turned.

'Well, there's a bit more to it than smashing up the motorbike,' I said.

The door opened a little.

'Ellie?' Lee asked.

'Like what?' Gavin said.

The door closed again and the footsteps went away.

Gavin sensed that I'd been distracted. He stiffened a little, lifted himself up on his elbow and looked towards the door. Perhaps he had felt the draught of air. 'What?' he asked.

'Nothing.'

I waited till he'd lain back down. I traced the worry lines on his forehead with the tip of my index finger. I remembered the words on a postcard my grandmother had sent me from Paris once. I think it was by a writer called Gide. 'To be loved is nothing; it is to be preferred that I desire.'

'You're the most important person in my life,' I said.

He didn't say anything.

'You're my brother,' I said.

He didn't say anything.

'I love you, you little ratbag,' I said.

He smiled, snuggled down in the bed, and closed his eyes. I think he was asleep within fifteen seconds. I turned off the light.

CHAPTER 16

TWO DAYS LATER came the fortnightly cattle sales on the edge of Wirrawee.

I sat in the kitchen with the bills spread across the table. I jotted down the figures as I turned each new page. Later I'd MYOB all this in the computer but for now I just wanted a rough total so I knew how much I could spend. It was pretty frightening. Electricity, rent on the gas bottles, telephone, bolts for the cattle yards, worming tablets for Marmie, penicillin from the vet, a letter from Gavin's school wanting the 'voluntary' fees, doctor's bill for Gavin's earache . . . By the end of it I figured I could afford about the rear end of one small steer.

But, I went anyway. Before the war there must have been six hundred to a thousand head yarded each fortnight at the Wirrawee cattle sales, now there were usually three hundred to six hundred. Today was a big day, just over eight hundred. I wanted steers and I didn't care if they were in light condition. It was pretty obvious looking at them that, like most of the cattle in the district, they'd had setbacks but if they were well-boned and had length I thought we could fatten them up OK. I still had plenty of hay and some good feed left in the paddocks. If I got them at 220 to 230 kilos I could double that and sell them off at around 450 or so.

It was good being at the sales again. It made me feel that some things hadn't changed. Sure the sun still rose every morning and set every night. I knew that. But the sun doing its thing didn't impress me much. You could be rotting away in a prison cell and the sun would rise and set every day. What I really liked, and what meant the most to me, was that every second Thursday at the Wirrawee Saleyards, Barry Fitzgibbon would be up on the rails slapping his papers into his left hand and yelling, 'As lovely a selection of yearlings as I've ever seen yarded at Wirrawee, ladies and gentlemen,' and Morrie Cavendish'd be on his haunches smoking a rollie and whingeing about what a pack of dogs had done to his lambs, and Sal Grinaldi would be telling another terrible joke about someone having sex with donkeys or blondes changing light bulbs or an Englishman, a Scotsman and an Irishman playing golf.

The people at the sale were pretty nice to me. I hadn't seen many of them since the funeral, and I'd been so out of it that day that I wasn't sure who'd been there and who hadn't. Before the war if something awful happened, like your parents getting killed, the whole district would rally around and visit every day, and help with everything from fixing your fences to getting in your lucerne. Now, there was plenty of sympathy but not much else, for the simple reason that so many people had suffered similar disasters and there just wasn't enough lovin' and carin' to go around.

So an occasion like this was good because it gave everyone the chance to come up and ask how I was doing and to say they were thinking of me and could they help in any way. This made them feel better and didn't do me any harm, so everyone was happy. And from some people it was nice, because it was genuine, but from others it didn't mean an awful lot.

It was also a bit distracting because I needed to pay attention to the pens and the prices. And the prices were unbelievable. I got in early, tearing myself away from the well-wishers, and I bid while people were still arriving, which seemed like a good idea seeing how many cars were there already. I picked up twenty-four steers for $825 a head, which was expensive compared to prewar prices, but not bad the way things were now. It felt a little weird though, to think I had just spent twenty thousand bucks.

But soon $825 was looking cheap. By the time half the yarding was sold I was getting scared. A pen of cows went for $1550 a head. They were beauties, sure, but no better than the ones we were turning off regularly from our place before the war. I was determined that one day we would be known for quality cattle like these again.

I had my eye on a pen of twenty Poll Herefords. I thought I could make a quick profit on them. I was hoping to get them for $950, maybe a thousand. By then red-faced Jerry Parsons was doing the auctioneering. Like most people he'd returned from the war looking pretty thin but already he'd got his gut back and I must admit he looked more comfortable with it. He was in uniform. The R.M. Williams heavy check shirt and the R.M. Williams white moleskin trousers and the Akubra hat. His voice was sounding thinner and older but it was still strong.

He got to my Herefords and called for a bid at $900, and got it straight away, which was a bit of a shock. Normally no-one bids till the auctioneer's forced to go down to, I don't know, quite a bit less than the first price he asks for. I looked around to see who was bidding, and figured it was Don Murray, judging from his serious expression.

Then Mr Rundle came in with $925, Polly Addams went to $950 and Don Murray touched his glasses for $975. I was sweating. This had all happened in about twelve seconds and I hadn't got a bid in yet. Jerry Parsons didn't have to work too hard. Polly called $1000, Mr Rundle went to $1025, and Don offered $1050.

They hesitated a moment then. 'Ten fifty, ten fifty,' Jerry yelled, 'dirt cheap, they're an exceptional draft for the money, not much more than two dollars a kilo at this price.'

Pretty much none of that was true, but I asked him, 'Take ten?', and he nodded and I nodded back and suddenly I was in the bidding, starting at a level that was already way past what I wanted to pay. But I needed these cattle. I had to get some more stock so that further down the track, if everything went according to plan – and nothing else in my life was going to plan – I'd be able to make some impact on the huge loans from the bank.

'At ten sixty,' Jerry yelled, striking his hand with his rolled-up receipt book. 'At ten sixty, and I'm taking tens.'

Mr Rundle shook his head, Polly gazed away across the car park as though she were trying to remember a dream she'd had about the Taj Mahal or wombats or mango ice-cream, but Don Murray didn't hesitate. A quick nod and we were up to $1070.

I didn't know Mr Murray too well. I'd barely seen him since I'd arrived at Simmons' Reef, on a big quest to find my mother, what seemed like years ago, just as the war ended, and he'd been nice to me when I at last had the big reunion with Mum. I know Dad respected him and thought he had good judgement. He managed 'Blackwood Springs' for a plastic surgeon who lived in the city and only got to Wirrawee every three or four months.

Don was an old guy, with white hair and sharp blue eyes. He was a bit overweight. He was one of those people who gets dressed up for the sales, with the blazer and tie. But he looked really posh anyway, the way some people do no matter what they're wearing. He wouldn't like being beaten by a girl, I was sure of that.

I felt the sweat oozing out of my skin, somewhere around my eyebrows. 'Oh well,' I thought, 'if he wants these cattle he'll have to pay for them.' I nodded again. 'Ten eighty, ten eighty, ten eighty,' Jerry went, 'it's against you, Don, ten eighty, it's with Ellie Linton on my right.'

For the first time Mr Murray hesitated. I hoped we could quit there. I was never sure how much these auctions were to do with getting the right price for the stock and how much they were to do with power struggles. In the past I'd watched my father caught up in these little dramas, I'd stood by his side and felt his tension as he went hammer and tongs with one of his neighbours or someone from three hundred k's away for a ram or a bull or a pen of calves.

Now I was in that position myself. It was harder than I'd expected. I was attacked by so many doubts. It seemed like Don Murray and I were the only two people at this sale who thought these cattle were worth $1080 each. In a few moments one of us would stand alone: the only person who thought he or she could turn a good profit on these twenty beasts.

I'd always liked the sales before; I wasn't so sure that I liked them now. It was the ultimate test of my judgement and knowledge as a primary producer, and I was no way ready for it.

Don twitched his sunglasses and Jerry was away again. 'At ten ninety, ten ninety, ten ninety, and they still represent great buying. You've all seen the market, ladies and gentlemen, and it's got quite a way to run yet.'

Before I could think too much I nodded again. Eleven hundred bucks. At last Mr Murray turned away. What a relief. I'd paid far more than I wanted. I'd be buying armchairs for these beasts and hiring a nanny for them. But I still thought I could make it work.

I glanced down at Gavin. He looked as nervous as I felt. Then out of nowhere I heard another female voice.

'Eleven ten,' she called out clearly and firmly.

No need to look. I knew that voice. Polly Addams was back. Well, the good news was that someone else thought the Herefords were worth around twenty-two thousand dollars the lot.

That was the only good news though. I went right back into full sweat mode. My first instinct was to yell 'No fair', as though I deserved these cattle because I'd worked harder through the bidding than anyone else. My second instinct was to commit homicide, out of sheer frustration. I had the ultimate weapon right beside me too. I'm sure if I told Gavin to go and buzz that lady with an electric cattle prod he wouldn't have stopped to ask questions.

Still, no time to think about that. I hunched up my

shoulders. Could I make these cattle pay? It was a gamble, like so much of life on the land. If prices kept going up, OK, yes. If they went down much I would be wiped out. But I couldn't run a property with no stock. And there weren't many pens left at this sale. I gritted my teeth and nodded at Jerry again.

'Eleven twenty,' he called, on my behalf. 'Eleven twenty, come on, Polly, what do you say, I'll take fives. Yes, it's against you now, Ellie, eleven twenty-five.'

Gavin tugged anxiously at my sleeve. 'Lot of money,' he said. He'd got that right. I'd long ago forgotten the idea of turning a quick profit on these steers. I nodded again, and so did Polly a moment later. I bid eleven forty, trying to look confident, but I knew this had to be my last go. If Polly wanted them for $1145, they were hers.

She stared straight back at Jerry. About an hour passed, or that's what it felt like. I half hoped she'd bid again, so she could have them. Then she turned away and Jerry knocked them down to me.

'See if you can find Jack Edgecombe,' I said to Gavin, wiping my face with my hand. 'Ask him if he can take forty-four head for us.'

Jack was an old-timer with a cattle truck. He attended the sales every fortnight, along with half a dozen other truckies hoping to pick up work. Jack had been moving stock for us since the invention of the internal combustion engine. I think Gavin would have loved to adopt him as a grandfather. Mind you, Gavin would have happily adopted anyone with a truck or a bulldozer. He ducked away through the legs of the crowd and disappeared towards the trucks.

In the end we had a bit more than forty-four head.

The second last pen of the day, fourteen cows in calf, looked reasonably cheap on the prices people were paying. I was watching the bidding and next to me was Mr Young. Turned out they were his cows. When the bidding stalled at $990 he whispered to me, 'Look, Ellie, you could do worse than this lot. They've had an excellent bull over them, and they're all good mothers. I'm only selling them because I've got to make more room for the stud.'

He was a good guy, someone I trusted. So I put my hand up just as Jerry was about to knock them down to Wingaree Pastoral Company and that turned out to be the winning bid, at a thousand bucks. I had fifty-eight more cattle than I'd had at the start of the day and I'd spent nearly sixty thousand dollars. Then there was Jack's bill for bringing the stock out to my place, not to mention all the taxes and other excuses the auctioneers found for adding stuff to the bill.

I was still shaking when I got home.

CHAPTER 17

THE NEXT DAY started early, like so many of them do. Right on dusk the night before I'd noticed a cow with a prolapsed rectum, so we moved her into the cattle yard. Before going out to the school bus I nicked into the yard with a sleepy and complaining Gavin.

Dad had taught me what to do with prolapsed rectums and uteruses but it wasn't nice before breakfast. There was too much of it to push back in so I got a piece of poly pipe, about thirty centimetres, and drilled a hole halfway along it. Then I had the fun job of finding the actual hole in the cow, through all the maggoty mess of intestines.

'Hope you wash your hands after this,' Gavin mumbled.

Once I'd found the bum, with a bit of careful pushing and experimenting, I got the pipe in, up to the hole which I'd drilled. Gavin gave me the needle and the twine and I got stuck into my needlework. A bit different from the needlework all those elegant ladies had done in the nineteenth century. Basically I was tying the twine round and round the prolapsed part, using the hole in the pipe, until I could tie it off and let the cow go back to the paddock. After a while the prolapsed part would drop off, because I'd cut the circulation to it. And the twine would rot away too. The pipe would drop out and the cow could go on with her life, able to mix with her friends again without the embarrassment of poly pipe sticking out of her bum. In the meantime she'd have to poo through the pipe.

We only just made it to the bus but I didn't dare miss another day of school. Gavin and I must have had the worst attendance records in Wirrawee. I didn't like it for me, because I didn't necessarily want to spend my whole life on the farm. I wanted to go to university, at some stage, and although I couldn't begin to think how to manage it, I didn't want to slam the door on the possibility. But I'd have to do a bloody lot of work and get some serious passes in some serious exams.

And I didn't want Gavin to miss any more school, because he too was way behind. It wasn't just the war. I don't think he was the most academic person in the Wirrawee area, and being deaf made it harder because it took him longer to get the instructions. Plus he didn't get as much information as other students. I got the sense that the teacher would give the class a five-minute speech about something, much of which Gavin would miss, and then she'd give Gavin a twenty-second summing up of his own. So he got about a tenth of what they got. I was too distracted by everything that was going on in my life, most lately of course Liberation, but I kept thinking I had to do something about Gavin and school. The trouble was that it kept getting pushed down the list of priorities.

Anyway, at least this day we arrived on time. I watched Gavin get off first, when we stopped at the primary school. He hated for me to wave to him or acknowledge him in any way. So he usually ignored me. This day though, our eyes met, and I smiled, and he even gave me a glimmer of a fraction of a tiny grin back. That was extremely rare.

I felt guilty that I hadn't talked about school with him much lately. In the old days, from what he told me, on the rare occasions when he talked about the old days, he had a special aide in the classroom most of the time. Now the government couldn't afford such luxuries and he was on his own, in a classroom of thirty-five kids. And apart from his naughty little mate Mark, he probably was on his own. He certainly sat on his own in the bus, but there were only eleven primary kids on our bus, and five of those went to Our Lady of Good Counsel, and four of the others were girls. I had a feeling the girls would be cautious of Gavin.

Our Lady of Good Counsel. Catholic schools always have such poetic names. In Stratton there was Saint Joseph the Worker, and Our Lady Help of Christians. In the city I saw a Catholic high school called Star of the Sea. And I went to Wirrawee High School. Why didn't they rename it? 'Place of Learning Among the Pines.' 'School of Wisdom and Enlightenment.' 'Saint Ellie the Irresolute.'

I saw Jess as soon as I arrived. It was my first day back since the raid on the guerilla camp and I could tell the moment Jess looked at me that she knew. She had a little secret smile. 'Nice one, Ellie,' she said offering me a Tic-Tac. 'It's true what they say about you.'

'What do they say about me?' I asked. I was off-balance.

I wasn't sure these days if I still liked Jess, but I thought I probably didn't.

'Oh well, you know, all that stuff about you being such a war legend. I didn't know how much of it was exaggerated. But you sure saved Homer's ass.'

'Well, Lee and Gavin managed to give a bit of help from time to time. So, who told you?'

'Homer. But don't worry, I'm safe with secrets.' She pulled a newspaper clipping out of her pocket. It was already wearing away through being folded and unfolded, even though it was only a day old.

I guessed what it would be about.

Unconfirmed reports suggest that missing agricultural consultant Nick Greene has been rescued by the guerilla group calling itself Liberation. Greene, who had been accused of distributing Christian literature across the border, was taken hostage nearly two months ago, and grave fears were held for his safety.

Greene is a member of Cross-Country, a group committed to reconciliation between the two countries. A spokesperson for Cross-Country said only that 'Greene's circumstances had changed', and a further statement would be made within forty-eight hours.

No comment could be obtained from Liberation, who are a notoriously secretive group. Greene is thought to be recuperating with family members in the Stratton–Wirrawee area.

I shrugged and gave it back to Jess. 'Did you do the Legal Studies?' I asked her.

She looked at me. 'God, it's true, you do have ice in your veins,' she said.

It sounded like she was quoting someone else and I wondered who it was. Would Homer have said a thing like that about me? I didn't have ice in my veins when it came to wondering what other people thought of me, but then I was a teenager after all.

I headed for my locker but just as I got there I ran into Ms Maxwell. She was our Year Coordinator these days and every day she looked more harassed. Her hair looked wilder and her face was thinner and her glasses were further and further down her nose. 'Oh, Ellie,' she said, 'I'm so glad you still remember where your locker is.'

'Ha-ha very funny, Ms Maxwell,' I said.

'Well, I need to talk to you about your attendance, Ellie. What about you come and see me at the staff room at recess?'

'OK, Ms Maxwell,' I said. Great start to the school day. As if a cow with a prolapsed rectum wasn't enough. I wondered how Ms Maxwell would go stuffing a bit of poly pipe up a cow's bum at seven o'clock in the morning.

The day didn't get any better. We had double English, which was another reason I'd made an effort to get to school today. I don't mind the occasional English lesson. This year we had Mrs Barlow. I'd had her in Year 7 for English and Year 8 for Social Studies. That's another problem with a small school, you get the same teachers over and over again. Still, as you get higher up, things improve. Teachers treat you more like a friend, kids are nicer to each other, the atmosphere improves about a thousand . . . something. What do you measure school atmosphere in? Kilos? Metres? Degrees? I don't know.

We'd been doing some quite good stuff in English, including literary archetypes and fantasy novels. Mrs Barlow is a bit of a fantasy freak. She's always got some twelve hundred page epic under her arm. But this time I got the fatty end of the brisket. 'Would have been better to stay home and hoe out the early thistles,' I thought. 'Would have been better to get involved in another border raid with Liberation. Would have been better to watch re-runs of "The Nanny" on TV.' Because for one hour and forty minutes all we did was listen to a taped interview with a guy called Joseph Campbell. Unbelievable.

I did all the things you do when you're bored in class. Redecorated my folder. Wrote a letter to Fi. Kicked Homer when he made stupid remarks, which he still did with about the same frequency as he had in Year 8. For example: the guy on the tape is talking about mandalas, and how they represent harmony and balance within the self, so Homer deliberately hears it as Mandelas and announces that Nelson Mandela is so balanced he can sit on both ends of a seesaw at the same time. Like, not very funny, but probably better than listening to the tape.

At lunchtime I sat with Homer and Jess and Bronte. It was awkward having Bronte there because I wanted to talk more about Liberation, and even the raid to get Homer and Nick back. Sure I'd been extra cool with Jess, but that was showing off really. I did want to talk about it. It's natural: after riding up to the gates of death on a four wheel motorbike and then racing away again, you want to go over and over it with anyone you can. But I couldn't talk about it in front of Bronte, although for all I knew she could be a member of Liberation too. Watching her sitting there all calm and peaceful I realised how much I really did like her. Even if she was a year behind us at school she seemed as mature as anyone in my year. More mature than Homer, for a start.

I asked Jess about Jeremy, just to turn the tables a bit. I was pretty casual. 'So, have you seen Jeremy Finley lately?'

She did go quite red. She leant back in her chair and fixed her strong eyes on me. 'Oh, yes, at the weekend. Just for a barbecue. We should have asked you.'

It had already struck me that no-one was asking me to anything these days, I suppose because they were still nervous of me after Mum and Dad's death. Maybe they thought I was too busy? I kind of hoped these were the reasons. I'd hate to think it was for anything more personal, like I had a bad dose of BO, or my sense of humour didn't rate anymore, or I was too up myself.

'So how's Jeremy?' I asked.

She'd got back her cool. 'Sexy as ever.' She laughed. 'I'm making some progress. I'll keep you posted.'

Bronte opened the lid of her lunchbox. It looked pretty interesting in there. Riceballs and something a bit sushi-ish, and silver beet and something light green. Not the typical contents of a Wirrawee lunchbox. 'What's that stuff?' I asked, pointing to one of the vegetables.

'Celeriac,' she said.

'Celeriac.' Nice word. Up there with insouciance, tissue and alligator.

When the first bell rang I walked back with her. But as we arrived at the lockers I saw Ms Maxwell striding towards me. My heart suddenly sagged inside my chest.

'Oh, Ms Maxwell,' I said.

'Ellie, you were meant to come and see me at recess.'

'I'm sorry, Ms Maxwell, I clean forgot.'

'Well, you can come and see me now, thank you.'

'But Ms Maxwell, we've got Drama.'

'I'm sure Mr Elliot can do without you for twenty minutes.'

I followed Ms Maxwell along the corridor, staring gloomily at her back. She wore one of those tailored suits, an olive green pattern that looked like wallpaper. It made her bum look big. One side of her bum was having a pillow fight with the other side.

In her office she settled herself comfortably at the desk. I settled uncomfortably on the other side. She checked a file then looked over her glasses at me. 'Ellie, I know life has hardly been easy for you lately.'

She seemed to expect an answer so I nodded obediently. 'Yes, Ms Maxwell,' I said, not really thinking much, because people said stuff like that to me so often these days that it no longer had an impact.

'And we have every sympathy for you, and every desire to help you.'

'Yes, Ms Maxwell.'

'But at the end of the day we have to operate within guidelines laid down by the Department.'

'Yes, Ms Maxwell.' Teachers mentioned the Department in the same way that priests mentioned God.

'And, Ellie, I have to say that I can't see how you are going to meet the Department's minimum requirements for a pass.'

I sat there numbly. So much to deal with, and now this.

'You've missed so many classes, you're way behind on assignments, you're scoring failing grades right across the board.'

I'd given up saying 'Yes, Ms Maxwell.'

'There is one thing. You can plead special circumstances. Certainly in your case there are a lot of special circumstances. There's your wartime experiences – and of course nearly everyone can claim some kind of special circumstances as a result of the war – but more particularly there's the death of your parents.'

I nodded.

She waited quite a while but I couldn't think of anything to add. So she went on: 'To tell you the truth, Ellie, I'm a traditionalist. Yes, if you put in for it, I have no doubt you'd get special consideration. But where does that leave you? You'd get a pass without earning it. You'd get a pass even though you don't have the same knowledge other students have. And what happens next year, and the year after that? For how many years would you keep getting special consideration?'

She leaned forward and looked at me earnestly. 'I know a lot of people would say I'm being hard on you. And I'm not saying you should "get over" your problems and "get on" with life. You can't force that, believe me, I know. It will only happen when it happens. I am saying that if you can't pass this year you should repeat the year, and see how you go the second time around. Better that than to get credit you haven't earned, better that than to go on to university and have lecturers assume you know things you don't.'

I left her office in a state of confusion. I thought the idea of special consideration was that you would have passed the exams except for some disaster. That seemed fair enough. I mean, if I got that and eventually went to university, I might have problems. But not in all subjects. I didn't think it would matter so much in English or History, for example.

I didn't want to seem like I was looking for excuses though. Maybe Ms Maxwell was right. I didn't know. It was awfully confusing having to think a problem like this through, to work it out on my own. I wanted to sit with someone at the kitchen table for hours, exploring it inside out and upside down, then taking it on a long walk through the paddocks. But instead it just had to take its place in the queue.

CHAPTER 18

I COULDN'T BELIEVE how quickly the court case snuck up on me. So much had happened since the first one, and I'd almost forgotten Mr Sayle was doing his level best to get control of my farm, my money, and my life.

Two days before the next hearing I rang Fi's mum in the city and was devastated to hear that she couldn't come.

'I'm sorry, Ellie, but I've got a meeting of the Advisory Council. Did I tell you I'd been elected to the Advisory Council?'

'No, congratulations.'

I felt bitter. I hardly heard my own voice. All at once the death of my parents, always so close at hand, welled up again, and I was filled with anger at the way I'd been deserted. At the same time as I knew 'deserted' was a desperately unfair word I felt it pounding inside my heart and aching in my head. I'd had the same feelings when I thought Homer and Fi and the others had been killed in the attack on the petrol station during the war.

'To be loved is nothing; it is to be preferred that I desire.' So many times since my parents died I'd wanted to have the total undivided attention of a large number of people, including Fi's mother, Homer's parents, Homer, Fi, Lee, and half the teachers at Wirrawee High. Now, as I leaned against the kitchen bench, glaring at the Aga, the phone hanging off my ear, holding a mental rollcall of all the people who had betrayed me, Gavin wandered past, grabbed a banana, peeled it and sat there grinning at me and eating it like he was a monkey.

I couldn't help grinning back. For better or for worse he was still around.

'So what do I do about Mr Sayle?' I asked Fi's mum.

'It seems to me that the main issue for the magistrate was that she didn't have much confidence in Mr Yannos to look after your finances. So you've got to convince her that she's wrong about that.'

'How?'

'Now come on, Ellie, you're one of the more resourceful young people I've ever met. I'm sure you can think of ways. References, evidence of successful financial activity, whatever. I've got to go. That bank loan you got, the one Mr Sayle didn't like, if you can prove that was a good move, it'd help a lot. Sorry, Ellie, I really have to run.'

The following night I went over to see Mr Yannos. While Mrs Yannos fussed over Gavin, giving him cupcakes, which he loved, and Turkish delight, which he didn't love, I sat down with Mr Yannos. He was very methodical, but slow. He wrote everything on a pad of green writing paper. He took ages, and I got quite frustrated waiting for him to finish each point.

I explained how we needed evidence that he was a

good manager, with sound financial sense. He immediately got insulted at the idea that anyone would think he wasn't. I had to keep calming him down. But eventually he said, 'OK, I get the bank manager. He tell everyone I am no fool with money.'

'That'd be a great idea. And I'll try to get my bank manager, to say the loan I took out was a smart move.'

He pointed his pen at me. 'You know what? You get Mr Jerry Parsons and he say you bought cattle good at the sale. What you pay for those cattle?'

I told him.

'Ah!' he said. 'Already you up a hundred dollars a head.'

'You think so?'

'Sure! Where you been? You not looking at prices? Prices are crazy. Them cattle, you up a hundred bucks easy.'

Even so, it wasn't until we were standing outside the Courthouse waiting to be called that Mrs Yannos dropped her bombshell.

'I don't know why Mr Rodd want your place,' she said. 'What he want more land for? He got enough.'

'Mr Rodd? What are you talking about?'

She looked at me doubtfully.

'You know Mr Rodd!'

'Yes of course I do. He's a pig.'

Mr Rodd lived down the road. Somehow he'd kept virtually all his land after the war. There were ugly rumours going around about how he'd managed that, but I'm not going to repeat them here, the reason being that my dad had got really mad when I tried to tell him about them.

Mrs Yannos was still looking at me in puzzlement.

I frowned back at her. But you have to be patient when you want to find out stuff from Mrs Yannos.

'Are you saying Mr Rodd wants to buy my place?'

She pressed her lips together and shook her head. 'I know what I know,' she said. 'But maybe I wrong about this.'

'Well, maybe you're right.'

She raised her eyebrows and shrugged her shoulders.

'He'd be a very difficult neighbour,' I said, trying to tempt her into talking.

'Is not for me to say who you should sell to, Ellie, if God forbid you sell at all.'

'I don't want to sell to Mr Rodd.'

'Yes, and what I say is, why his brother-in-law tell you what to do? Is not right I think.'

'His brother-in-law?' I was getting more and more confused.

'Well, you know Mr Sayle is brother-in-law to Mr Rodd.'

'Mrs Yannos! Who have you been talking to?'

But I'd scared her off again. 'Just what people say,' she said.

A moment later my case was called. I walked in with my mind spinning. Already things were tough enough. Both the bank managers and Jerry Parsons had been unavailable. I'd asked them for written statements, and got them from Mr Yannos's manager, and from Jerry, but my bank manager, although she'd promised to have it ready, had gone to Stratton for the day and her assistant couldn't find any trace of it in her office.

Mr Sayle stood up and said pretty much the same things he'd said last time. I handed up the statements from Mr Yannos's bank and the letter from Jerry saying my cattle had gone up in value, but the magistrate only glanced at them. She seemed to be in a bad mood. 'Great,' I thought. 'My future gets decided by a judge with PMT.'

I told her again how much I wanted Mr and Mrs Yannos to look after me, how I didn't know Mr Sayle, and I added that I thought it was good to have three different points of view instead of just one. I knew I couldn't say anything about Mr Rodd because I'd only just heard about it, and I didn't know whether it was true. I wasn't sure if there was anything wrong with him being Mr Sayle's brother-in-law anyway.

When I'd finished, the magistrate wrote a lot of stuff. She seemed to take forever. I knew Mr Yannos would approve. Finally she looked down at me.

'Ellie, I know this is difficult for you to understand, but at your age you don't require the amount of parenting a young child would need. The main function of a guardian for you is to look after your financial interests. It seems to me that Mr and Mrs Yannos, who are obviously very good friends and good neighbours, will be there for you no matter what order I make today. But I'm not convinced they have the financial sophistication to look after your parents' estate. Therefore I am going to assign Mr Sayle as your guardian. Obviously your parents felt comfortable with his judgement, to make him trustee of their estate, so I'm sure they would approve of his having the legal care of you as well. And in the fullness of time you will appreciate that this is in your best interests.'

I didn't hear the rest of it, just sat there gaping at her. How could she? How dare she! How dare Mr Sayle! What kind of stupid morons made up these laws anyway?

My eyes stinging with rage I followed Mr and Mrs Yannos outside. Mr Sayle came up, looking as smug as a bull who's fetched top price at a stud sale. 'Well, there you are,' he said. 'I have to say it's a very sensible decision, Ellie. As she said, you'll soon realise that it's the best solution. Now why don't you give Mrs Samuels a ring and arrange an appointment and we can have another look at your affairs?'

I couldn't even answer him, and after an embarrassed silence he went off again, saying, 'Oh well, I can see you're a bit upset, but you'll soon be over it.'

I was meant to go back to school but I couldn't face it. I said goodbye to Mr and Mrs Yannos, who were looking bewildered and upset, and I got a cafe latte at Juicy's, in Barker Street. I was meant to be saving money but I didn't care at that stage.

The cafe was half full of soldiers. That was another thing we were slowly getting used to, soldiers everywhere. Conscription had started a month ago. Only limited at this stage. There would have been more but the Army couldn't cope with hundreds and thousands of new recruits yet. By the time we left school there was a fair chance they'd be ready to take us, although because of our family circumstances both Lee and I would get exemption. Special consideration again. If we wanted it.

To my surprise I saw Bronte hurrying along the street. I called to her and she came over straight away. 'What are you doing here?' I asked.

'Hi,' she said. 'God, so many soldiers.'

'Yeah. It's giving me the creeps.'

'Hey, careful.'

'Sorry,' I said automatically. Then I wondered why I

had to be sorry. 'What, are you connected with the Army or something?'

'My parents are both in the Army.'

'Really?' I realised how little I knew about her. 'What do they do?'

'God, how would I know? What does anyone in the Army do? I don't think it's anything very exciting though. They seem to spend their time with piles of folders and reports. And they both look pretty bored when I go onto the base to see them.'

'You don't live on the base?'

'No, it's all so new out there, and there aren't many houses. But eventually we'll move, if we're in Wirrawee long enough.'

'So what rank are your parents?' It was a relief to have something else to think about.

'They're both majors. I call them Major Major.'

I must have looked a bit blank because she added: 'It's a joke from a book. *Catch 22*. It was about the American Army in World War II, and there was a character in it called Major Major, because that was both his rank and his surname.'

'I get it. Like Doctor Doctor. You want a coffee?'

She looked at her watch. 'Sure.'

'So what are you doing out of school?' I asked again, when I'd finally fought off half the Army and come back with a black coffee and a latte.

'Oh, I just had to go to the doctor. Nothing much.' She brushed her hair from her forehead. 'I get dermatitis and I was picking up a new prescription. I keep hoping for the miracle cream to turn up and cure it but I think I'm stuck with it. I get rashes and stuff all the time. Then I scratch them and make it worse.'

'So where did you live before the war?'

'Before the war. That's our benchmark for everything now, isn't it? Well, we lived everywhere. Typical Army kid. I've been to eight different schools. Mostly with other Army kids, depending on where we were stationed. Sometimes we went to normal schools. It was good in a way, because you'd turn up at a new school in, say, Darwin, and there'd be three kids you'd been in Grade 3 with in Holsworthy and two you'd been in Grade 4 with at Puckapunyal and one you'd remember from Grade 1 in Townsville, and so it went on.'

'The paths kept recrossing?'

'Exactly.'

'Have you got any brothers or sisters?'

'I had a brother but he was killed in the war.'

'Killed?'

'We were being evacuated to New Zealand by helicopter. He was in the one ahead of me. We got separated at the last minute. I tried to switch to his one but they wouldn't let me so I just called out to him, 'Don't worry, you go on that one, I'll meet you at the other end.' I thought he'd be OK. He was with his friends and he'd been on a helicopter before. He just waved back. There was such chaos.' She shrugged.

'So what happened?' I was gripping the cup as my latte got colder and colder. She seemed so calm.

'It hit powerlines, just after take-off. Pilot error I guess. The weather was good enough. It fell on its side. And of course it was full of fuel so it exploded. We weren't even allowed to get out of ours. We took off about two minutes later.'

I tried to imagine how that would be, going up in one

helicopter as you saw your brother killed in another one. I tried and I failed.

'How old was he?'

'Twelve.'

'Was he a nice brother?'

Her face broke into a huge smile. 'Oh he was so cool! I know you're meant to fight with your brother and say he's a nuisance and all that stuff, but Michael and I were the closest friends you could ever be. He was so gentle and kind. He played guitar and he'd just started writing his own songs. I think he would have been famous one day. The songs were great. It was like someone a thousand years old had written them.'

Her eyes were moist now, but she shook her head and had a long sip of her coffee.

'Anyway, what are you doing out of school?' she asked.

'It seems almost insignificant now,' I said.

'Is it insignificant to you?'

'No.'

'Well?'

'This lawyer who's in charge of my parents' money, he wanted to make himself my guardian as well. I didn't want him, I wanted Homer's mum and dad. But this morning the court handed me over to him.'

'They did? Even though you didn't want him?'

'Yeah. Seems like that's the way it works around here.'

'That sucks.'

'You mind going down to the Courthouse right now and saying that to the magistrate?'

'What about the little boy, Gavin, who's his guardian?'

'Well, you know, I'm not sure. I think it was my mum

and dad. I think they got some sort of court order about it. No-one seems to care much about Gavin, I mean no government department. No-one's asked about him since my parents died. His school just acts like I'm suddenly his mum and dad rolled into one.'

'So it sounds like this lawyer guy might now be Gavin's guardian as well as yours?'

'Maybe. Sheez. God, that's terrible. This gets worse every minute.'

'But can't you do something about it? Come on, Ellie. You're a fighter. That's the way to be. I did boxing before the war. When you get knocked into the ropes you bounce off them and come back twice as hard and twice as fast. You use the ropes to work for you instead of against you.'

'You did boxing? Real boxing?'

'Sure. I mean mainly with the bag, but some practice rounds too, with real people.'

This girl was full of surprises.

'Can't you appeal?' she was asking. 'Or go to the papers? Or get some dirt on this guy? Tell them he dragged you behind the filing cabinets and felt your boobs? Why don't you fire-bomb his office?'

'Bronte!' I thought for a minute. 'There is one thing. Mrs Yannos said she thinks he and Mr Rodd are brothers-in-law. Mr Rodd's a farmer who lives near us. He's a real bastard, and Mrs Yannos reckons he wants to buy my place. So if Sayle – that's the lawyer – has complete control he could sell to Rodd at a cheap price and get me out of his hair.'

'Well, that's got to be illegal, surely?'

'I don't know. You'd think so.'

I kept thinking how generous she was to care about

my problems after what she'd been through. We finished our coffees and walked back to school. By the time we reached the gates there wasn't much school left for the day. I sighed. Another day for Ms Maxwell to mark off on her calendar as a backward step in Ellie's education.

CHAPTER 19

THE CONVERSATION WITH Bronte gave me some heart but by that night I was really down about it again. The situation seemed hopeless. There were too many forces on too many fronts to battle against. It was all very well for Bronte to say 'Fight', but I'd never had enemies like these before.

I needed someone else to talk to so I rang Lee. He wasn't always the first person I called when I was up to my neck in mud, but in my life there were Lee-times and Fi-times and sometimes even Homer-times, and this felt like a Lee-time.

His little sister, Pang, answered. I'd only met Lee's sisters and brothers a couple of times but I'd talked to Pang a lot on the phone, and she was my favourite. She was nine, and as bubbly as Lee was still, as noisy as he was silent, as funny as he was grave.

'Hi, Pang,' I said, 'how's life? Is Lee being good to you?'

'No, he's being horrible. He's always yelling at us and he picks on me and he's the worst cook in the world.'

'Why, what'd he give you for tea tonight?'

'Tonight. We had burnt newspaper and bits of old carpet, and . . . um . . .' Pang was obviously looking around the room for inspiration. 'And then we had the budgie for dessert.'

'You did? What's that I can hear singing in the background?'

'He was reincarnated.'

I could hear Lee saying, 'C'mon, Pang, is that Ellie? Give me the phone,' so I said a quick goodbye as she handed it over.

But when Lee came on I suddenly dried up. It had been an effort to be light and chatty with Pang. Now I couldn't keep making the effort. I heard Lee gradually getting more concerned. 'Ellie, are you OK? . . . Hello, Ellie . . . Ellie, what's wrong?'

Finally I whispered, 'I think I'm going to lose the farm.'

'What do you mean? Why? Are you broke?'

'No, not yet.'

'Was today the court case?'

'Yep.'

'Oh sorry. I would have rung. I thought it was next week.'

'Well it wasn't.'

'And you lost?'

There was another long silence. I said, 'Why is the world so awful?'

'Is it?'

'Everyone's so greedy. Everyone only looks after themselves. They're just out for all they can get.'

'Are they?'

'Well, take Mr Sayle for instance.'

'Take Robyn Mathers.'

'Take Mr Rodd.'

'Take Mr and Mrs Yannos.'

'Take the women in the prison ward, when I was shot. During the war.'

'Take Mrs Xannides.'

'Who's she?'

'The lady in the next apartment. She comes in and looks after the kids when I'm going to be late home.'

'I still think I'm right though. What about Hitler?'

'What about Nelson Mandela?'

'Stalin.'

'Martin Luther King.'

'Pol Pot.'

'I'll see your Pol Pot with Mother Theresa and raise you a Pastor Neimoller.'

'Who?'

'He was in a concentration camp in World War II and he volunteered to take the place of a guy who was about to be shot, because the other guy had a wife and kids.'

'God is there anything you don't know?'

He ignored that and ripped off another string of names, most of which I'd never heard of: 'Ralph Nader. Gandhi. John Lennon. Paul Robeson. Marie Curie. Bob Brown. Lassie.'

'Oh I don't know, Jack the Ripper. Stop being so annoying.'

He laughed, and I did too.

I rang Mrs Yannos and got loads of sympathy but when I started asking about any relationship between Mr Sayle and Mr Rodd I got nowhere. She just went all vague again. So I took a bit of a risk and rang Mrs Sanderson. I was really working the phone that night. I guess it was my way of fighting back, a little bit at least.

Mrs Sanderson was new to Wirrawee but she already knew ten times more about the district than I did. We talked about rainfall, cattle prices, and government rules and regulations, which had all become compulsory topics around here. After a while I got onto the subject of Mr Rodd's life and times, and just asked her straight out: 'Is his brother-in-law Mr Sayle, the lawyer in town?'

'Well, not exactly. No, there's no real relationship there. Mr Sayle's wife has a sister and she lived with Mr Rodd for a while. But that broke up pretty fast. I think it only lasted a couple of months.'

'That seems to happen a lot to Mr Rodd.'

'Yes, he's not my favourite person.'

I was exhausted after talking to her. I don't know why shopping, sitting in class and talking on the phone are all so tiring, but they are, especially shopping. Still, I wasn't ready to give up yet. My last call was to Fi's mum. I told her everything that had happened, including the bit about Mr Sayle being connected to Mr Rodd.

At the end she said what I expected: 'It's not looking good for you, Ellie.'

'But there must be something I can do.'

'Oh yes, you can lodge an appeal. But to be honest I'd be surprised if they agree to hear it. Appeal courts decide for themselves which cases they'll hear. I mean, the courts are so clogged and you haven't got any new evidence and I doubt if the magistrate's made any errors in law.'

'What about the connection between Sayle and Mr Rodd?'

'That's nothing by itself. His sister-in-law . . . And she and Mr Rodd aren't even together anymore. You'd have to prove a conspiracy, and you won't be able to do that. Look, I'm not sure of the law in this area, but I suspect that as your guardian he can probably sell the property to Mr Rodd at any halfway fair price. If he sells it at twenty cents a hectare obviously you can stop that. But as long as it's in a reasonable range he'd probably get away with it.'

'This is so wrong,' I wailed. 'It's so unfair.'

'Ellie, have you ever thought that maybe you're being a bit paranoid? He may have no intention of cheating you. After all, your father obviously trusted him. You're not going to like this, darling, but he may be right about the property. It may not be possible to keep it. He may just be acting in your best interests.'

Nothing in my heart or mind would let me accept this idea. I went to bed feeling that the only person on my side was Gavin, and I hadn't even been able to tell him what happened in court yet. I couldn't bring myself to do it.

I was so caught up in the whole thing, worrying myself into a coma, that I could have completely missed what was going on the very next day at the Youngs' place.

'Adderley' was about six k's from us. The Youngs had three kids: the twins, Shannon and Sam, and their younger brother Alastair, who was ten. All the kids were funny, which in itself was funny, because Mr and Mrs Young had as much sense of humour as a John Deere four wheel drive tractor. They seemed constantly baffled by their children. Mrs Young's brother had owned the property next door but he'd been killed in the war, on the first day. The Youngs inherited it but it was taken off them again in the redistribution, so they basically ended up back where they started.

'Adderley' was a small place but it was on the river, so it had good soil. It was well fenced, with a famous old shearing shed that hadn't been used for decades, and the biggest machinery shed I've ever seen. Mrs Young's family had owned it since the fifteenth century or something like that.

You had the feeling that nothing ever changed on 'Adderley' which is why, the day after the court case, I should have noticed that something was different. But it took Gavin's sharp eyes to pick it up. We were both on the school bus, sitting three seats apart. Homer and we were the only kids left on board. The first footy match between Wirrawee and Keating since the war was happening back in town, so a lot of people had stayed on for that. But Homer hated team sports and I had too much stuff to do back home.

I was three-quarters asleep and Homer, behind me, was completely asleep. Suddenly Gavin was standing next to me. He looked puzzled.

'What's wrong?' I asked.

'The Youngs' house,' he said, nodding backwards.

'What about it?'

'There's a light upstairs. It keeps going on and off.' He demonstrated with his hands.

'It what?'

'On and off. All the time.'

'What do you . . . ? But that's weird.'

He stood back while I got up and went over to the other side of the bus, but of course the house was already out of sight.

I only had a moment to make a decision. I didn't have a clue what might be going on. It was probably Alastair, mucking around, but we'd been warned so often to be on guard. There'd been lots of ads saying things like 'Every bell is an alarm bell.' 'Be super alert.' A light turning on and off was probably nothing. But ignoring it seemed like a bad idea.

I told Gavin to wake Homer, which I knew he'd enjoy, and I ran forward to stop the bus. Barry was driving. He was pretty easygoing and when I told him we wanted to get off he just shrugged and pulled over. I didn't tell him why, because I was already feeling a bit stupid. I mean, what were we doing? Getting off in the middle of nowhere because the Youngs' house had a problem with electricity? How were we meant to get home?

Homer was really grumpy, like a bear who's just come out of hibernation. The bus galumphed away down the road. 'What's this all about?' Homer asked.

'Gavin said there's a light upstairs at the Youngs' place that keeps going on and off.'

'So what?' He hesitated, then relented a bit. 'Oh well, I suppose we'd better check it out, seeing we're here now.'

'We're getting like Nancy Drew or the Hardy Boys or something, solving mysteries.'

'Well, it does sound a bit odd. The light, I mean.'

We walked quite quickly down the road. As we went Homer pulled out his mobile and dialled a number. To me he muttered, 'I'm going to tell Liberation what we're doing. We need to tell someone.'

'Good idea.'

I couldn't hear who answered, though I wished I could. Homer did all the talking anyway, then the other person said something, and that was the end of the conversation.

'You could ring the Youngs,' I suggested.

'OK.'

I looked up their number in my little address book. We were already at their boundary.

Homer dialled and waited for a bit.

'Just the answering machine,' he said, cutting the call off.

'What about ringing the cops?'

It seemed funny suggesting that. We'd never before been in a situation where ringing the cops was an option. Times had changed.

'Yeah right, and tell them what? That they should get out here fast because Alastair Young has been playing with a light switch?'

I didn't bother answering that, just said, 'Well, we'd better not go through the front gate. Let's cut across the paddock here.'

We made our way along the ploughed furrows, trying not to break too many ankles. From a row of trees we could at last see the house. There was no movement. And no light going on and off. Homer and I both looked at Gavin. He spread his hands out, palms up.

'Hey, don't blame me.'

'What do you think?' Homer asked me.

'We've come this far. Might as well finish the job.'

It was difficult in broad daylight to work out a good approach. We took the obvious route, towards the massive machinery shed, which would put us reasonably close to the house.

We were being a bit casual, not casual exactly, but I imagine we all thought the same thing, that nothing was wrong and we were on a wild-goose chase. And we reached the machinery shed with no drama. By then Homer was getting embarrassed.

'Shannon and Sam are going to give us heaps about this,' he complained.

I just shrugged. We were committed, for better or for worse.

Unlike most machinery sheds this one had a side door. And unlike most machinery sheds this one was spotlessly clean and tidy. Put ours to shame. We snuck in through the side door. All was quiet, except for us. No matter how careful we tried to be, our footsteps echoed a bit. I kept to the shadows and went past the work-bench. I stood there, hidden by a big yellow Kubota.

By then I was starting to swing back to thinking that Gavin might be right. It was one of those 'nothing is wrong and that's what's wrong' situations. Both the cars were in the carport yet the place was dead still. And I hoped I didn't mean 'dead'. At this time of day, in this kind of weather, the Youngs should have been zigzag-ging all over the place, from the house to the machinery shed, from the shed to the fuel pumps, from the bowsers to the dumpster, from the dumpster to the chooks, etc etc etc. Instead, if a blowie hadn't been buzzing past me in the machinery shed, nothing would have moved.

Gavin came up beside me, touched my elbow, and pointed down. I looked. There was a fresh red line of blood drops on the concrete floor.

I felt a lurch at my heart, like someone was trying to pull it out of position. I looked at Homer and he looked back at me. I suspect his face was mirroring mine: a kind of sick expression of 'No, please, not again'. He may have been a member of Liberation and he may have enjoyed the excitement of war, but at that moment I think he'd had enough. I know I had.

'It mightn't be human,' he muttered.

I shook my head and turned my attention to the house. I wanted to try to get in the upstairs part, because I thought it would be safer. Whoever had flashed the light had done it from upstairs, so for a time at least they had felt safe up there. And going that way would give us the advantage of surprise. General Finley had sometimes used the word 'hostiles' to describe enemy soldiers. I quite liked it as a word. If there were hostiles in this house the last thing they would expect was visitors through the upstairs windows.

I looked at Homer and said, 'Let's get in through the first floor.'

His eyebrows shot up. 'What do you want?' he asked. 'A trampoline?'

I didn't answer, just kept looking, impatient to start moving, but reminding myself that reconnaissance was three-quarters of any battle. 'Time spent on reconnaissance is seldom wasted.'

There was a triangle of water tanks immediately beside the house, and they had flat tops. That had to be the route. This wasn't like some old house in an Enid Blyton story, with ivy conveniently growing up the wall. The Youngs' place was quite English looking, in a slightly fake way: one of those brick houses with a tiled roof. At least all the upstairs windows that I could see were open.

I gave Homer a look that was meant to say 'I don't know about this but do we have a choice?'

I'm not sure if he understood the look, but I was not happy. In spite of our conversation about the agony and ecstasy of these combat episodes, taking a majorly dangerous route into a potentially lethal situation wasn't how I wanted to spend the afternoon. It was an afternoon that had been going along in a quiet and straightforward fashion. Maybe I'd find nothing in the house more shocking than Alastair watching 'South Park'. Sure hoped so.

CHAPTER 20

WE CHOSE A wooden stepladder because it would make less noise than a metal one. I had a quick look out the door and the coast seemed clear. Now was as good a time as any other. I swallowed hard and did a dash to the tank. I felt incredibly exposed. At least the ladder was light. I reached the first tank and leant against it, trying to get some oxygen into my lungs, which felt empty of everything. At the same time I tried to press myself so far into the corrugations that I would disappear.

Homer and Gavin arrived at speed beside me. Immediately they started peeping around the sides of the tank. I left them to do the looking, but really, what was the point of looking anyway? If hostiles suddenly turned up and Homer and Gavin saw them, well, it would give us extra time to hold our hands up and surrender, but that would be about the only advantage.

As soon as I had some breath I turned towards the tank, propped the ladder against it, and scrambled up.

Putting my head over the top, I was aware again that

I was totally exposed. I got up there anyway. The top was all muddy and covered with leaves and dead insects, like the top of every tank in Wirrawee I'd guess. But I wasn't bothered by that. I crouched down and waited for Homer and Gavin.

When the three of us were there Homer and I hauled the ladder up, as quietly as possible. Unfortunately complete silence wasn't possible. It knocked and banged against the tank a couple of times, and to make it worse the tank sounded empty, so there was a booming echoing effect which probably wasn't all that loud, but to me could have been a tenpin bowling alley on a busy day.

There was no point waiting though. We tiptoed to the part of the tank roof closest to the house and set the ladder against the wall. I looked up at it and swore quietly to myself. There seemed like an awful big gap between the top of the ladder and the window, and I'm not that fond of heights anyway. But I knew if I waited any time at all Homer would try to beat me up there and I didn't want that. Only because the suspense would have killed me if I'd had to watch him go into the house first.

I gulped again, put my foot on the bottom rung, settled the ladder a bit more, nodded at Homer to thank him for holding it, and started on up.

Standing on the second rung from the top was difficult. I had to try to get a grip on the bricks because there was nothing else. I was so close to the wall that I couldn't use the lean of my body for balance. And what was worse, I still had to get onto the very top rung, and even then it would be a stretch to the sill.

I forgot the famous advice about not looking down, glanced in that direction, saw Homer and Gavin's anxious faces, and wished I hadn't. I knew I had to get onto that top step fast. To keep my balance I needed a lot of energy. I couldn't hang around until I got tired. But I'd be pressed flat against the wall and then have to try to reach the windowsill. I wasn't sure if that would be possible: in fact I thought it probably wouldn't. But I knew I had to try it.

Suddenly into my imagination came an image of me reaching for the window, failing, and falling backwards, breaking my spine in a dozen places when I hit the unforgiving top of the tank.

Sometimes I hate having an imagination.

I hoped Homer was holding that ladder with maximum power. I had nothing to grip with my hands, so all I could do was press them against the bricks. I slid them up the wall inch by inch, feeling the rough surface scrape my palms. As I did I brought my right foot out and, trying to keep perfect balance, trying not to let my leg tremble too much, I eased it up.

Slow slow slow. It would have been hard enough doing this under any circumstances, but to know that at any moment an armed hostile might appear below me, or even at the window above, made my whole body tremble, not just my leg. That phrase of my father's, 'Time spent on reconnaissance is seldom wasted', floated into my mind again and became like a litany, till it was a meaningless jumble. 'Time spent on reconnaissance.' Stay calm. 'Seldom wasted.' Nice and calm.

I got my right foot onto the top step. 'Time spent.' I was surprised at how I rose. I'd now moved about twenty or twenty-five centimetres higher. 'Reconnaissance.' The sill was still an awful way above though. Pressing my sweaty hands hard against the wall, but not too hard, I kept going. 'Seldom wasted.' It wasn't easy to take that left foot off its rung. It hadn't been feeling too safe on that rung but it was a lot more comfortable there than it was in mid-air.

The trembling was getting worse. I broke into an all-body sweat. The ladder gave a jolt. I bit my lip, cursed Homer and every molecule in his big stupid body, but knew it was too dangerous now to look down. My left foot got to the top step and I tried to stand straight and tall, even though I didn't want to.

I stretched higher and higher. 'Reconnaissance seldom wasted.' Oh God where was that windowsill? My face was pressed into the wall and I didn't dare look up.

'Time seldom.' My fingertips brushed the bottom of the sill. And that was at full stretch. This was my worst nightmare. I knew exactly what it meant. The only way I could reach was to take a jump and try to hang on. If I missed I was dead. OK, not dead, just a paraplegic. My hands were now so sweaty that I didn't know how I could hang on to the windowsill even if I did catch it. The danger was that I'd just slip off. Funny, I'd survived aerial bombing, a train wreck, a bullet, and captivity – and now a few centimetres between my fingertips and a piece of painted wood could kill me.

But I had to go, and I had to go now, because every moment I waited would make it harder. 'Seldom reconnaissance.'

I reminded myself that I had to reach right in and grab all of the windowsill, not just the edge of it. I crouched as much as I could – which wasn't much – to get a bit of spring. 'Wasted.'

I took off.

I seemed to fly upwards for an amazing period of time. Yet I knew I wasn't getting much height. My fingers touched the windowsill. I couldn't tell which part of it. It didn't seem like enough. I scrabbled for another inch or so. Like I'd feared, my palms were so wet that they slipped, slipped, slipped. I grabbed harder. I felt every little crack and bubble in the paintwork. It too was rough but very different to the bricks of the wall. I grabbed again for the last time and gripped.

I hauled myself up. The muscles in my arms were bulging. My armpits were as sweaty as my palms. I got my head over the sill, my right shoulder, wriggled the left shoulder over, and at last knew I'd made it. I still hadn't been able to give a thought to what might be waiting. Enemy soldiers with guns? No good thinking about that until I was safe from falling. Sam Young with a camera trying to focus, at the same time as he was rolling around laughing? No good thinking about that either. In a truly stupid and bizarre way I would actually have preferred to find enemy soldiers than Sam Young laughing at me.

I was in a bedroom. I realised it was Shannon's. I took it in with just one glance but even that was enough to appreciate how good it looked. Three walls were light mauve, the other lime green. The cornices were dark purple, good enough to eat. Doesn't sound like it should have worked, but it did. She had a big bed made of some reddish-brown timber, maybe jarrah, and a desk to match. There were some fascinating paintings on the walls. One of them was a face of great beauty, a woman who looked at the same time peaceful, wise and worried. Shame I didn't have time to look closely.

It seemed almost too serious a room for Shannon, because she was always laughing, but still, it had to be hers. I knew that because, as I ran to the bed and ripped a sheet off it, I saw a drawing I'd done for her just a week ago: a kind of tangram thing. She'd pinned it to a curtain, right next to the bed. I was pleased about that.

I rushed back to the window. Peeping out I saw Homer and Gavin, looking up anxiously. I trailed the sheet down the wall so they'd have something to hang on to as they came up the ladder, then hung on to it myself as hard as I could.

Gavin came up first. It wasn't a problem holding him – he weighed about as much as a newborn calf – but Homer was more like a Grand Reserve bull at the Wirrawee Show.

Homer came through the window, grunting with the effort. As soon as he was in the room I said, 'Grab my legs,' and started going back out again, head first. He got the idea fast enough. I felt his strong hands grip me around the knees, then the ankles, as I dangled down. Down and down I went, like I was on an elevator. 'Don't drop me, Homer,' I pleaded silently as I got closer and closer to the top of the ladder. On my first swing towards it I missed by a couple of centimetres. On my next, my fingertips brushed against it. I still needed a few more centimetres. I tried to look up, but couldn't very well. It wasn't comfortable, with the blood running to my head. I had a sense of Homer leaning dangerously far out of the window. I hoped he didn't overbalance. I hoped no enemy soldier grabbed him and suddenly took him away.

Somehow he found another centimetre or two because I lurched down again. I tried not to panic, and grabbed the top rung. He waited a moment, I guess to be sure I'd got it. There was no way I could give him a signal. Then he started hauling.

It was heavy for me. I don't know what it was like for

him. And somehow I had to get in through the window without dropping the ladder. Homer ended up on the floor with me off-balance and the ladder sticking out from the house at ninety degrees. Gavin came to the rescue, holding it till Homer and I got our balance back enough to take it from him.

We manoeuvred it in. Seemed like Shannon now had another piece of furniture for her bedroom. I left Homer to move it away from the window and turned around to see what Gavin was up to. Typical. He'd already opened the door and was peering down the corridor.

'Geez, Gavin,' I said, which wasn't a lot of use as he couldn't hear me.

I raced to the door. Standing above Gavin I did my own peering.

My eyes had to get used to the light but I couldn't see any movement. I tapped Gavin on the shoulder. He looked up. I gestured 'Do you see anything?' and he shook his head.

Between us we eased the door open. We took our first step. By now Homer was right behind us. I thought this was a bad idea. If a soldier suddenly appeared he would be able to take all three of us with no trouble. I turned around and whispered to him, 'You should hide. Just while we check out this floor.'

He thought about it for a moment. He looked disappointed but he knew I was right. After all, he'd forced us to make some tough decisions in the past. Now he made a face, looked around, and then opened a door right next to me. It was a kind of hall closet, where they stored their suitcases and winter clothes. With a little smile at me he shrugged, disappeared in among the coats, and closed the door behind him.

Gavin and I tiptoed forward. I didn't want to do much, didn't want to take on an army of hostiles. I just wanted to know what was going on. I could see the head of the staircase and I moved carefully towards it. I thought the stairwell would amplify any sounds from downstairs.

In fact the first sound I heard would have reached any corner of the house. A door opened downstairs, to the left, and a roar of laughter came out. I grabbed Gavin by the arm, hard, and we both stopped dead.

Maybe the Youngs were having friends for afternoon tea? I didn't think so. I snuck closer to the edge and peeped over. I caught a glimpse of the man. He didn't look like one of the Youngs' friends. He walked across to a pot plant in a big blue and white tub, unzipped his daks, and started pissing in the plant.

I grabbed Gavin's arm again, just as he tried to grab mine. As the man sprayed all over the broad green leaves he kept talking in a loud voice to other people in the room he'd left. Someone answered him and there was another shout of laughter, even louder.

I couldn't believe him. I hated him, the way he was so calmly and arrogantly taking over my friends' house. Plus my most hated thing is people spitting in the streets and here was this guy going about a hundred degrees worse.

The pungent smell drifted up to us and I wrinkled my nose. Seemed like these guys urinated every time I got near them. I thought of yelling out 'You're killing the flamingo flower', just so I could see his expression.

The man finished and started back to the room. The door closed and everything went quiet again.

I looked at Gavin and shook my head. He looked at me. His eyes were the size of my watch face, which is big.

Without saying a word we both snuck back a metre. Then we tiptoed down the hall to the cupboard. I knocked on the door, which might seem stupid, but I didn't want Homer bopping me with a walking stick. I opened the door and Homer emerged from the coats, brushing them away from his face.

'They're here all right,' I whispered. 'Downstairs. Sounds like they're having a party.'

'How many of them?'

'I don't know. We only saw one. They're in a room to the left, the sitting room I think.'

'Any sign of the Youngs?'

'No.'

'We should check the rooms up here, don't you think?'

'Yes, absolutely.'

We knew Shannon's bedroom was clear, so we started with the next one. We didn't go about it like the professionals – well, the professionals we'd seen on TV anyway, the ones who bust down the door and cover each other while they search. We didn't have any weapons to speak of, so we quietly turned the knob of each door and let it swing open, then waited a minute. If nothing happened we snuck in and had a good look.

There were four bedrooms and a bathroom and a sewing room. Each of the kids had a bedroom. Occasionally as we slipped from one to the next we heard more noise from downstairs. There were shouts, laughter, even, once, breaking bottles. They had occupied the house and were enjoying themselves. I was sure they were getting well and truly into the grog supply.

I just wished I knew what they had done with the Youngs, and I had the worst fears about that.

We ended up in Alastair's room. He had a poster of Terri Boswell on the wall, and a few photos of her on his cupboard, and more sports equipment than I've seen outside a branch of Rebel Sport. Apart from that and the basic bed, desk and dressing table, there wasn't much else. It was such a boy's room.

'So, what do you think?' I asked Homer as we crouched in a corner.

I'd been thinking desperately and hadn't come up with the beginning of a plan. But I knew we had to act fast, because if the Youngs were still alive, we had to get to them soon. Their chances would be lower with each minute that passed.

Homer pulled out his phone. 'Call the cops,' he said.

'Oh yeah!'

It seemed so obvious. But I was really startled. For so long we'd lived in a world where police did not exist. I'd gotten out of the habit of thinking of the police: I was used to a life where either you solved your own problems or you died. I rather liked the idea of handing this over to the cops.

I should have known it was optimistic though. No sooner had I said 'Oh yeah' than I heard someone coming up the stairs. I made a face at Homer. He went white and put the phone away. I made the same face at Gavin but there was no need – he was always so quick to pick up on what was happening.

I grabbed Alastair's cricket bat and Homer and Gavin each took a stump. We tiptoed to the door. Homer took one side of it, with Gavin behind him, and I took the other. I had the wardrobe behind me, which wasn't so good as I wouldn't be able to get a good swing.

The footsteps outside sounded confident. And they

sounded like they were coming straight towards Alastair's room. I had the horrible feeling that it might be Alastair and we were about to knock him into another dimension, but the steps sounded too old and heavy for Alastair.

The handle turned. I have no idea why an enemy soldier was coming into this room, unless he'd suddenly decided on a game of cricket with his mates, but he didn't hesitate. The door opened and he started to enter. Homer took a swing straight away, before the man was right inside, which was a mistake as it gave him an opportunity to back out again. Nevertheless Homer got him across the forehead, with a hell of a crack. The man put his hands to his face and staggered backwards. Blood spurted between his fingers. But now he was out in the corridor again. He was having trouble standing but he let out a noise, a sort of cry and yell at the same time. I'd followed him but I couldn't stop him doing that. There wasn't time for much of a backswing there either, but I belted him as hard as I could, on the top of his head. There was a terrible clunking noise, like I'd hit a solid rock. His eyes rolled and his mouth opened and he dropped to his knees. Homer hit him again with a full backswing, this time to the side of his head. The whole thing was pretty disgusting. I hauled off Gavin, who was sneaking round to my other side so he could have a go. Gavin had been corrupted by the war enough already; I didn't want him to get even worse.

The man fell sideways and lay on the carpet. Blood poured from his scalp. You could see the stain, the lake, quickly spreading across the carpet. His eyes were now closed.

We waited anxiously, watching over the stair railing,

to see if anyone had heard. The door downstairs was still shut, so that was in our favour. But I saw it open again. I darted back. I heard a man's voice, in a foreign language, calling out what sounded like a name. And he was aiming his voice right up to us.

'Oh geez,' I thought. 'He's calling for his mate.' The same mate who was lying on the floor to my left, bleeding so freely that the carpet was already wet and soggy.

I glanced at Homer. He'd picked up my cricket bat and was on the other side of the stairwell. It seemed like a huge gulf suddenly stretched between us. We all retreated a bit, Homer towards Shannon's room, Gavin and I towards the door of Alastair's room. A floorboard creaked under me and I shuddered at the sound. The man called again. This time he seemed puzzled.

Still going backwards I got a better idea. On hands and knees I scuttled back to the unconscious body. I knelt beside him and checked his pocket, the one I could reach. Just a packet of cigarettes and some coins. I tried to roll him over. He let out a low groan. Gavin helped me. I glimpsed the triumph in his face as we saw, at the same time, a big bulge in the left pocket. Either this guy was glad to see . . . but no. He was unconscious. It had to be a gun.

I worked it out of the pocket. I wasn't sure if the man downstairs had heard the groan. But I had to assume the worst. I mightn't have much time. Thank God the war had taught me how to use a hand gun. It was all right for Gavin to think our troubles were over, now that I had a revolver, but it wasn't that easy. I didn't know if the thing was loaded, let alone how many bullets were in it, how many enemy soldiers were down there, whether the gun even worked.

Homer was next to the hall cupboard again. Gavin had retreated to the doorway of Alastair's bedroom. I thought I heard a creak, a step, on the staircase. I gestured for Homer to go into the closet and Gavin into the bedroom. Neither boy moved. I heard another sound from the staircase. I gestured at the two boys again, furiously, and this time they seemed to take some notice.

I couldn't waste any more time on them. I had to know about the revolver, whether it was loaded or not. I pulled back the slide as quietly as I could, and felt relieved to see the dull gleam of the shiny little metal cap. But the noise as I closed it again sounded like a car door slamming. I glanced up. The man was almost there already. I could see the top of his head. He didn't seem too suspicious yet – he was just walking up the stairs. Well, he was about to become suspicious as hell. If only we'd had time to move the body. But the patch of blood would have been there. Anyway, the whole war was full of 'if onlys'. Couldn't think about them, not now.

I was crouched over the body when the man reached the top of the stairs. He looked to his left first. Luckily Homer had disappeared. It gave me time to see that the man had a gun in his hand. I had been thinking of something like 'Put your hands up'. Now I decided I'd say 'Drop your gun'. But as he turned towards me and I tried to speak, I couldn't. The words stuck in my throat. My throat felt like a rusted-up hinge. And I had no WD40. I knew no sounds would be coming out of there.

I saw the light of understanding flame in the man's eyes. Understanding and fear. He started to leap to his left. He didn't have much room to move. He raised his revolver.

That's when I shot him. I didn't mean to shoot more than once, because I knew I might need every bullet in the magazine, assuming there were any bullets in the magazine, but my finger kind of spasmed and I let off two shots before I could get control again.

The guy spun around to his left, almost a complete revolution. His mouth opened but his eyes seemed to open even wider. He fell backwards, landing on the top couple of steps. His knees were sticking up and they stopped him from sliding down the staircase. His head suddenly fell to the left and the life went out of him. You could see it go.

I was still frozen, still kneeling on the carpet. I think I would have stayed there half an hour but Gavin burst out from Alastair's bedroom and grabbed me by the shoulder. I'm sure he heard the shots.

At the same time the door of the room below opened, and a cacophony of voices flooded out. There were shouts directed upstairs and a scrabble of boots across the polished floor. I assumed they were calling to the two missing men. I suppose at that stage they didn't know whether the shots had been fired in error, from one of their friend's guns, or whether someone like me was in the house and cutting loose.

When no-one answered their calls they figured out that things were not going according to their script.

By then Gavin and I had moved quickly, as quietly as we could, down the corridor. We were outside Homer's closet. I opened the door a little and whispered, 'They're coming, we'll go in Sam's room,' and closed the door again. We went on a few steps. We were now opposite the bedroom. I pushed Gavin in there and I stood in the doorway, trying to keep him behind me, and at the same time keeping a watch down the corridor.

Now I had time to check the magazine and the chamber. Three rounds. Sheez. It sounded like at least three men were coming up the stairs. But the revolver was all we had. Suddenly those other little weapons, the cricket bat and stumps, seemed a waste of time.

CHAPTER 21

A LONG WAIT followed, maybe four minutes. I heard a murmur of voices at one stage: I think when they saw their dead buddy lying on the top steps. I knew they were still making their way up the stairs though. I heard occasional whispered comments, and the slow 'urrrhhh' noise of a step as the weight was gradually taken off it.

A head suddenly appeared, almost at floor level, looking along the corridor both ways then quickly withdrawing. It was like a tortoise sticking out its neck, but just for a moment. It happened at a speed no tortoise would have recognised. I was left wondering if I'd imagined it.

I didn't think he'd seen me. I eased back a little further into the doorway. Gavin prodded me. 'What?' he asked, with a whisper. It intrigued me that a deaf kid was so good at whispering and moving quietly. Maybe he'd learned it during the war.

'One soldier,' I mouthed back, holding up a finger.
'One?'

'I saw one. There are more.'

I took another peep. Lucky I did. I was just in time to see a guy dart across the corridor, crouching low. He went straight into the main bedroom. Another one dashed across almost immediately afterwards. He seemed to be covering the first man. They were both inside the bedroom now. I heard shouts from in there. It seemed like the classic stuff, straight from the manual of how to enter a room which could be full of people with guns.

Sweat was pouring off me, and I mean pouring. I thought my shoes would squelch if I tried to move. I was having trouble seeing through my wet eyelids, wet hair. I shook my head. I tried to control my sweating by a simple act of will. Could I turn it off just with the power of my mind?

I kept peeping. The two men came out of the bed-room. At the same time another guy joined them at the top of the stairs. One guarded the left-hand side, facing my way, the other the right-hand side, towards Alastair's bedroom, the third knelt by the guy we'd whacked with the cricket stuff. If they were drunk, it wasn't showing. Maybe fear sobers you up pretty fast.

I didn't dare peep anymore for a while because of the man looking our way. Instead I glanced back at the window, wishing it were open, like the ones we'd seen from the tank. I wondered what we could do if and when they came for us. Could Gavin and I leap through the glass? A spectacular head-first dive? I nodded at Gavin and then at the windows and I think he got the idea. I left him to try to get them open and had another sneak look out the door.

This time I got down low to do it. As I extended my

head a few centimetres I heard a crash. I dared the snatched glance which was all I could allow. One of them was bouncing out of the door of Alastair's bedroom looking bloody scary; I think another was just behind him. The third was getting up from where he'd been kneeling beside the guy we'd hit. Something about the way he moved made me think that his unconscious friend wasn't going anywhere for a long time. Or to put it another way, he had already left for a long journey.

And I figured that while one was doing the quick medical inspection the other two had checked out Alastair's room and found it empty. Now they knew we were down this end of the corridor.

I heard a longish squeak behind me. I whirled around and gestured at Gavin. He was trying as hard as he could, but the window was stiff and difficult. I waved him away; it was too dangerous.

I had to look again. The men might be right outside the door and about to burst in to the room. I pointed Gavin towards the bed and made wild hand movements to tell him to go under it, but I didn't have time to see if he obeyed.

I lined up with the frame of the door and slowly let myself lean out. My flesh crawled. I saw only one of them and he was all of three metres away. I shrunk back in to the room. I ran on soft feet to the bed and took a position on the other side. It had come to a shootout then. I'd get one of them for sure, and maybe a second one if I were lucky, and I generally had been lucky since the war started. But the third one would get me and then Gavin. Homer would have to take his chances, would have to look after himself.

Suddenly one of them flashed past the door. I knew

what he was doing. I could see it in my mind so clearly. He would now be standing on the other side of the doorframe, gun held high, waiting for his mates to take up their positions before two of them burst in, with the third backing them up.

As I saw it happen in my mind, so it happened in real life. Two of them, guns ready, appeared in the doorway, gazing into a room that to them looked empty.

And in the next second, the next instant, they swung around instead.

I heard it too, the sound that had distracted them. The telephone ringing. The mobile telephone. It played 'A Whiter Shade of Pale'. It was Homer's mobile phone. And as they both, with a single movement, like they were choreographed, pointed their hand guns at the cupboard door in order to riddle it and Homer with bullets, I shot them both in the back.

It was the perfect accidental ambush. I saved Homer's ass. He maybe didn't deserve it, but I saved him. And Gavin's ass, and mine with it.

The third guy took off. I heard him leaping down the stairs three, four at a time. I felt too weak to follow him. A door banged. Suddenly the house was silent. From the window Gavin must have seen him because he suddenly called, 'Ellie, shoot him.'

He pointed down into the yard. I had a bullet left but I wasn't going to use it. A moment later I heard a vehicle start up and take off. They must have hidden it nearby.

I stepped over the bodies, getting blood on my shoes from the pools that were already puddling on the corridor floor. I opened Homer's door, being careful to warn him in advance: 'It's me. Don't smash my head in.'

I'd got that right. He had a golf club at the ready.

We went downstairs.

We found Shannon first. She was in the sitting room, tied up, not in good shape. Homer saw her, went white, looked away, folded his arms. I was angry with him, not for any logical reason. I said, 'I'll look after her. Go find the others.' He muttered something I didn't hear, and skittered out of there, collecting Gavin on the way.

I undid Shannon. She rolled onto her side and covered her face. 'It's OK,' I said, one of those meaningless remarks, not at all true, and not much better than 'You'll get over it', or 'I know just how you feel'. At least I didn't say those things.

I wondered what I would feel in that situation and what I'd want done for me if an Ellie-type person dropped in out of the blue, so I ran to the kitchen, got a big bowl, filled it with warm water, picked up some face flannels and towels and soap from the bathroom, and hurried back.

I was getting worried that I hadn't heard from Homer about Shannon's parents and brothers. 'Oh God, please don't let them be dead,' I prayed as I knelt beside her.

I cleaned her up and dried her, as gently as I could. There was a bit of blood but I couldn't see much sign of injury. Physical injury, that is. Then Mrs Young rushed in, pretty much hysterical, as you would be, but that didn't worry Shannon, although she hadn't said anything yet. They hugged and hugged. Once I realised I couldn't do any more, I went out.

When Homer told me that the other Youngs were OK – he'd found them in the basement – the thought went through my mind: 'That's what I prayed for. There is a God!'

But then I figured 'If there is a God, why did he put them through that in the first place? And in particular, why did he put Shannon through what she suffered?' It's like, if one survivor gets pulled out of a coalmine three days after it's collapsed, trapping a hundred blokes, everyone shouts, 'God be praised,' but you've got to ask, 'What was God thinking to have buried the other ninety-nine?'

Homer had called the ambos and the cops already. His mobile had been pretty useful, all things considered.

Once I knew they were on their way, I headed for the open air.

Open air feels good sometimes. I sat gazing at the big machinery shed, wondering who'd called Homer on his mobile at the critical moment. Maybe that was God, using the Royal Telephone.

CHAPTER 22

DURING THE WAR no-one held us to account for the stuff we'd done. That figured. Back then there wasn't anyone around asking us to fill in forms. Now I found that things had changed a lot. The three of us were at the house for hours, answering questions in between turning down multiple offers of counselling. Finally I chucked a bit of a tantrum and told them we were tired and had done enough for one day and they suddenly reversed direction. Next thing we were on our way home in a police car.

It took a long time to get Gavin to bed. He reminded me of the cow who'd been on Ecstasy. I just hoped he survived it as well as she had. She was in great shape. But Gavin was like a puppy on Ecstasy, jumping around, running around, zigzagging through the house. He broke a cup and a pot-plant holder. It was only when he fell against the window beside the front door and cracked it that he calmed down a bit, and that was only because I got so mad at him. I didn't want my parents' house trashed as soon as I took it over. I felt every break, every bit of damage as a failure on my part.

Poor kid, he couldn't help himself. I made him take a bath instead of a shower and I did Milo for two, and toast with Vegemite, then said, yes, he could sleep in my bed if he didn't take up all the room.

By the time I got to bed he was asleep big-time, like, unconscious. I stood looking at him. He seemed so relaxed, half on his back, his right arm flung out, breathing long and slow. I was glad he could find a peaceful place in sleep at least.

I was in my pj's and had one knee on the bed when I realised, almost calmly, that I was about to fall apart. I also realised I couldn't do this in my bed when Gavin was there. I went back out towards the sitting room but only got halfway when I started trembling and sobbing and hugging myself. I leaned against the wall then slid down until I was on the floor. It seemed like something outside me had taken control. It shook through me like I was a washing machine. I knew what it was of course. The image of Shannon, lying there naked and tied up, her blood, the death that I saw in her eyes: where was I supposed to put that? What was I supposed to do with it? In what part of my body was I supposed to store it? Please tell me. Because whichever part it was, I knew that part was full. It had been full for some time. Since the death of my parents in fact. I had my arms around my knees and I was shaking so hard that it hurt my teeth, as I tried to find a place for all this horror.

Gradually Shannon's blood gave way to my parents' blood, her damaged body made room for my parents' terrible wounds. The enormity of what had happened hit me at last. Sitting there on the corridor floor in the house where my mother died, I howled for my mother and father, howled like a dog, gasping for air between the howls. At the same time crazy torn-up pictures of our lives seemed to blow down the corridor towards me, as though someone had literally pulled out thousands of photos from the family albums and confettied them, so that all I saw were my mother's gloves tied to her stocks when we were waiting to go skiing, my father's moustache when he grew one for a few months, the scar on my mother's wrist that she wouldn't talk about – and now I would never know its origin and I would never see it again – her amused expression when my Stratton grandmother commented on the new curtains: 'Do you think this style will *last?*' The little black dress my mother wore to the opening of the grandstand at the racecourse, my father's pencil stub writing down the golf scores, his laugh, her fine fingers, his grunts when he was absorbed in a job and I was asking questions, her big brown nipples that she didn't like but I loved, his long soft penis and its curious head, her pubic hair so dark and mysterious, his pubic hair so thick and curly, him planting a kiss on the new tractor while I, at the age of eight, took a photo, her laughing and saying, 'So you'd like me better if I had four wheels and a power take-off?', him saying, 'I'll show you a power take-off,' and grabbing her and them kissing kissing kissing, passionately, as I ran around them laughing and squealing and grabbing at them, the two of them kissing, hugging, and the love between them, the love the love, always the love, the wild beautiful love that somehow survived the fights and the stresses and strains and worst of all the monotony of everyday life and I understood then what it means for a human life to end prematurely and arbitrarily, how each human being is an accumulation of wonderful and unique details, and in destroying a human being you destroy 'all the thousand million memories' as well as the bent little finger on his left hand and the stubble on her legs and the smile and the grimace and the frown and the way they use a spatula and the way they chop an onion at arm's length or place the jumper leads on the car battery or hold a baby at the school fete while the mother has a go at the 'Putt for Prizes'. 'Does anyone really appreciate life while they have it?' For a few moments there I think I became one of the philosophers and poets and infants and even Monets, a member of the exclusive club of those who do.

It seemed so unfair and lonely and cold as I lay there on the floor and realised after a while that no-one was going to come and get me, no-one was available to help me, no-one would put me to bed. The house was cooling fast – we couldn't afford to have a heater on all night – and it always lost its temperature quickly.

So I put myself to bed, after a while, a long while, and I lay there feeling Gavin's warmth and listening to his breathing. At the end of each breath I waited for the next one, scared that it might not come. 'Please keep breathing, Gavin,' I begged him, 'please don't stop. Keep reaching for that next breath, little one.'

I was thinking about my parents' love. Where was it now? What happened to it? It had to be somewhere. A force as powerful as that doesn't just disappear. Didn't they teach us in science that matter can't be destroyed? It only changes form. If that were true for an orange or a rock or a Falcon ute, surely it had to be true for the bond that my father and mother had. Maybe that's what bound this house together, kept the farm going, caused Gavin and me to be lying here together tonight. As I drifted into sleep I imagined I could feel it whispering down the corridor, slipping in and out of the rooms, circling the bed and finally holding us both safe in its arms.

CHAPTER 23

THE NEXT DAY brought more of the questions and answers and paperwork. It seemed that the Youngs had probably just been unlucky. A group of renegade soldiers from across the border, out to see what they could get, in the same way that people like Jake Douglass might go out on a Saturday night in Wirrawee – not that I'm saying for a moment Jake Douglass would do anything like these scumballs – had probably picked out the Youngs' house at random.

Maybe that's what had happened at my place.

These guys had stacked up everything valuable they could find and even divided it into five piles, one for each of them I suppose. It's good to share.

And then they'd shared Shannon.

Alastair heard them coming and hid in his room. They'd locked Mr and Mrs Young and Sam in the basement and after a while Alastair started turning the light on and off. Then he decided he wasn't achieving anything so he tiptoed downstairs to try to get to the phone. Pretty brave I reckon. But they'd grabbed him.

I don't think the Youngs' life expectancy was looking too good when we turned up.

It seemed ages before I had time to think about my own situation again. But in fact it was only two days later that I found myself back in the office of Mr Sayle, or, to be more accurate, in the waiting area. That mightn't sound like an important difference, but it turned out to be all-important.

Mrs Samuels was there again of course. I glanced at her as I came in. This time she had a newspaper open and she seemed to be grappling with the crossword. She hadn't done much though: I think she'd only got one word.

Once again I wasn't in the mood for Mrs Samuels. She could be so over the top. I mumbled, 'Hello, Mrs Samuels,' as I headed for the scruffy out-of-date magazines on the coffee table in the corner.

But there was something about her voice when she answered, 'Hello, Ellie.' I don't know quite what it was. She sounded off-key, awfully off-balance, for someone just doing a crossword.

I looked at her properly then, not sure what I'd see. She had dropped her pen and was staring at me like someone with a fever of forty-two. She even had the little red spots on her cheeks.

I couldn't help staring back. Her hair was a mess, like she hadn't washed it in a week; either that or she'd been doing a lot of sweating. Instead of not wanting to look at her, now I couldn't take my eyes off her. It was, well, to use another word I don't mind, perplexing. I was perplexed. This went on for forty seconds maybe. Then, sounding even more unusual, she said, 'Ellie, I just want to say again how sorry I am for causing you so much trouble back in Camp 23.'

'That's OK, Mrs Samuels. It worked out fine in the end.'

Mind you, I didn't mention the young doctor, Dr Muir. As far as I could find out, no-one had seen him again after he'd helped me escape.

She nodded. She lifted up a folder and put it on the edge of her desk, where I could see it easily. Then she said, 'Mr Sayle's running a bit late. He rang to say he's down at the Council office and won't be here for another ten minutes or so.'

'That's OK, I can wait.'

'And I have to go across to the chemist. I'll be ten minutes too.'

'Oh. OK.'

Without looking at me again she went out the door, shutting it firmly behind her.

I sat there, puzzled. Perplexed. Why had she been so keen to let me know where she was going and how long she'd be? Then I noticed the folder again. Why had she put it there like that, so conspicuously, drawing my attention to it? Surely she didn't mean me to . . . ?

I got up and went over to her desk, nervously. I saw my name on the folder. I hesitated a moment. Then I opened it.

It took me a while to work out what the first sheet of paper was all about. It was some sort of document for the Council, a planning application, but it was so complicated, and the longer I kept looking at it the more nervous I got, so that made it harder and harder to concentrate. I recognised the name of our property, and the map on the third page was definitely our place, but it seemed to be called something else: Kelsey Resort, the Gateway to the Mountains.

I couldn't make any more sense of it, and I skipped anxiously to the next lot of papers. I tried to concentrate. Riffling through them I saw one that caught my eye, because it was handwritten. It was signed Murray, and addressed to someone called Kelvin. Mr Rodd's first name was Kelvin. The first sentence was 'Don't worry about it mate, I've got her wrapped up tighter than a Sumo jockstrap'.

I'd lost any sense of how much time had passed. Over against the wall was a photocopier. I grabbed the letter and the next few pages and rushed to it. Might as well be hung for a sheep as a lamb. I've never understood that expression. Why is a sheep more guilty than a lamb? I thought it should be 'Might as well be hung for a wolf as a lamb'.

I slapped the first page onto the copier and stabbed at the green button. The machine took forever. The light slowly slid across, blinding me for a moment. I did four more but although I still had a few pages in my hand the tension was too much. This was worse than being upstairs in a house watching gunmen coming along the corridor to kill you. I raced back to the folder and shoved the papers in, trying to get them into some vaguely neat shape.

I heard a voice from outside, and a footstep. I sprang away from the desk, trying to get as close to the opposite wall as I could. The door swung open. Mrs Samuels came in, followed immediately by Mr Sayle. He looked cross, she was red-faced and apologising. She didn't look at me; her eyes went straight to the folder. Mr Sayle, however, came across to me with both arms out.

'Ellie! Very nice to see you. I've been hearing about your heroics. Well done. Come in.'

He ushered me into the office. As we went in I suddenly realised that in rushing to put the originals back in the folder I'd left the copies on the tray of the machine.

I know I went white, and my mind went blank. I sat numbly in the chair and I hardly heard the first two or three minutes of what he said. How could I get the papers back? What if Mrs Samuels found them? Had she meant me to see that folder? But even if she had, it didn't mean I was allowed to photocopy them. Geez, I was in a tough spot. And I couldn't think of a single way out of it.

Then Mr Sayle caught my attention. He was pushing some papers at me. 'The company's called Kelsey Pty Ltd, but don't take any notice of that. It's just a private company who'll take it off your hands and let you live in town with your debts paid and enough left over to rent a place.'

My mind still racing furiously, I took the papers and tried to read them.

'What is this?' I asked stupidly.

'Well, as I said, it's a contract of sale. Just a copy for your records. You'll have the money in ninety days.'

'What money?'

He frowned and sat back in his big swivelling leather armchair. 'Ellie, I'm very busy. I can't keep repeating myself. All you need to know is that the property has been sold, not for the kind of money that we would have liked, but beggars can't be choosers.'

I stood and hurled the papers back at him.

'I'm not a fucking beggar,' I said.

I started walking out, then decided that I really

needed the contract after all. Without looking at him I went back and picked up the pages from his desk. He stayed sitting there, rigid. From the corners of my eyes I saw his white knuckles. I thought, 'At least I can get out and try to grab the stuff from the photocopier.' But just as I got to his door he jumped up and came after me.

'Look, Ellie,' he said, 'this is ridiculous. There's simply no need for this kind of unpleasantness. I'm sorry I used the word "beggar". It's just an expression.'

By now we were out in the reception area. Mrs Samuels stared at us like her eyes were ping-pong balls. She had such a guilty expression that I thought, 'If Mr Sayle takes one look at her he'll know she's been up to something.' I probably looked pretty guilty myself. I just had to get to the photocopier. I couldn't leave that office with the papers sitting in the out tray. It'd cost Mrs Samuels her job. And I needed whatever information was in the documents to try to stop this stunt Mr Sayle was pulling on me.

All I could think of was a completely outrageous bluff. I got myself close to the copier then rounded on Mr Sayle. In as angry a voice as I could manage I yelled, 'I've got one thing to say to you and I'm going to put it in writing!'

I grabbed a sheet of blank paper from the feed tray for the copier, took a pen out of my pocket and, using the copier as a desk, started writing as fast as I could. I had no idea what I was going to say and I knew it didn't matter much. I scrawled something like 'You are never to sell my property, never, never, never'. I signed it Ellie Linton, then screamed at him, 'And I'm going to take a copy home with me, to prove it.'

I don't know what I was supposed to be proving, but

using my body as a shield between Mr Sayle and the out tray I ran the note through the photocopier. Then I opened the top again, threw the original at Mr Sayle to distract him, grabbed the whole pile of papers from the out tray, trying to make it look like it was just one sheet, and stormed out through the door so fast that I was just a blur of movement.

I have never in my life been so totally embarrassed, but I also knew I'd got away with it.

CHAPTER 24

GAVIN WAS IN tantrum territory, and looked likely to be there for quite some time. What is it with guys and tantrums? I mean, not counting me with Mr Sayle, most girls have grown out of them by the age of four. I think for boys it's around twenty, maybe: best case scenario.

The problem was that Homer had officially invited me to join Liberation, but he'd done it in front of Gavin. Gavin hadn't quite figured out who or what Liberation was – neither had I for that matter – but he knew they were to do with fighting the enemy, and they were to do with Homer and Lee, and it was a secret society where either you were in or you were out.

That was enough for him. But to make matters worse, when he asked if he could join, Homer said, 'No, you're too young.'

This was not helpful, and not really fair, as Gavin had proved time and time again how brave and useful he was. But other people wouldn't understand that, and I could see how Gavin might lower the average age of the Liberation members by a year or so.

Homer had delivered the invitation as we sat around the kitchen table after lunch Saturday afternoon. 'They'll understand if you don't want to,' he said, 'but they'd love it if you did. Face it, you've been involved in exactly half the stuff they've done in the last couple of months.'

'Would I get to find out who the Scarlet Pimple himself is?' I asked.

'Hmm, maybe. You might be that lucky,' he said, smiling like there was a secret joke going on. I wondered, not for the first time, if Homer himself was the Pimpernel.

That's when Gavin announced that he wanted to join, and Homer brushed him off with the 'you're too young' bit.

The kitchen table was the place for so many of our – wait for it, another of my favourite words coming up – confabulations. Gavin stood up, shoved the chair back, looked for a moment like he was going to cry, then kicked the chair over, swept everything within reach onto the floor and headed for the door, pausing only to chuck a half-empty jar of SPC raspberry jam at Homer, who caught it one-handed without blinking.

'That was tactful of you,' I said.

From the other end of the house I heard a door slam as Gavin sealed himself off from the world.

Homer shrugged. 'It's the truth. Anyway, he just proved he's not old enough. Anyone who acts like that isn't ready for what we do.'

'Oh, cut him some slack,' I said, getting up. 'He's done more in his short life than most people do in a hundred years.'

I went down the corridor and tried to open his door. It's difficult when someone's deaf: it's a waste of time knocking, so you keep violating his privacy by charging in. Only a week before I'd violated Gavin's privacy big-time, and caused him great embarrassment. I backed out thinking, 'God, he's starting young.' I thought it was pretty funny but Gavin was red-faced all morning and I didn't dare mention it or make jokes about it.

I thought that maybe it was time I bought him a book and left it lying around, because I couldn't see myself actually giving him the big talk, but someone had to do something, and who else was there? I could have asked Homer, except Homer would have taught him that 'Get over here', 'Sit', 'Heel' and 'Beg' were not just for cattle dogs but for girls as well. If Gavin grew up with the same attitude to girls as Homer had, I'd be seriously worried.

Anyway, this time Gavin had used a wedge or something to stop me getting in. I rattled the door a few times, hoping it would let him know I was there, then wrote him a note and slipped it underneath. There wasn't any more I could do, short of shooting the door down. There were times when Gavin made me feel like doing stuff like that, proving again that I was perfectly capable of having my own tantrums.

Back in the kitchen I asked Homer some more questions about Liberation but I didn't get very far.

'You know me,' he said, holding his big hands out, palms up, and making a face. 'I keep secrets. I'm not like you girls. If someone asks me not to repeat something, I don't repeat it.'

'Stop doing all the Greek body language,' I said, flicking his nearest hand with the flyswat. It was true though, he didn't repeat stuff. You could trust him that way. You could trust him most ways actually. 'So what happens if I join? Do I have to practise the secret hand-shake? Learn the passwords? Dress up in uniform and go to a weekly meeting?'

'Yeah, all of the above. You wear a mask and go as your favourite superhero, so no-one knows your true identity.'

'Who do you go as?'

'I'm the Phantom, Ghost who Walks. Phantom never die. Phantom King of the Jungle. You can go as Princess Cattle-drencher. You get to wear an Akubra and a Driza-Bone and a flynet over your face.'

'Yeah, that's me, Princess Cattle-drencher, does a hundred bullocks an hour, all on my own. But I want some corks for my hat.'

Homer made himself another coffee.

'Drink it fast,' I said, 'and then you can help me move those steers to Burnt Hut. Now that you've taken Gavin out of the running for the day, it's the least you can do.'

As we walked up there and I looked across at the farm, the cattle cropping at the short grass in Park-lands, the patches of bracken in Nellie's, the blackberry at the back of the barn that should have been sprayed months ago and was now a nice little suburb for snakes, the heap of firewood waiting to be stacked, I made my decision about Liberation.

'I don't want to join,' I said. 'Not yet anyway. There's too much else going on, keeping this place afloat, trying to get some school work done, looking after Gavin. Once this thing with Sayle has been sorted out, then I might give it a go. But even so, even though we agreed that it's a buzz, I don't know how much more I can take.

Walking on the edge of death all the time, it gets a bit unnerving. I haven't slept too well since I saw what they did to Shannon. And you know, it worries me with Gavin. I thought I'd be able to protect him from all this once the war ended, give him a normal life, let him grow up away from the violence.'

'Just what my parents wanted for me. Just what your parents wanted for you. Shame life can't be a choose-your-own-adventure book, where if you don't like the way it's going you pick a different path.'

'Choose-your-own-adventures'd be the only books you've ever read,' I said. 'Oh, sorry, plus *The Scarlet Pimpernel*.'

'No way. I'm reading *Alibrandi* even as we speak.'

'You are?'

'Sure. Good book. That Josephine needs a good smack though.'

I just laughed but I was impressed that he was reading so much. You never knew with Homer. I mean, the guy was wearing a T-shirt with the words 'Tomorrow is just a fiction of today'. I didn't even know what it meant and I'm pretty sure Homer didn't either.

After we'd moved the steers we hung on the fence for a while and talked. 'So are you going to tell me what's happening with Sayle?' Homer asked. 'I mean, the full story.'

'Don't think I'd better tell you the full story. I don't want to get someone in trouble. Let's just say I got access to stuff he didn't want me to see. I don't know whether it'll change things but I think it will. I've been trying to talk to Fi's mum but now she's on the Advisory Council it's bloody hard to track her down. Poor Fi, she's going crazy trying to get her mum to ring me. She keeps apologising to me and feeling guilty and I tell her not to worry, but of course she does.'

'So what kind of stuff have you got exactly?'

'Some papers. I can't understand all of it, but what I can understand is pretty nasty. You want to see them?'

'Oh yeah.'

I went back to the house. Gavin had emerged and was in the kitchen. That was pretty good for him. I don't know what his record sulk was, but there were times when you could go climb Everest, come back and write a novel, then diet and lose ten kilos before Gavin would come out of his bedroom. Or maybe he was amusing himself in there and it was nothing to do with sulking at all.

I said, 'I told Homer I'm not joining Liberation because there's too much else to worry about at the moment,' but he didn't react, although I'm sure he understood.

I went back to Homer with the papers. I was glad I'd photocopied that handwritten note. The full wording was nasty all right.

> Don't worry about it mate, I've got her wrapped up tighter than a Sumo jockstrap. The magistrate is all for me, and the courts are that clogged up it'd take a Scud missile to get an appeal through. She's a tough little bitch but mate, I wrote the book on tough. You'll have the place in three months, and it'll cost you about five bucks for her and a slab of stubbies for me.

'Charming,' Homer said.

'I thought you'd approve. "Tough little bitch." That'd be your wording, wouldn't it?'

He gave me a funny look but didn't say anything.

The Council document was definitely a planning application, like I'd thought. I'd had a proper look through it now, and it seemed that a company called Kelsey Developments Pty Ltd was going to turn our property into a luxury hotel called Kelsey Resort, the Gateway to the Mountains.

'What is it with that "Pty Ltd" stuff?' Homer asked. 'They're all called that. Even our family company.'

'I don't know. But what do you think about it all?'

'I think you've been right all along, and that he's a giant bullshit artist. But that's no surprise. What else have you got?'

I only had two other documents, one of which was just a typed summary of the stuff he'd said in court. I think it was the notes that he'd used to make his speech. The other one was a photocopy of something from a law book, about guardianship. It was from a case in the Supreme Court, called *R v. Ellis*, which apparently said, from what I could make of it, that the principles a magistrate uses for choosing guardians can be different for older kids than for younger ones, which I thought was pretty obvious anyway.

We wandered back to the house. 'What do you do now?' Homer asked.

'Stuffed if I know. Keep trying to get Fi's mum on the phone and see what she says.'

'Why don't you ask Bronte's dad?'

'Bronte? From school? Her parents are in the Army, aren't they?'

'Yeah, but her father's a lawyer in the Army.'

'Is that right? OK. Gosh. I might ask her on Monday.'

CHAPTER 25

BRONTE'S FATHER WAS a bit of a surprise. For one thing he was really young, compared to the parents of my friends. Compared to the age my parents had been for that matter.

It had been difficult getting in to see him. I didn't think a major was as important as all that, but by the time I'd talked my way in there I was quite nervous. The security was full-on. It was like when Mr King was on bus duty after school.

Major Gisborne wasn't all that friendly at first; not exactly unfriendly, just acting like he was too busy for this. I was already uncomfortable enough, after being interrogated about twenty-six times by men and women with guns, having to stand around while they rang each other to check that I had an appointment.

Eventually I got to the biggest building on the place, a concrete hangar half the size of Wirrawee, and was interviewed by Major Gisborne in a room the size of a washing machine. Life's full of contrasts, that's what I love about it.

There was no small talk, just, 'You've got some papers? Let's have a look,' and then I sat there wondering what I could do while he read everything. The choice was between studying the heavy wire mesh on the window, the light globe on the long cord from the ceiling, the scratches on the old brown desk, or the poster on the wall headed 'EVACUATION PROCEDURES'. There were a lot of posters like that around these days, but somehow it seemed funny to see one on an Army base. I'd figured Army people would know how to do that stuff without needing to be told on a poster, like the rest of us.

Major Gisborne took another piece of paper out of the inside pocket of his uniform jacket. I recognised it as the summary I'd done for Bronte, of what had happened since my parents died. Bronte had told me to be brief. 'My dad says the Gettysburg Address was two hundred and seventy-two words long, so nothing else needs to be longer than that.'

'That's a long address,' I said. 'What state did they live in?'

But it turned out the Gettysburg Address was a famous speech by Abraham Lincoln, and all Bronte knew about it was that it included the words 'government of the people, by the people, for the people'.

Major Gisborne read through my sheet of paper, taking another three or four minutes. This time I stared at the top of his head, trying to count the number of hairs. For a guy who looked about twenty he was pretty bald.

Suddenly he looked up, catching me staring at him.

'So let me get this straight,' he said, gazing at me over the top of his glasses. 'You wanted your neighbours as your guardians, and the court appointed the executor instead, but you've taken a dislike to him.'

I was already a bit red and now I blushed more. Put like that it all sounded pathetic. 'Well, yes, but when I got this stuff, it made it look like I was right.'

'This is illegally obtained evidence,' he said. 'Not admissible in court.'

'How do you mean?'

'You opened his files, took papers from them, copied them on his paper using his chemicals in his photocopier powered by his electricity. That's theft. You might think it's silly, but courts have sometimes convicted people for stealing a couple of sheets of paper, or a few cents worth of electricity, when they can't get them on any other charge.'

'Really?'

'For instance, if an employee steals an idea from his employer but there's no law covering the situation, it might be possible to get him for stealing the sheets of paper that the idea's printed on. And that then gives the employer a legal remedy.'

I gaped a bit at that. 'Well, I don't want to be arrested for stealing a few sheets of paper.'

For the first time he smiled. 'I don't think you're on the "Most Wanted" list.'

'So, what can I do? Surely I can do something.'

He launched into a long speech about what he recommended, which included going to the Law Society or Law Institute or something, and making a complaint about Mr Sayle's behaviour, or lodging an appeal with the court against him being my guardian. Or, I could ask him for the contents of my file and sue him if he wouldn't hand it over. But he didn't have to give me his personal notes anyway. Then he explained that any of those remedies might take years and that wasn't the only problem.

'If you appeal against the guardianship order, you have two main grounds,' he said. 'One is that your friend Sayle seems to have prior knowledge of a development plan for the property, and what's worse, a plan in which he may have a financial interest. And the second is that he seems to have malice towards you, as demonstrated by the handwritten memo, which he'll never let you get. You need to find admissible ways of proving both those points in court. A lot would depend on the secretary you've mentioned being prepared to give evidence.'

'I don't know if she'd do that,' I said.

He stood up and handed me back the papers. 'I can see it's a lot to take in,' he said. 'I'll write a summary and send it via Bronte.'

'That'd be really nice of you,' I said. But before I could thank him any more he'd gone again, straight out the door.

I was a bit off-balance after this. He sure didn't muck around. He seemed so cold compared to Bronte.

I went back to school, counting the number of periods I'd missed this week. I was nowhere near my record but I wasn't doing badly. So many missed periods. I should have been pregnant.

I looked for Bronte but couldn't find her till the next day. When I did, she was in the library, in the middle of a Chemistry lesson with Mr Bracken. I don't know why they were doing it in the library. Bronte gave me a wink and gradually sidled over to where I'd sat myself at a computer.

To my amazement she already had a letter from her father.

'Wow, that was quick,' I said.

'He's Major Action Man,' she said and sidled back to her class.

I stayed there and read the letter. It spelt things out pretty clearly, although it was longer than 272 words. The only part that was fuzzy was the bit about how I got the papers. He'd written: 'The origin of the documents is uncertain'.

But most of the time he was outlining the different strategies I could use. They all seemed incredibly long and incredibly legalistic, not to mention expensive and not even guaranteed to work. A lot seemed to depend on whether Mrs Samuels would testify. He didn't spell it out, but it was obviously because I'd got the papers illegally, and he was saying that if she testified it'd solve that problem.

I didn't think Mrs Samuels would testify. She seemed scared enough when she left that file out. If she testified, she'd lose her job, for a start, and she might find it hard to get another one.

I didn't realise Bronte had been watching me, but as soon as I put the letter down she appeared again.

'Finished?' she asked.

'Yeah. It's all a bit depressing.'

'That's what he said you'd think.' She gave me another piece of paper. 'This is from him too but he didn't sign it, because it's kind of unofficial.'

I opened it. It was a brief message, all typed. 'Forget the legal approach, Ellie. You know how effective direct action is. You've proved that often enough. Use your brains and your imagination and you'll come up with better solutions than these.'

I knew what he was getting at. Even before the war I guess I was pretty straightforward. I preferred to go at life full-on, not to sneak around the edges. I got sick of people at school who got into corners with their friends and bitched about how Chelsea had said something to Ilka about the way Meg had treated Simone. I preferred to march over to Chelsea and demand, 'Has Meg been getting up your nose?'

Maybe it's just another of those farm things. When you find a cow who's decided to have her calf halfway up an eroded cliff, and the calf has fallen into one of the cracks and he seems like he's only got minutes to live, there's not much point going for a walk around the paddock and thinking that God can be very cruel sometimes. You go as fast as you can to get a shovel and you start digging your butt off, and the only thanks you get is that the cow licks your arm all the time you're doing it, and later, when you see them together in the paddock, you get a nice warm feeling.

In the war we had times when we had to be sneaky, sure, and times when we planned attacks, but mostly we made it up as we went along. And mostly that meant fighting flat out, going at the enemy with everything we had, whether it was on an airfield or up among the rocks of Tailor's Stitch or on a train-ride to hell.

So that approach does kind of suit me I guess.

I still couldn't think of a direct solution. But later that morning I was sitting in History while Mr Baddiley went through his overheads, doing a big number on the Korean War. Because of the shortage of projectors he told Jake Douglass to pretend he was an overhead projector, and Jake sat there holding up each bit of plastic while Mr Baddiley talked about it.

It was boring, but the thing about Mr Baddiley was that if you got him distracted he could be quite interesting. That particular day I was so inattentive that I don't know who got him distracted or how he could jump from the Korean War to France in 1898, but I realised suddenly he was talking about a guy called Dreyfus, and a writer called Emile Zola.

As far as I could put the story together, what happened was that a French Army officer called Dreyfus had been outrageously framed as a spy. The real spy was a member of the ruling classes but they didn't have the guts to go after him, so they blamed Dreyfus instead, partly because he was Jewish. Dreyfus got kicked out of the Army, which had been the great love of his life, God knows why, and he was sent to an island prison to live on cockroaches and his own fingernail clippings.

OK, OK, I made that bit up.

Anyway, as time went on, some people in France got more and more convinced that Dreyfus had been ripped off. It didn't matter what they said though, the government wouldn't listen, wouldn't do anything.

Well, along came this writer called Emile Zola. He was mega-famous, like, we're talking Charles Dickens, Tim Winton, J.K. Rowling. He wrote this letter called 'J'Accuse'. He called it that because he was French. If he was English he probably would have called it 'I Accuse'. 'The most famous letter ever written,' Mr Baddiley said, which was a big call when you think of Princess Di's love letters to James Hewitt.

'J'Accuse' was a public letter, saying stuff like 'I accuse the three handwriting experts of making lying and fraudulent reports . . . I accuse the War Council of deliberately and dishonestly convicting an innocent man . . .'

It created a huge storm. Zola got chucked in prison for it. But it did build up such pressure on the government and the Army that eventually they gave in and held an enquiry that found out the truth and Dreyfus was brought back and everyone said sorry and kissed him on both cheeks, many many times, the way the French do.

So I listened to this with a lot of interest. The roar of the pen, I thought. Louder than a submachine gun or a B52 or a surface-to-air missile. I picked up my pen and, as Mr Baddiley went back to the Korean War, I tried writing my 'J'Accuse'.

I kept it short and simple. It was less than 272 words, but it was no Gettysburg Address.

When I'd finished I sat there figuring out what to do with it. Then I nicked off to the library and tried to negotiate a low price for multiple photocopies with the new library assistant. Didn't have any luck though. Their rates weren't as cheap as Mr Sayle's.

It was so annoying that Mrs Fisher was off sick, with jaundice. I could twist her around my pinkie with one easy twirl of the fingers. As it was I had to spend most of my cash, the money I was saving for chicken, and oyster sauce and tomatoes and snakes. Looked like dinner would be out of the freezer tonight. But now I had some ammunition. Unfortunately I had no confidence about using it, and no confidence about it working.

At lunchtime I had to go down to the supermarket. I couldn't afford much, except the essentials: milk and bread and spuds. The way it worked was that I shopped at lunchtime and they kept the stuff in the coolroom till I picked it up after school. In the afternoons I got the bus from school like normal, and Barry dropped me at the supermarket while he went to Our Lady of Good Counsel, the Catholic primary school, then he picked me up again as he went past to get Gavin and the others from the state school. It was a good system.

The walk downtown was right past Mr Sayle's big

dark red door. I scowled at it as I went past, but on the way back I did more than scowl. I stopped in my tracks.

Parked right outside was Mr Rodd's Audi. I knew it almost as well as I knew our vehicles. He'd had it a long time and after the war he'd found it dumped in Stratton with a couple of bullet holes in the driver's door and a lot of dried blood on the floor. No-one knew what the car had been through, but it had no other damage, so unlike a lot of people Mr Rodd got his car back.

I stood there looking at it and the longer I looked the madder I got. I thought about the long letter from Bronte's father and the long conversations with Fi's mother and the court hearings about my guardianship and I realised that, yes, I really was sick of it and, yes, it was time to take action.

It would have been nice to sit down with a counsellor and work out a win-win solution that would leave all of us feeling good about ourselves. To share our feelings so we could work together better. To understand how to turn our weaknesses into strengths and our obstacles into opportunities. But at this stage I was more into the idea of invading Sayle's office with an AK-47 and detonating him to kingdom come.

I thought about the little typed note from Major Gisborne.

Unconsciously maybe I was planning to do something this very lunchtime, because I did have my 'J'Accuse's with me, in my backpack. I grabbed my pen and wrote another note, the one I needed Sayle to sign.

Mrs Samuels was blowing her nose. I saw her eyes go big and wide over the top of her handkerchief. I knew how awkward it was for her, and I could guess how frightened she was at the thought of being busted by Mr

Sayle for what she'd done. I wasn't in the mood to hesitate but I realised I'd have to tread a bit more carefully than I'd planned.

'Ellie,' she said, sniffling a little. 'How are you, dear? I'm afraid Mr Sayle's busy at the moment . . . Ellie? Oh Ellie, you can't –'

That was the last I heard of her voice as I opened his door and marched in. I probably wasn't feeling quite as confident as I hoped I looked. But at the same time I was mad enough to take this all the way, and to hell with the consequences.

Mr Sayle was sitting at his desk. He was leaning back with his hands behind his head, elbows out like wings, telling a joke I think, because the words I heard were: 'So then Napoleon hits his shot, and it goes straight in the hole.'

He didn't move when he saw me, just stopped speaking and gazed at me, still with his arms behind his head. I think he knew straight away that this was going to be ugly.

After a long pause he said, 'Hello, Ellie.'

Only then did Mr Rodd turn around. He wasn't as cool as Mr Sayle. He heated up real fast. I could see the red rising in his face. His eyes went narrow and he glanced back at Mr Sayle. A lip-reader couldn't have read his words, 'cos his lips didn't move. All you needed was a bit of telepathy. 'Get this girl out of here' wouldn't have been far off the mark. I was trembling but I tried to stop my body ratting on me. I had to keep it fixed in my head that these guys were the ones who'd called me a tough little bitch. Might as well prove them right.

I pulled out the note I'd just written outside.

Before I could do anything more, Mr Sayle spoke

again. No-one else had said anything yet. He was still off-balance; he didn't know what I wanted, what I had on him. That was good. I had to keep him like that. I sensed that Mr Rodd was out of his depth; it all depended on my being able to fake out Mr Sayle.

'What can I do for you, Ellie?'

'I'm here with your resignation as my trustee,' I said as evenly as I could. I looked at the note. My father had told me that courts like plain language, even though they never use it themselves. He'd said that if you don't have a lawyer you just use the simplest words possible.

I read it to both of them. 'I, Murray Sayle, resign as executor of the Linton estate and as guardian to Ellie Linton.'

I could see Mr Sayle lean back a little more, relax just a little. I could see the smile start to break out. I had to go in fast. I ripped the pile of photocopied sheets out of my bag. These were my ammunition and I needed to blow this office up, with both these men in it. I had to make every shot count. I kept one and threw the others onto the desk. My single reason for spending all that money to copy so many was so they would make a big thump when they landed. They did. It had been worth the sacrifice of the chicken and the oyster sauce.

After a moment Mr Sayle leaned forward and picked one up. After another moment Mr Rodd took one too. Fifteen-love to me. As they started reading I said: 'I've done four thousand of these. My friends are going to distribute them tonight. They'll go into every letterbox in Wirrawee, and then some. Tomorrow afternoon kids who live out on properties will take them home and spread them round their districts. They'll go like a wildfire.'

'I'll get an injunction,' Mr Sayle said, but it was kind of automatic, like he wasn't even listening to himself. He was too busy reading.

He was reading these words:

My name is Ellie Linton and I live on a cattle and sheep property twelve kilometres from Wirrawee.

My parents were murdered earlier this year.

Before they died they appointed Mr Murray Sayle, a solicitor in Wirrawee, as executor of their estate.

When I was orphaned Mr Sayle got permission from the court to be my guardian as well.

Since that time Mr Sayle has set out to steal my property from me.

I knew when Mr Sayle reached this part. He suddenly stood up. He went quite white and said, 'You can't say this.'

But he didn't even look at me. I didn't reply, and he kept reading.

He and Mr Kelvin Rodd, also from Wirrawee, have a plan to set up a resort on my place, offering luxury mountain holidays. They have a company called Kelsey Developments Pty Ltd. They made a secret agreement for Kelsey to buy my place at a dirt-cheap price. Because Mr Sayle is my guardian I can't stop him. Then the two of them will set up their resort, and make a huge profit.

These men are criminals. What they are doing is illegal. If you deal with them, expect to be ripped off. If you've had any dealings with Mr Sayle, you should get another lawyer to check what he has done, in case he's stolen from you too.

At the bottom was my signature and the date.

Well, there was no shit to hit the fan, and no fan. But it seemed for a few moments that everything else hit everything else. Mr Sayle threw the sheet back at me. Mr Rodd tore his up. Mr Sayle started around the corner of his desk but then stopped again. It was like he suddenly realised it mightn't be a good idea to stomp me to death on the floor of his office. Instead he grabbed the pile of papers I'd put in front of him and threw them at me too. He followed up with a newspaper and a couple of finance magazines. Then he started shouting at me. It was hard to understand some of it but in general he was saying that he would sue me for defamation, that he'd ruin me, that I could even go to prison.

I didn't think prison was too likely, given how old I was, and that I was an orphan, and assuming that Mr Sayle's behaviour wouldn't look too good under close examination. Zola yes, Ellie no.

I had thought this through quite a bit, even in the short time since I'd had the idea of doing it. So I took a step forward, trying to stay calm. I've noticed a few times now how powerful it is if you stay calm when someone else has lost his temper.

'Sure,' I said, 'go ahead and sue me. If you can sue a minor for defamation.'

That rocked him right to his Reeboks.

I followed up fast. 'I don't know if you can or not. But suppose you can. What happens then? Either you win, and you get some money from me, but I won't have much left anyway by the time the case is finished. And your reputation will be shot and you'll have a stain the size of California on your name. Or you'll lose, and your reputation'll be even more shot. And face it, you're a good chance of losing. There's nothing in my letter that isn't true.'

Mr Rodd sneered at him: 'I told you what she's like.'

'I'll get an injunction,' he said again.

'We'll ignore it,' I said. 'We're teenagers. We don't do injunctions. We'll scatter these notices like confetti. By tomorrow morning you won't be able to walk down the street. You'll need an umbrella to keep the spit off your head.'

I've got to hand it to myself, he was definitely white-faced. I decided Zola was a pretty good role model. He'd known what he was doing.

I couldn't give Sayle any more time to think. I pulled out my pen. 'Sign it,' I snarled. 'And then I'll try to get to my friends and stop these papers going out. But I'll have no hope of doing anything after three thirty. It's now or never.'

Mr Rodd was still sitting there sneering. Then he suddenly saw the look in Mr Sayle's eyes. 'Don't sign,' he said, jumping up.

'I have to, Kelvin,' he said. 'Her family's been here forever. Everyone knows them. Especially after that stuff she did in the war. These local yokels are going to read her bit of paper, the ones who can read that is, and it'll be the end of the story. No-one's going to listen to us.'

With the signed statement in my hand I turned and headed for the door. I didn't think it would be a good idea to run but I expected at every step to get a letter-opener buried in my back or a wastepaper bin shoved down on my head. I couldn't believe it when I got to the door without a word being said, and I couldn't believe it even more when I opened the door and left, and nothing and no-one followed me down the street. It had been as bad as any encounter with enemy soldiers in wartime. All the way back to school I shook like a tissue in a typhoon.

EPILOGUE

BLOODY HOMER. How often have I put those two words together? It's like the official adjective for Homer is bloody. Or, to put it another way, there are two words for Homer, and the second is Homer. And the first one needn't necessarily be bloody, either.

He really wasn't interested in my great victory over Mr Sayle and Mr Rodd. Oh, he listened of course, because he knew he was expected to, but because it wasn't about him he only half listened, and the moment I was finished he went back to talking about Liberation, which was all he seems to care about these days.

I suppose if you weren't there you wouldn't realise how difficult it was, and how it felt so dangerous, and how much it meant to me to have succeeded. Not only for the obvious reason that it looked like I'd saved the farm, for a short time anyway, but also because it proved that I could win my battles in the adult world of post-war Wirrawee, against the movers and shakers and lawyers and developers and sharks.

It gave me more hope that I could make a go of things by myself.

I shouldn't say by myself, because Gavin was doing it too, and it was Gavin who seemed to understand how much it meant to get that letter of resignation from Mr Sayle. When I showed it to him he ran around the kitchen three times waving it in the air and making noises like a train that's trapped in a tunnel.

He then kissed me, which shocked both of us I think.

So now I'm in the kitchen looking around, one minute thinking, 'This is mine, I'm in charge, I own it all, it's my kitchen, my house, my farm,' and the next minute I'm, 'Oh my God I'm too young, this is the scariest thing that's ever happened, I can't do this.'

Can I do it? 'I think I can, I think I can, I think I can.'

Well, I'm not a train, and anyway, even a train can be derailed by a landslide. Or blown up. I'm just me, just Ellie, sitting at the kitchen table, trying to make my life work, barely holding it together some days, some days feeling too big a flood of grief for the house to hold, but some days feeling pride and strength.

I know my life's different to other people's but everyone's life is different to everyone else's. All I can do is keep living it, keep moving it forward every day I can. Lots of days it's three steps forward, four steps back. If at the end of every month I'm a step or two ahead – well, I'll settle for that.

WHATEVER BOOK YOU'D LIKE TO READ, JOHN MARSDEN HAS WRITTEN IT.

Comedy

The Great Gatenby is the joke-a-minute story of a teenager in a co-ed boarding school. Erle Gatenby isn't scoring great grades but he's a swimmer with the potential to break records, and he's doing OK with the beautiful Melanie. Two out of three ain't bad!

Cool School takes you on a wild and funny ride through your first day in a new high school. It's a short read or a long read – that's up to you – but it's maximally entertaining! More fun than a Game Boy.

Creep Street has gore, ghosts, spiders, more gore and gratuitous violence. Funny funny funny from start through to . . . whatever finish you choose. A quick and light read when you can't be bothered with *Romeo and Juliet*.

Staying Alive in Year 5 is a twister ride through Scott's first few months with his Year 5 teacher, the legendary Mr Murlin. 'I couldn't find a boring sentence in it,' said one reader. It's the way you didn't even dream school could be. Maybe it's the way school should be?

Looking for Trouble is John Marsden's favourite of his own books. Hour by hour Tony tries to figure out a few truths about life, school, girls, and the strange new family living down the block. Funny, yes, but at the same time moving and real, *Looking for Trouble* is a warm and alive book.

Human interest

Winter is the story of a sixteen-year-old girl who decides it is time for action. With courage and strength, offending others and scaring herself, Winter sets off on an epic search. Winter is intelligent, wealthy and spirited, but she has no parents – and she wants to know why. A gothic mystery, a human interest story and a compelling account of a girl with courage and brains, this is about a teenager who takes charge of her own life.

Dear Miffy is short but devastating. Too powerful for some, who are horrified by its violence and street language, and the hopelessness of Tony's life, *Dear Miffy* is an unflinching journey into darkness. Readers who make the journey with Tony will not emerge unaffected. A compelling and honest book.

So Much to Tell You, the first John Marsden novel, is Marina's diary. In primary school Marina was popular, proud and successful. A sudden event changed her life. It was an event so devastating that no-one around her can cope with it. No-one has a solution. But a few friends start to gather. And a teacher and a counsellor . . .

Ultimately, though, it is for Marina herself to try to overcome something so terrible that it is almost outside the human imagination.

Take My Word For It is the sequel to *So Much to Tell You*. Lisa, cold and strong, successful and admired, shares a boarding school dormitory with Marina. Through her eyes we observe Marina and we observe Lisa herself. Behind the mask is the real Lisa, passionate, beautiful and unhappy. Her story is compelling, alive and real.

Checkers explores the world of a teenager from a powerful family. With brilliant intimacy it takes you into the lifestyle of the wealthy and famous. From the outside everything glitters but on the inside things are starting to break up, to come apart. What happens to a teenager when everything she trusts crumbles away? What happens when she has no-one left but herself?

Fantasy

Out of Time combines the psychological dramas for which John Marsden became famous with a startling story of time travel. James is a lost child who has lost his sister. Many people in *Out of Time* are lost. James will never see his sister again. But by taking great risks, by undertaking dangerous journeys, he may find himself. Soon to be released into the American market, *Out of Time* is a story that turns its readers inside out.

The Journey is for readers willing and ready to make a journey of their own. An engrossing story of a boy who at fourteen knows he is ready to move forward. Here is the place where he starts and here is the place to which he must return. It is what happens in between that matters. A strong, tense, wise and even funny book, *The Journey* takes its readers into new territory.

The *Tomorrow* Series

'The feeling of reality you bring into your work is extraordinary. It makes you feel as if you are running along the dangerous streets with Ellie, tense and alert, about to blow up a bridge, or a couple of houses, or waiting quietly inside a container in the bottom of a ship, about to do the biggest thing of your life.'
KIM, MOUNT GAMBIER

'We have bags under our eyes thanks to your books, because we can't put them down long enough to sleep!'
COURTNEY AND DIANNA, YORKETOWN

Readers across Australia are unanimous: this is the greatest series ever published in this country.

Seven books charged with high emotion, drama, action and even a dash of romance.

When you open the first page of *Tomorrow, When the War Began* you'll enter a world that'll change you forever.

A world of danger, risks, challenge and self-discovery.

A world that will stay with you, through all the years of your life.

Tomorrow, When the War Began is the first of the *Tomorrow* series, and is followed by *The Dead of the Night, The Third Day, The Frost, Darkness, Be My Friend, Burning for Revenge, The Night is for Hunting* and *The Other Side of Dawn*.

PRAISE FOR THE *TOMORROW* SERIES

'. . . compulsively readable'
NEW YORK TIMES

'. . . without a doubt the best series for younger readers that an Australian writer has ever produced'
DAILY ADVERTISER

'. . . makes for reading as exciting, disturbing, provocative, as we have had for many years'
JUNIOR BOOKSHELF (UK)

'Like ancient myths, the stories confront the purpose of life, death, betrayal, killing, love, hate, revenge, selflessness, sacrifice and, in the most recent book, faith'
THE AGE

THE *TOMORROW* SERIES

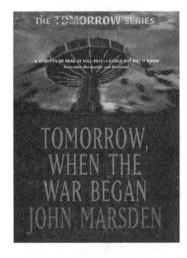

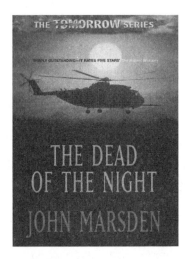

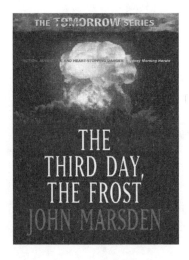

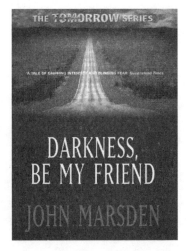

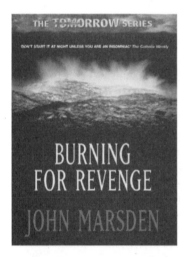

THE TOMORROW SERIES

'DON'T START IT AT NIGHT UNLESS YOU ARE AN INSOMNIAC' The Catholic Weekly

BURNING FOR REVENGE

JOHN MARSDEN

THE TOMORROW SERIES

AN ELEVATION OF ADVENTURE LITERATURE TO HEIGHTS THAT ARE ONLY ACHIEVED ONCE OR TWICE IN A GENERATION

THE NIGHT IS FOR HUNTING

JOHN MARSDEN

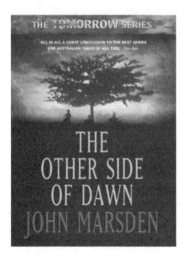

THE TOMORROW SERIES

'ALL IN ALL A GREAT CONCLUSION TO THE BEST SERIES FOR AUSTRALIAN TEENS OF ALL TIME' The Age

THE OTHER SIDE OF DAWN

JOHN MARSDEN

Learn great new writing skills
with John Marsden

You are invited to spend a few days with John Marsden at one of Australia's most beautiful properties.

The Tye Estate is just 25 minutes from Melbourne's Tullamarine Airport, and is perfectly set up for writing camps and other activities.

Every school holidays, John takes writing and drama camps, where you can improve your skills, make new friends, expand your thinking, and have a huge heap of fun.

Accommodation is modern and comfortable, meals are far removed from the shepherd's pie they gave you at your last school camp, and supervision is by friendly and experienced staff.

Between the workshops with John, you can explore the surrounding spectacular bush, looking out for rare and highly endangered species like Tiger Quolls and Powerful Owls, as well as koalas, platypuses, wedgetail eagles, kangaroos and wallabies.

Activities including bushwalking, mountain biking, tennis and orienteering are also available, to help you enjoy your stay at the Tye Estate.

For details, write to:

The Tye Estate
RMB 1250
Romsey VICTORIA 3434

Or fax: (61) 03 5427 0395
Phone: (61) 03 5427 0384
Email: johnmarsden@bigpond.com
Web: www.johnmarsden.com

The Tye Estate writers' conferences

At the Tye Estate writers' conferences, you work face-to-face with senior editors from major publishers, as well as prominent Australian authors.

- Workshop your manuscript with leading editors, from Australia's biggest publishing companies.
- Panels, small group discussions, author talks.
- Workshops with leading authors, including John Marsden.

In the beautiful surrounds of the 1100-acre Tye Estate, just outside Melbourne.

More than twenty writers have been contracted by publishers and editors at the unique Tye Estate writers' conferences. Accommodation packages are available.

The Tye Estate
RMB 1250
Romsey VICTORIA 3434
Phone: 03 5427 0384
Fax: 03 5427 0395
Email: johnmarsden@bigpond.com
Web: www.johnmarsden.com